A FAMILY BETRAYAL

BOOKS BY EMMA TALLON

ANNA DAVIS AND FREDDIE TYLER SERIES

Runaway Girl

Dangerous Girl

Boss Girl

Fierce Girl

Reckless Girl

Fearless Girl

Ruthless Girl

THE DREW FAMILY SERIES

Her Revenge

Her Rival

Her Betrayal

Her Payback

Her Fight

Her Enemy

Her Feud

STANDALONE NOVELS

Snow Going Back

EMMA TALLON
A FAMILY BETRAYAL

bookouture

Published by Bookouture in 2025

An imprint of Storyfire Ltd.
Carmelite House
50 Victoria Embankment
London EC4Y 0DZ

www.bookouture.com

The authorised representative in the EEA is Hachette Ireland
8 Castlecourt Centre
Dublin 15 D15 XTP3
Ireland
(email: info@hbgi.ie)

Copyright © Emma Tallon, 2025

Emma Tallon has asserted her right to be identified as the author of this work.

All rights reserved. No part of this publication may be reproduced, stored in any retrieval system, or transmitted, in any form or by any means, electronic, mechanical, photocopying, recording or otherwise, without the prior written permission of the publishers.

ISBN: 978-1-83525-285-7
eBook ISBN: 978-1-83525-284-0

This book is a work of fiction. Names, characters, businesses, organisations, places and events other than those clearly in the public domain, are either the product of the author's imagination or are used fictitiously. Any resemblance to actual persons, living or dead, events or locales is entirely coincidental.

*For my bright ray of sunshine and my wildfire princess
Christian & Dolly
I love you both so much.
You are my reason for everything.*

PROLOGUE

It was the kind of day that suited a funeral. Steel-grey skies and the miserable onslaught of constant drizzle that made everything and everyone thoroughly damp, no matter how effective their umbrellas promised to be.

Maria Capello stood by the graveside silently working her leg muscles to keep her slim heels from sinking into the sodden ground, her head respectfully bowed as the vicar said his final words. In a calf-length black dress and long black coat, the only colour she'd added was the splash of red on her lips.

A thin arm wound around hers clutched tighter as the casket was lowered into the ground, and Maria patted it gently with her free hand, offering what little support she could to the grieving widow. The older woman looked up at her with a sad, watery smile.

'Thank you for being with me today,' she said quietly.

Maria shook her head. 'There's no need for thanks, Margaret,' she murmured back. 'You know how much I think of you. How much I thought of John.'

Margaret nodded, tightly clamping her mouth as fresh tears began to fall.

Maria gripped the widow's hand in hers. John had been a good man. A good husband to Margaret, a good friend to all who'd known him, and to Maria, for the last three years. He'd been a barrister on the parliamentary council, comfortably seated in one of the most coveted legal roles in the country. Maria, though a barrister herself, hadn't quite reached those heights. Nor would she ever. Her background would be scrutinised far too closely, should she ever try to get that close to the government. But through her friendship with John, she'd made some incredibly lucrative connections, and her association with him had given her a lot of sway in important legal circles. He had opened up the world to her and her family in more ways than he had any idea of. In ways that if he *had* had any idea of, he would have been horrified about. But Maria had always been careful to stay two steps ahead in her dangerous game, ensuring that John remained safely blindfolded. Now that he was gone, it was going to be tough keeping the power she'd so carefully gained. But she should be able to do it. One way or another.

The vicar called Margaret forward to throw the first handful of dirt, and her grip tightened again on Maria's arm. Maria gently released it and gave the grieving woman a small nod of encouragement. Margaret reluctantly moved forward, and Maria's strikingly bright hazel eyes slipped across to the ornately carved oak coffin. She'd always found it odd that so much detail and expense went into the wooden box used to encase a dead body before it was buried six feet underground, never to be seen again.

But as she stood and watched the polished oak and gleaming brass handles disappear under the shower of dirt, inch by inch, it was no longer John's dead body she was thinking of. It was the body of the man she'd had buried two feet beneath where his coffin now lay, late last night. The body she'd had buried without a specially carved box, or the parting words of a priest, or the eyes of the people he knew watching. The body that, now, thanks to John and the general common decency shown to the *officially* dead in graveyards, would never ever be found.

ONE

The low buzz of electricity from the bright strip light illuminating the small, clinically white room broke the tense silence as the three men sitting around the small table stared at each other. As one of the two policemen sat together on one side sighed and moved his gaze away, the man they were interrogating smirked.

'Something funny, Antonio?' the other officer snapped.

Antonio relaxed back in the hard plastic chair. 'Not yet.'

'Not *yet?*' the officer repeated with a frown. 'What do you mean by that?'

Antonio's gaze flicked up to the clock. *She would definitely be here by now.*

'You'll see,' he said calmly, the smile still playing at the corners of his mouth. 'Any minute now.'

He regarded the officers unwaveringly, but his focus was on the small red dot on the CCTV camera behind them.

The first officer sighed and leaned forward, the hard-etched lines on his forehead deepening with annoyance. 'I'm not interested in riddles, Antonio. You're just wasting my time – and if you waste much more of it, I'll happily add *that* to your charges as well.'

'What charges are those exactly?' Antonio grinned, unfazed by the threat.

His dark brown eyes glinted with amusement, and his smile widened as the small red light suddenly disappeared.

Go time.

The officer ignored him and tried to push forward with the interview. 'Tell me where you were last night around eight thirty.'

'I don't think I will,' Antonio replied calmly, not missing a beat.

'And why's that?' the officer asked.

'Because I don't have to.' Antonio paused, waiting for the sound of her approach in the hallway outside.

'Actually, yes you do,' came the irate response.

'Or what?' Antonio asked, lacing his fingers behind his head and stretching back. The rhythmic thuds of footsteps hurrying down the hall finally sounded, at first faintly but quickly growing louder as they drew nearer.

'Or I'd be happy to find you a nice, uncomfortable bed for the night,' the officer threatened. 'You don't want to play ball, that's fine, Capello. I won't either.'

'Oh, I think you will,' Antonio replied. He stood up and trained his eyes on the door as the footsteps slowed to a stop.

'Hey, sit down,' the officer demanded. 'We're not done h—'

The door flew open, cutting him off, and a short, balding man in a suit that slightly strained across his middle stepped inside with a grim look on his face.

'Chief?' the officer questioned, looking surprised.

The chief superintendent faced Antonio for a moment with a steely, unreadable expression then released a long breath through his nose. He gestured towards the door with an irate flick of his hand. 'Mr Capello is free to leave,' he said curtly.

'What?' The officers exchanged a shocked glance and then looked back at their boss. 'But—'

He silenced them with the same hand and a sharp look. 'This came from special ops. I can't say any more. Destroy the file and discuss this with no one. You understand?' He eyed them both until they reluctantly nodded their agreement. 'Good. Mr Capello, I'll see you out.'

One of the officers slumped back and threw his pen lid across the table in frustration. Antonio chuckled as he buttoned up his jacket and walked past them.

'See you later, boys. Actually, no, I *won't*, will I? It looks like you'll just have to admire me from a distance from now on.'

He swaggered out into the hallway, and his grin widened as they cursed behind him.

'I wouldn't get too cocky if I were you, Antonio,' the chief superintendent growled under his breath. 'You're lucky your sister is who she is and that I owed her a favour, but this is the last favour she's ever getting from me. Next time you're on your own. I don't care who you're connected to.'

They reached the exit, and Antonio stopped and turned to face him. 'I'll get as cocky as I like, *Chief*.' He leaned in and lowered his voice. 'Because you and I both know that if my sister comes knocking again, you'll have no choice in the matter. You see, that's what real power is. The ability to remove any obstacle in the way, no matter what that is. And if you become someone that won't move when my sister asks? Well... there are other ways to take you out of the picture. Ways I don't think you'll enjoy – at all.' He watched the man's eyes widen and then turned away, calling back over his shoulder as he exited the building. 'But please, do feel free to fuck about and find out.'

TWO

Catriona Holden sat at her round, wooden kitchen table, staring straight through the pile of condolence cards in front of her until they were no more than a blur of muted colours. She'd meant to read them and respond in the polite way she knew was expected, but she just couldn't. She couldn't seem to do anything today, except sit there, feeling numb.

Over the last few days since her father had died, there had been things to do. A funeral to arrange, people to coordinate. It had kept her busy. Kept her going. But now the funeral was over. Her father had been buried the day before, the service delivered, everyone's goodbye said and all the mess cleaned up expertly by the caterers before they'd left her alone in her spotless, orderly home. Looking around the place this morning in the painfully empty silence, it was as if the wake hadn't even happened just the day before. As if it hadn't been filled with people and memories and grief.

It felt unsettling to Cat, just how swiftly it had all gone away. How quickly it had been back to just her and her three-year-old daughter, Orla, again. Her husband, Greg, had mumbled some excuse and slipped away as soon as he could after the wake. Most wives in the same position would probably be upset about that. They'd probably have been angry, too, about the fact he hadn't returned home all night. But Cat was glad. With everything she was already dealing with, he was the last person she wanted around. Though she would have to deal with him at some point. And, much as she dreaded it, she knew that the sooner she did that, the better. For everyone.

Pulling in a deep breath in a half-hearted attempt to revive herself, Cat tipped her face to the ceiling and pushed her hands back through her mid-length dark brown hair. It cascaded down over her shoulders as she lowered her gaze again, and the ends curled gently, which served to soften the harsh angles of her face that had appeared over the last few months. After her father's terminal diagnosis, she'd lost what little weight she'd carried, through grief and stress. Her pale skin had lost its usual rosy glow and her warm brown eyes had dulled. But still, none of these recent changes, nor the tiredness that seemed to now permanently cloak her face, could hide the fact that Cat was a very beautiful woman.

The front door slammed, the sound reverberating from the other end of the house, and Cat turned her head towards the doorway with resigned expectation. Her stomach tightened, as it always did when her husband entered, and she briefly closed her eyes, steeling herself for the conversation she knew it was time to have.

A man of moderate build and height, wearing a slightly crumpled black suit, walked into the kitchen and halted just inside the doorway, his expression surprised. He raised one eyebrow and then slicked back his slightly too long, dirty-blond hair with the palm of one hand, in an attempt to tidy it.

'I thought you'd be out by now,' he said, in the overly exaggerated public-school-boy accent Cat had grown to loathe.

It was the sort of exaggeration he usually only put on for work or for situations when he wanted to make it clear he thought himself superior to whoever he was talking to. She idly wondered at what point he'd started using it with her. It had been so long she couldn't remember, now.

'It *is* Thursday, isn't it?' he continued.

Cat felt a prickle of pain in her chest and swallowed hard. 'I buried my dad yesterday, Greg,' she reminded him. 'You really think I'm going to the hospice today, when he's no longer there? When he's no longer *anywhere*?'

'Well, I thought you liked volunteering there, setting up those board games for people,' he replied in a bored, flat tone. 'You've spent your Thursdays there for months.' He loosened his tie and pulled it off, crossing the kitchen to the fridge.

'Because it was time with my *dad*,' Cat responded sharply. 'Seriously, what—'

She stopped and bit her full bottom lip. It was a pointless conversation and she wasn't going to waste her energy on it. She released a long, slow breath.

'Did you make me anything to eat?' Greg asked, searching the fridge shelves for a second time.

Cat just stared at him, unsure whether the bubbling feeling in her core was because she wanted to scream, laugh or cry. In the end, she didn't do any of those things. And when she opened her mouth to speak, she was surprised at how calmly her next words came out.

'I want a divorce, Greg.'

'*What?*' He spun round, his attention now acutely focused on her.

'I said I want a divorce.'

As she finally let out what she'd been biting back for so long, Cat felt a wave of relief wash over her. When she'd made the decision to leave Greg, her father had broken his awful news before she'd had a chance to break hers. She'd decided, upon hearing that his condition was terminal, that she would stay quiet and keep up appearances until he'd passed. She couldn't let him depart this world worried about her and Orla's future. It had been better to pretend she was happy and secure in her marriage to Greg, and let him pass in peace. But he was gone now. And so was the last of her ability to pretend anymore.

'You must be joking,' Greg scoffed, looking incredulous and amused.

That look sparked a small flare of anger inside, and Cat clamped her teeth together. Who did he think he was, mocking her like that, after all he'd done?

'The only joke I can see right now is the fact I've stayed in this marriage so long,' she replied. 'I should have left you a long time ago. I should have left when you stopped showing me even the slightest element of care and respect, but I didn't. I stupidly stayed, thinking it was a phase. I put it down to work stress, for a while. Then I put it down to you finding it difficult, adjusting to fatherhood. I even thought maybe it was *me*, that I wasn't doing enough. But it wasn't any of that, was it? It was just you.' Cat looked at him tiredly, taking in the bleary grey-blue eyes, the stale smell of last night's alcohol and the rumpled shirt beneath his suit jacket, and wondered how she ever fell for the façade. 'It was you dropping the act and showing your real colours.'

Greg stared at her for a few moments before answering, his expression unreadable. 'You've had a long few days,' he surmised. 'This has all got to you more than we'd expected it to, that's all this is. Maybe I have been a bit distant lately, and we'll talk about that, but all the rest, that's all in your head, Catriona. This is just your grief talking. What you really need is to go to bed and sleep this off. Go head on upstairs for a rest, OK? And once you wake up with a clearer head, we'll forget this ever happened.'

'No,' Cat replied firmly. 'This isn't my grief, and I won't be swayed by your mind games anymore. I'm done. I was done a long time ago. This isn't a decision I've made lightly. I was ready to tell you back in the spring, but then Dad told us he was dying and I couldn't put that stress on him. So I decided to wait until he was gone, and now he is. This has been a long time coming, Greg. Surely even you can see that.'

Greg was frowning now, his gaze sharpening as he realised she meant business. 'I'm not playing mind games, Catriona. I'm simply trying to stop you making a huge mistake. Do you really want to throw away all we've got together for... well, for what, exactly? Is this really what you want to do to our daughter?'

'You mean the daughter you have practically nothing to do with? The one you have me keep out of your way six days of the week, barely interact with on the seventh and who you're only interested in when it's time to show off a trophy?' Cat asked sharply.

It was one of the most painful things she'd ever had to come to terms with, Greg's lack of interest in their child. His irritation whenever she sought out his attention. His refusal to help Cat with nappies or night feeds or meltdowns or pre-school runs. As a spoiled man-child, he had no interest in giving Orla any of the attention he believed should be solely spent on him. And it had utterly and completely broken Cat's heart.

A muscle in Greg's jaw twitched. 'Look, marriages go through rough patches,' he said, changing tack. 'They require a little more effort as time goes on. Effort and hard work and better communication.'

'Right.' Cat nodded slowly, as if considering his words. 'And which of those would you call Rachel, exactly? Is she the effort, work or communication that you've added to our marriage?'

Greg's face paled as Cat mentioned his young lover's name – a girl of no more than twenty, if that. God only knew where he'd picked her up. That was the only detail Cat didn't know, and at this point she didn't care enough to even ask.

He swallowed, his Adam's apple bobbing, before he spoke. 'Who? What are you talking about?'

'Oh *please*, save the pretence,' Cat told him, standing up

and pushing the chair back into place. 'I found your second phone months ago, and I followed up on all the details. Rachel Morris, the blonde *child* still at uni, studying media and film. The one you've been screwing for nearly a year. The one you went to stay with last night after leaving my father's wake.'

Cat crossed her arms defensively. Although she didn't love Greg anymore, Rachel's existence still stung. It still stung that no matter how hard she'd tried, Cat hadn't been enough. It still stung that the girl was so young. But most of all, it still stung to realise she'd been a fool, wasting so much of her life on this man.

'I—' Greg began.

'No, you know what, don't.' Cat halted him with her hand and shook her head. 'I can't. I don't have the energy for whatever excuse or argument you have. I just want you out.' She broke her gaze away and walked towards the doorway. 'Pack whatever you need for the next few days and leave. I'll send the rest on to you later. And just to be clear, I mean *today*. From tomorrow, you will no longer be welcome in this house ever again.' She glanced back at him one last time and saw the shock register on his face as he finally understood that she was serious. 'Goodbye, Greg.'

She wondered, as she made her way to the front door, whether he would try to fight for her. Fight for their marriage. But he didn't. And as she unlocked the car and cast her gaze up to the skies, she felt a little of the weight on her heart lift. She'd done it. She'd finally done it. From the end of this day, it would all be over. Greg and the dark shadow he'd brought into their home would be gone for good. And she and Orla could finally breathe and start living the brighter, happier lives they deserved.

THREE

Alex Capello sat behind the wide antique walnut desk that had once belonged to his father, and his grandfather before him, and thrummed his fingers on the red leather top. He watched his sister, Maria, pace the room. They were unmistakably siblings, even through the eyes of strangers. Alex had the same olive skin and naturally obsidian hair as his sister, although hers was now expertly streaked with rich caramels and golds, lightening it somewhat. They had the same straight nose and generous mouth, but where Maria's eyes were an unusually bright shade of hazel, Alex's were a deep brown, like their younger brother Antonio's.

Their large brown eyes were inherited from their mother, and the brothers also shared the strong jawline of their father, but other than this, they didn't look much alike at all. Of the two, Alex was taller and broader. At six foot four, he towered over most men, including Antonio, who stood at six one. They both worked out, but whilst Alex's muscles were large and obvious in his broad frame, Antonio's were lean and neat. Alex's face was more squared and Antonio's longer. If a stranger had been asked to guess *their* relationship, they might have been more likely to ask if they were cousins.

The three siblings ran the criminal firm their father had built and that they'd inherited when he died. But Maria's involvement was discreet, her presence in their ranks only known by those they truly trusted. She'd worked hard to become a barrister and to move up the social ladder. It had taken her years, but she'd infiltrated the circles of those with real political power, making genuine friends out of some of them and waiting with baited traps to force others, rather unwillingly, into her pocket. She couldn't be publicly associated with a criminal firm. Even if nothing was proved, mud like that would stick. And she couldn't afford to give any of those she'd blackmailed the chance to use her background against her. This was why she was so angry at Antonio now. He'd revealed her hand, used her to get himself out of that police station.

Maria took a long drag from her cigarette before blowing it out in a sharp, angry burst.

'He's getting too cocky, Alex,' she warned. '*Far* too cocky. He needs to be put on a leash for a while. No, actually, he's too *wild* for a leash. What *he* needs is a fucking *muzzle*.'

Alex sighed, unable to disagree with her on this point. Much as he loved their brother, Antonio had been pushing the limits to the extreme lately. On all fronts.

'I'll talk to him,' he assured her.

She turned away from the window and sat down on one of the stuffed leather armchairs flanking the room. 'Talking doesn't work with him, Alex. Not anymore.' Resting her head back, she rubbed her eyes with her free hand tiredly. 'If he's not poking whatever bears he can find with a pitchfork and putting *my* arse on the line in the process, he's off his nut on the gear and causing trouble with our dealers. Joe's had to calm down *two* of them already this month and pay them extra for their troubles.

If he carries on causing this much grief, *no one* is going to work for us. And then what?'

'Hey, Maria, don't stress, OK? Leave it with me. I'll make sure he stays away from our dealers moving forward,' Alex promised, already not relishing the task.

Antonio had been helping himself to the drugs they imported and sold on through a carefully cultivated network of dealers, more and more recently. Alex had been worried for a while that it was much more than just a sociable dip in their plentiful pool of narcotics. In fact, it was starting to look much more like a dark and gripping addiction problem. But Antonio didn't – or perhaps just refused to – see it that way. In his eyes, as he liked to tell anyone who cared to listen, he simply had *a nose for the good stuff*.

'Fine,' Maria agreed. 'But get that in hand *quickly*, Alex. Because he really will be the undoing of all of us soon if you don't. And I can't afford to keep stepping in to fix things. I got *far* too close to the fire, clearing up this last mess of his.' Her strikingly bright hazel eyes moved to meet his gaze, the warning in them clear.

Alex nodded. 'Is the grave filled in and sealed now?'

'It should be. I'll wait until tomorrow, then I'll go back and check. It's too soon today. There may still be a police presence around the graveyard, out of respect for his position,' Maria replied.

Alex nodded again.

A freelance photographer, who routinely sold his findings into several of London's smaller newspapers, had recently stumbled across one of their illegal operations and had taken it upon himself to get as many pictures as he could for both the press and police. Fortunately for the Capellos – and *unfortunately* for him – Antonio had caught him in the act and destroyed the evidence. From that point, it could have been a civil conversation in which both parties benefitted and walked away unscathed. He could have enjoyed a hefty payout and gone about his life with a wealth of powerful new friends, in return for no more than his silence. But the photographer decided to take things in a different direction. He'd told Antonio that he'd already uploaded most of the images to the cloud and that, the moment he could, he was going straight to the police.

Had Alex been informed, he would have taken over and tried to reason with the man, and the situation would have been dealt with quietly, whichever way it went. But Antonio had been as high as a kite, itching for somewhere to release his pent-up, drug-fuelled energy. So he took matters into his own hands. From the accounts later whispered to Alex and Maria by the men surrounding him that day, Antonio hadn't attempted to reason with the man at all. In fact, he hadn't said another word. He'd simply beaten him to death, partially with his own camera. It had been a mess on many levels, and Maria had had no choice but to step in.

John had just died, and as soon as the grave had been prepared for his funeral, she'd had some of their men dig a few feet deeper, in the dead of night, and bury the photographer there. No one would think to look for him under another body, in the graveyard. At least not without just cause. But it had been a tense few days as they waited, with the dead photographer's body, for the grave to be dug, and the police had started looking for him much sooner than they'd thought. Someone had told them he was missing and that he'd taken an interest in Antonio, and when some CCTV footage caught him heading Antonio's way the day he disappeared, that was when their brother had been arrested.

The sound of a car rolling up on the wide gravel drive pulled Alex's attention to the window, though his gaze almost instantly shot back to Maria when he realised who it was. She sat bolt upright, her hard gaze trained on the door.

'Try not to kill him *straightaway*,' Alex suggested casually.

'I can't promise anything,' she replied. Outwardly, her tone was calm, but he knew her better than to believe that.

The front door opened and shut, then a second later the door to the large office-cum-library swung open to reveal the source of all their current stresses. Antonio paused, looking at them both as if to assess their moods, then he slowly walked over and took a seat facing Maria, on the opposite side of the room. He leaned on the arm of the overly stuffed chair and rested his forehead on his index and middle finger, studying her with a thoughtful expression.

For a tense few seconds, there was silence, until finally Antonio broke it.

'Well, what did you expect me to do?' he asked, briefly lifting his palms to the sky with a shrug. 'Book myself a room at Belmarsh for the next twenty years at His Majesty's expense?'

'What I *expected*,' Maria shot back, 'was for you to be smart enough to ride out a simple fucking interrogation without dragging me into it and potentially destroying *everything* I've spent the last few years building. You were *never* in danger of getting done for that murder, Antonio; it was *dealt* with. You were clean. But then you pulled me out like some dodgy ace card, showing our hand to people we don't know and can't trust. It was *stupid* and *unnecessary*. How am I supposed to be seen as clean in a courtroom when you're outing me as dirtier than the floor of a fucking night bus on a weekend?'

'They pulled me into a *murder* investigation, Maria. For a man I *did murder*. They must have had something,' Antonio countered. 'I needed out, and you were my best bet.'

'They had *nothing!*' Maria cried. She let out a growl of frustration and pushed her hand back through her long thick hair.

Alex sat forward, aware of how close she was to *really* losing it. 'Antonio, all they had was footage of him heading in your general direction and that someone *thought* they'd heard the guy say your name.' He looked at his brother intently. 'Even if they'd searched, they'd have found nothing. Everything was burned. The body was gone, the camera destroyed. Bill Hanlon scrubbed all trace of the images from the cloud. You were in the clear. And *then* you went and used Maria's position to get yourself out of there. If they weren't sure you did it before, they sure as hell are now. And that's gonna sting, so they're going to be watching you very closely now.'

He lifted his eyebrows accusingly, anger beginning to colour his tone. 'And hopefully the threats we left them with mean they'll steer clear, but if not, if it ever gets out that Maria used her influence to illegally pull you out of the line of fire for a murder charge, she's burned. Her career is over, our sway with council members and politicians is gone, and as this house of cards tumbles, she could very seriously be facing time. And we ain't talking a slap on the wrist; they'll eat her alive. Publicly. 'Cause they don't like being reminded that people like us sometimes slip into positions of real legal power. So you've *royally* fucked up here.'

Antonio thrummed his fingers on the edge of the chair and exhaled slowly. Alex could see, by the grim look on his face, that he'd truly had no idea the extent of the trouble he'd caused. But that was the problem with Antonio. He'd always had a tendency to act first and think later.

The three siblings had run the family firm together since their father had died, a decade before. It was a thriving firm in North London that dealt in cocaine, counterfeit money and various other criminal enterprises that linked in to their main endeavours. They were also known, through the murky depths of the criminal underworld, as *solution men*. This meant a vast variety of things, but it all came down to one general need from their clients – an inability to solve a tricky issue themselves. Most of the time, no one ever heard the details of these jobs. All that was shared between people was that however impossible a job was, if the Capellos took it on, they would pull it off with finesse and could be trusted to keep the secret.

The leadership rankings of the Capello family business were a complex situation, the view of which changed, depending on who was watching. In public, the two brothers were the faces of the firm, Maria choosing to stay hidden as she climbed the ranks of the legal world. Behind closed doors, the three siblings were equal leaders officially. But in the unspoken reality, it was Alex and Maria who their men looked to, first, for leadership. Mainly because of situations like this, when Antonio's hot-headedness took over ahead of all reason or logic.

Antonio cast his gaze downwards with a slow nod. 'I'm sorry, Maria. I really thought they had me. I didn't know Bill had wiped those pictures.'

Maria tutted, her anger not fully abated just yet. 'You really think I'd have left out something so vital? *Me?* Really, Antonio?'

Annoyance flashed over Antonio's face. 'I've said I'm sorry, Maria, what more do you want from me?'

'Several things actually,' she shot back, glancing pointedly over at Alex.

He resisted the urge to sigh, instead giving her a slight shake of the head. This wasn't the right time to talk about the drugs. Antonio could only take so much berating in one go before his quick temper would take over.

'Oh, I see,' Antonio said, his gaze cooling as he stared across the room at Maria. 'You're after a fight. Well, come on then. Let's fucking go.'

'Hey,' Alex intervened sharply. 'Watch yourself.' He glared at Antonio, who raised his hands in surrender and settled back in his chair. Antonio could talk however he wanted to those outside of the family, but when it came to their sister or mother, Alex wouldn't tolerate disrespect from anyone. Family or not.

Maria returned Antonio's look, still clearly furious, but she swallowed whatever she'd been about to say and looked away to the window instead.

Alex heaved a silent sigh of relief. The last thing they needed was to be squabbling between themselves. They had bigger things to think about. 'Look, it is what it is now. We just need to stay sharp and keep a low profile for a bit. See how—'

But the rest of his sentence was cut short as a resounding crash sounded through from the hallway. A loud scream swiftly followed, and Alex jumped up, his blood freezing in his veins.

'What the fuck is that?' Antonio breathed.

Alex grabbed the sharp steel letter opener on his desk and ran for the door. He had no idea what he was running towards. In their game, it could be anything. Or anyone. But he had no time to try and figure it out because that scream had been their mother's.

FOUR

For the first time in months, Cat actually slept through the night. She still didn't feel hugely energised, as the weight of her grief still hung over her like a thick, sodden cape. But she'd definitely felt something different when she'd woken up today. Not happiness exactly, but something good. Something that glimmered through the dark clouds she'd been living with for so long. Something she faintly recognised as... hope.

She'd played with Orla for a while after breakfast, then dropped her off at pre-school with a big smile and a hug before driving determinedly towards her father's old offices. Today was the start of a whole new chapter in her and Orla's story. It was a fresh new beginning, just the two of them, without the shadow of Greg hanging over them at every turn. Cat knew already that he wouldn't bother much, if at all, with Orla, now they'd split. He hadn't bothered with her much while they'd been together.

He'd been uninterested in Orla as a baby, barely helping Cat with their newborn, even as she'd lain recovering from an emergency C-section. As Orla had grown, so had Greg's annoyance whenever she made a noise or got in his way. And because of how detached he'd remained, despite the fact he was her father, Orla wouldn't miss him. She was too used to him not being around or, when he was around, being ignored. Cat couldn't decide whether she was saddened or glad about that. At least his absence wouldn't cause her pain. But Orla had deserved so much more from Greg. They both had.

Cat pulled into her father's old parking space at the front of his building, and her fingers momentarily tightened around the steering wheel as her eyes rested on the little plaque with his name on.

Richard Donahue, CEO

The letters began to blur and move as tears filled her eyes, but she quickly blinked them away. Not today. She wasn't going to cry today.

Stepping out of the car, Cat straightened the smart jacket she'd pulled from the back of her wardrobe and made her way to the wide double glass doors that fronted the building.

As she walked, memories of being here with her father flooded back and she had to work to keep her composure. The world just felt so empty without him in it. Now that he'd gone, Cat was painfully aware of how alone she was, other than Orla. And it really was just the two of them now. They had no one else. Her mother had died when she'd been a baby, and she had no other family. Her friends had all become distant over the last few years too. Sure, they'd catch up now and then. Maybe once or twice a year. But they'd all moved on, their lives going in different directions, and it had been difficult to stay close. Cat missed them, but she understood. That was just how life was, and she'd still always had her dad. He'd always been her very best friend. He'd been her village. And so the jagged, aching hole that he'd left behind in her life seemed almost all consuming at times.

Cat lifted her chin bravely as she entered the building and walked across to the security desk with a small smile for the guard sat behind it. He looked surprised to see her and smiled back, but with a strangely uncomfortable look in his eyes for someone who'd known her for the best part of twenty years.

'Hi, Caleb, how are you?' she asked, stopping as she reached the tall, white stone counter. 'How's the family?'

'They're good thanks, Cat. All good.' He scratched the back of his neck and cast his eyes away from hers. 'That was a beautiful wake for your dad by the way. He'd have been real proud.'

'Thanks,' she said, her smile faltering. 'Still doesn't feel real that he's gone. I know he got really sick these last few months, but I keep feeling like he's just going to pop up somewhere like he used to, you know? Full of life and laughing at his own jokes.'

Caleb chuckled. 'He was a real character, that's for sure.'

'He was.' Cat looked past him to the lifts. 'I'm going to start going through everything today, work out what I need to do to make sure there's minimum disruption here while I figure things out. Is Jeanie in?'

'Er, thing is...' Caleb trailed off with an awkward wince. 'I, er, well, I've been told I can't let you up there.'

Cat blinked, unsure if she'd just heard him correctly. 'I'm sorry, *what*?'

'I'm so sorry, Cat. I feel awful saying this to you – this is your family business. It's – it's... well, it should be *yours*.' He sighed a deeply unhappy sigh and fiddled with a button on his jacket nervously.

Cat frowned. 'Caleb, what are you talking about? It *is* mine. Dad left everything to me. What's going on?'

'I really don't know,' he told her, shaking his head slowly. 'We all got pulled into a meeting last night, were told the company's been left to Greg and that from now on you weren't to be let on the premises.'

'What?' Cat uttered, horrified.

This couldn't be true. It just *couldn't*. Her dad would never have done that. He'd given Greg a job here, yes, but it was purely because he was her husband, not because he'd been prepping him to take over. Greg was a marketing manager, for Christ's sake, not a groundbreaking technological engineer like her father – or even a good business manager! Not that *she* was either of those things, but her father had prepared her for what to do if this day ever came, and he trusted her to make sure the right people were in place to carry his work forward. It was his legacy. It was everything he'd built up to pass down to her. He'd told her that, more than once. No, he would never have handed his company over to Greg. There had to have been some mistake.

Caleb grimaced apologetically. 'I spoke up, but Greg insisted he's calling the shots now and said anyone who lets you in gets fired. Then Jeanie backed him up, said it was legit, so I don't know *what's* going on. And I would let you in anyway, Cat, you know I would, but—'

'No. No, it's fine, Caleb,' Cat interjected, halting him with her hand as she looked worriedly at the lifts behind him. 'You can't risk your job. You have bills to pay and kids to feed. It's ridiculous that you've even been put in this position.'

Caleb opened his mouth as if he wanted to say more, but then shut it again with a defeated expression.

Biting her lip, Cat backed away from the desk. 'Honestly, don't worry. This isn't your fault. I'm going to straighten this out.'

She walked back out of the building and over to her car, trying to work out what was going on. Of all the things she'd expected from Greg, post break-up, this certainly hadn't made the list. Why was he acting like this? Pretending to take over and kicking her out of her own father's building? Well, *her* building now. How long did he think he could keep that up? As soon as she showed everyone the will, this ridiculous game would be over. So what was he playing at? Was he panicking because he thought she was going to fire him? She looked across to his parking space and frowned when she found it empty. Where was he?

'Cat!'

She turned at the sound of someone calling her voice and saw Jeanie, the woman who'd been her father's more senior executive assistant, running towards her. Jeanie glanced back at the building anxiously as she slowed to a stop.

'Hey, Jeanie,' Cat began. 'Don't worry, I'm going to sort this all out—'

'No, Cat, you don't understand,' Jeanie said in a low, worried tone. 'I don't know what happened or when things changed, but it's true. It's all been left to Greg. He showed me the new will, and it states very clearly that everything has been left to him.'

'*What?*' Cat exclaimed. 'No. Dad would never...'

'I know – I thought the same,' Jeanie said hurriedly. 'But it's there in black and white. His signature's on it.'

Cat paled. 'No, it has to be a fake.'

Jeanie gave her a look of helpless pity. 'I wish I could agree with you, I really do. But I know your dad's signature better than anyone, and I went over and over it...' She trailed off, briefly raising her arms and then dropping them to her sides. 'I'm so sorry. It looks legit. However it came about, your dad made this new will. And...' She hesitated and bit her lip. 'Look, I wasn't supposed to tell you, but I feel like I should. It's *everything,* Cat. Not just the business. Your dad's house was obviously sold to pay for his care, but *your* house is still company owned.'

'*My* house?' Cat asked, her heart beginning to pound painfully against the wall of her chest. Her eyes darted back to the empty space where Greg's car should be. 'Shit,' she breathed. 'My *house!*'

Without pausing to say goodbye, she turned and ran to her

car, realising far too late *exactly* where her soon-to-be ex-husband would be.

FIVE

Maria exited the Royal Free Hospital with a deep sigh and walked quickly through the car park to where Antonio was helping their mother, Sophia, into his car.

'You'll be OK taking her home by yourself?' Maria checked, lifting one perfectly arched dark eyebrow in question.

'Will I be *OK*?' he repeated. 'Funnily enough, Maria, I have actually driven a car with a passenger before.'

Maria tutted. 'I just mean getting her out and settled the other end.'

'We'll be fine, Maria. Don't fuss,' their mother replied, waving her good hand dismissively.

Sophia Capello had broken her arm in a fall down the stairs the day before and had badly sprained her ankle along with it. This was what had prompted the scream that had sent the three of them rushing out of the library. They'd spent the night with her in hospital waiting for X-rays and treatment and appointments with the consultant, ignoring her near constant protests at being kept waiting for so long, until half an hour ago, when they'd finally been given the all-clear to leave.

Sophie had been carrying down the bedding from all five of

the bedrooms in the house when she'd fallen – most of which didn't even need washing, as no one had slept in the other four for a very long time. Her children had all flown the nest to their own homes long ago, but they all still gathered at the large family home each day, keeping the opulent office-cum-library as a hub for the firm, which was why they'd luckily been around when she'd fallen.

Sophia leaned back out of the car and looked up at the pair of them. 'I'll have to just throw together a carbonara tonight with some salad. I won't have time now to go—'

'No, you bloody won't!' Maria declared. 'You've broken your arm clean through, Mum! You need to lay off the cooking and cleaning for a while.'

Despite the fact they were grown up and living elsewhere, Sophia still cooked for them all, most days, unable to shake off her need to mother them completely.

Antonio looked disappointed. 'Well, if she feels up to it—' he began.

'*No,*' Maria insisted, shooting him a glare. 'Mum, you've got one good arm and you need it to hold your crutch to help you stay off your ankle. You can't be knocking around the kitchen *cooking.*'

'Well, who *else* is going to do it?' Sophia demanded. 'Maria, you all need to eat – and *not* that cardboard shit you can get delivered; you need *real* food. And before you offer to do it, *don't.* You know you can't. You're too busy.' Sophia gave her a stern look. 'This is nothing. It will just slow me down a bit, that's all.'

Maria sighed and shook her head. 'It's not nothing, Mum. Look, I'll get someone in to help you for a while with the cooking and the housework. Just until you're healed up.' She watched her mother bristle instantly and suppressed another sigh.

'*You will not!*' Sophia declared.

Maria and Antonio exchanged a grim glance, then he leaned in and pulled Sophia's belt around her with a smile. 'We'll talk about it later, yeah?' he offered.

'Over my dead body,' Sophia spat back, looking absolutely outraged by the idea.

'Nah, just over a cup of tea,' he replied, shutting the door before she could reply. He turned to face Maria. 'She'll come around.'

'She'll have to,' Maria said with a shrug. 'I'll look into it later, see if I can find someone.'

'Someone *trustworthy*,' Antonio said pointedly.

'Obviously,' she replied, already pondering the dilemma in her head as she bit her bottom lip. 'Leave it with me. I'll sort it.'

He nodded and walked around to the other side of the car, unbuttoning his suit jacket before slipping into the driver's seat.

Maria's phone rang and she glanced at the screen before answering. 'Yes?' She started walking towards her car.

'Those tourists that ended up near the compound. They checked out,' a gruff voice told her.

'You're absolutely sure?' Maria queried, glancing over her shoulder to check she was definitely alone.

'Yeah,' he confirmed. 'We followed 'em back and listened in for a couple of days. Clean and clueless.'

'And they're not curious? They don't feel the burning need to find out what they stumbled across?' Maria pressed.

'Nah. They believed the farm story. Ain't talked about it again.'

Maria slid into the driver's seat of her BMW and rested back in the seat for a moment, gently biting one neat red nail. 'Double the watch for now, just in case. And extend the perimeter. We don't need any other lost tourists driving up the track, wondering what we're doing.'

'Where do you want me after that?' he asked.

Watching her brother's car pull out of the car park into the stream of traffic beyond, Maria momentarily pressed her teeth down harder on her nail. 'I want you to follow Antonio for a while.'

'Antonio?' he repeated.

'Yeah,' she replied decidedly. 'Discreetly. Just keep an eye on him for a few days and report back to me on what he's doing. He's a loose cannon right now, and I can't afford any more fuck-ups off the back of this last one. None of us can.'

'Got it.'

The line went dead and Maria slipped the phone back into her bag. Another shrill ringing noise almost instantly began chiming from her handbag, but this was from a different phone. Her official phone. The one people on the legal side of her life had the number for. She looked at the screen and silenced it, ignoring the call. She didn't have time to talk right now. There were other, more urgent, matters to take care of. And her first port of call would be the graveyard to make sure the dead body she'd hidden there was still safely buried, never to be found.

SIX

Cat pulled up sharply outside her house, her mouth gaping as she took in the scene in front of her. Two large suitcases and a backpack were stacked together on the drive, behind Greg's car. A broad, burly man in a multi-pocketed navy boiler suit was kneeling at her open front door, a toolkit next to him. As she got out of the car, he stood up and dusted off his knees, then began packing up his things.

'Er, hello?' Cat called, hurrying up the drive. 'Who are you?'

The man sighed and muttered something under his breath that sounded a lot like *oh, here we go*. But he didn't answer her straightaway, and this just added to Cat's increasing sense of panic.

'Hello? Did you hear me?' she asked, her tone a little sharper now. 'I asked who you are.' She stopped just short of the front porch and looked around for Greg.

'I'm just the locksmith,' the man finally answered.

'Right, so why are you here?' she asked, a sickly feeling beginning to roll around the pit of her stomach.

'To do a job,' he replied bluntly. 'Look, if you've got any

questions, you're best off asking this guy. He's the one who hired me.'

He gestured to the open doorway, and Cat looked up to see Greg appear with a cold glint in his eyes.

'Greg, what the *hell* are you doing?' she demanded. Although she had an awful feeling that she already knew.

'I'm securing my house,' he responded in a flat, dead tone.

He stared at her with an equally empty expression, and Cat felt a sharp shiver run down her spine.

'This is *my* house, Greg,' she insisted, managing to sound much stronger than she really felt. 'Mine and Orla's. It's not yours – it's not even *ours*, and you know it. My dad bought me this house.'

He'd gifted her this house just before she'd married Greg, and in the carefully strategic way that he always did everything, he'd bought it under the company's name, rather than putting it into hers. It was supposed to have protected her. She was the only heir to the company, and if anything ever happened between her and Greg – as it had now – it should have meant her and Orla's home was protected from him. That's why none of this made any sense. What should have been guaranteed security was now turning into the complete opposite. This whole situation was becoming the worst nightmare imaginable.

'No.' Greg sauntered towards her, taking the set of keys from the tradesman's outstretched hand as he passed. 'The house was part of the *company*, and, as I'm sure you're aware after your visit to the offices just now, the company has been left to *me*.'

Tears stung Cat's eyes as she stared at Greg's cold, mocking smile. 'No. My dad wouldn't do that. I don't know how you've done this, but I *know* it's not legitimate. This is my *home*. Orla's home.' She wiped the tears away with the back of her hand, her mind reeling. 'Seriously, you need to stop this. Just give me those keys and get out of my way, Greg. *Now.*'

'Not a chance,' he said in a low, defiant tone. 'You were quite happy to do this to me last night, weren't you? Happy to cast me out and leave me with nothing. So I'm returning the favour. This is no more than you tried to do to me.'

The locksmith bowed his head uncomfortably as he walked past and hurriedly left.

'Greg, this is *absurd*,' Cat cried. 'This is *my house*. This is Orla's *home*, and she's three years old, for God's sake! Are you really going to do this to your own daughter?'

Greg turned away with a dismissive wave of the hand. 'She'll be fine. I'll pay you maintenance like every other cast-off father does. What you do with it and how you provide for her going forward is your own problem.' He walked back to the door and reached inside. 'And if you wanted more than this, you should have thought of that *before* trying to throw me out last night.' He walked to the pile of bags on the drive with a smaller suitcase and one of Orla's backpacks in his hand. '*You* set the bar. I'm simply playing the game you started, except I've won. Which you don't like, of course, but that's just tough luck. You should never play a game you aren't prepared to lose.'

He threw Orla's backpack to her, and she quickly wrapped her arms around it as it hit her stomach with a thud. She took a half step back in shock as Greg marched past her to the pile of suitcases and dumped the one in his hand next to it.

Cat's heart beat faster in her chest as she looked back at the house. He really meant this. He was turning her away from their home and had changed the locks. But it was *her house*. Everything she owned was in there. Everything of Orla's was in there too. God only knew what Greg had packed, but it certainly wouldn't be everything she needed – she was sure of it. She swallowed, trying to think.

'This is ridiculous. I'm going inside.'

Cat tried to walk around Greg, but he darted in front of her, blocking her path.

'Not a chance,' he told her firmly.

Cat frowned and tried to move around him again, but he grabbed her roughly by the forearm.

'Ouch! Greg, stop it!'

'*No*,' he snarled. 'You aren't stepping foot back in that house again. And go ahead by the way – call the police,' he added, already a step ahead of her as she opened her mouth to suggest just that. 'I'll simply show them the will. It's my legal right to decline you access. After all, this isn't a marital property. It's owned by the company. The company *I* now own.'

A slow, cruel smile spread across his face, and Cat felt her insides flash white hot. She took a step back and shook her head.

'I want to see the will,' she demanded. 'I don't believe you. I don't believe any of this.'

'Yes, I thought you'd say that. Here.' Greg reached into his inside jacket pocket and pulled out a rolled-up A4 envelope. He passed it to her with a triumphant flourish. 'I made you a copy. I'm sorry to say— actually, no, I'm not,' he corrected. 'I'm *not* sorry to say that your father clearly had a change of heart recently and had this drawn up. Maybe he saw how useless you really are. How weak and selfish and *utterly* inadequate. I don't know.' He shrugged. 'All I know is that he changed his plans. And you could have remained part of things, but as of last night you lost that privilege. So collect the bags I very kindly packed for you and get off my property.' He leaned in closer, his expression hard and cold. '*Now*.'

Icy shock flooded Cat's body as she realised he was deadly serious. Her hands began to shake as they clutched Orla's backpack a little tighter, and she suddenly felt light-headed. She blinked and tried to regulate her breath – tried to clear her head. Because she needed to work out what to do to stop this nightmare from going on any further. But before she could say or do anything, Greg turned and walked back to the house, then slammed the door firmly closed behind him.

SEVEN

Alex cast his eyes over the imposing front of the elegant boutique hotel nestled between two others on the long sweeping road in Paddington. White pillars stood proudly either side of the steps leading up to the glass front door, and the hotel emblem was emblazoned on the red-and-gold welcome mat.

Antonio rounded the car and stood beside him, letting out a low whistle. 'I'd bet this place brings in a pretty penny.'

'I'd bet you're right,' Alex agreed.

They walked inside and were directed to a small, empty lounge opulently decorated in muted golds and browns, with a nod towards vintage art deco. Piano music played quietly in the background, and Alex clocked the subtly placed sound system speakers. He also clocked the discreet camera in the corner of the room, filing that information away for another time. He wandered to the front window, glancing out at his car as he unbuttoned his suit jacket.

'It's well wired,' Antonio mumbled quietly.

'Mm,' Alex conceded. His brother was talking about the camera system.

Neither of them knew what this potential job was going to entail yet. The meeting had been arranged under a secure veil of secrecy, through a chain of people who would have vetted the person asking for the meeting, to ensure they weren't undercover law enforcement. All they had been told was the client's last name, and the time and the place to meet them. Other than that, the only thing they knew for sure was that this person had a problem that needed fixing – and the money to pay for it.

Alex looked at his watch. 'I hope this don't go on too long. I've got to get back.'

'I hope we're dealing with a fit lonely heiress myself,' Antonio answered. 'Maybe she needs someone to help her test the soundproofing in these rooms.'

Alex tutted. 'Keep your focus above your belt for once, would ya?' He glanced at the ceiling. 'And this ain't the kind of place that soundproofs rooms.'

The sound of approaching footsteps stopped Antonio from replying, and they both turned to see a short, slim man in his thirties enter the room. Antonio sighed, clearly disappointed. The man smiled as he approached them, the action creeping rather than spreading across his face, and Alex felt an instant inexplicable wave of dislike flood through him.

'Mr Capello?' the man checked.

Alex nodded, no trace of his feelings in his expression. 'Alex. And this is my brother Antonio. You must be Mr Sinclair.'

'Yes. Justin. Thank you for meeting me. Won't you take a seat?' He gestured to one of the beige sofas either side of a square coffee table. 'I'll order us some tea.' His genteel voice was thin and reedy, and somehow tinged with an arrogance it didn't sound strong enough to carry.

Alex sat down and shook his head. 'We ain't here for tea. How did you hear about us? And what's this problem you need sorting?'

Antonio sat down next to Alex as the other man took a seat opposite them both. Justin looked put out by Alex's curt response to his offer of tea, but after drawing in a deep breath, he crossed one leg over the other and began talking.

'Well, the crux of it is that I need someone taken care of. And when I approached an old associate who I thought might be able to help, he introduced me to someone else that he uses to do his... let's say *murky* work. That gentleman told me that he knew of some very effective *solution men* and that he could access the channels that would lead to them. Or to *you*, I should say. And here we are.' Justin spread his arms, and his grin momentarily widened.

'What do you mean – *specifically* – when you say you want someone taken care of?' Alex asked.

'Oh, you know,' Justin replied with an awkward scoff. '*Taken care of*. Ousted. Offed. However you want to put it.'

Antonio leaned in and gave him a hard stare, causing the other man to blink and pull back a little. 'We need to hear you say it,' he growled. 'Very clearly. So there can be no misunderstanding what you mean.'

Justin cleared his throat, eyeing them both warily. 'OK, fine. If we *must* be so vulgar. I want him killed. OK? Is that satisfactory for you?'

He'd lowered his voice and glanced towards the archway that led back through to reception, but he hadn't bothered to look at the cameras, Alex noted. They must not record audio.

'Why do you want this person killed?' Antonio asked.

Justin hesitated. 'Does it matter? I'll pay you whatever you want.'

'Yes, it does,' Alex replied, his tone low and sharp. 'We need to know who and why, and everything else of importance about the situation before we'll consider taking it on.'

Justin shifted uncomfortably in his seat. 'OK. It's the owner of this hotel. I, er – well, I just need him out of my way. That's all there is to it really.'

Alex narrowed his gaze. 'Is this a fucking joke to you?' He stood up and towered over the other man, anger suddenly clouding his features. 'Do you really think you can summon people like us and then give us the fucking runaround with the details?' He leaned over the quivering man with a dark glare. 'You can either answer the question properly, and in detail, or call this off if you've realised you don't have the balls for it. I don't care which, but you have exactly five seconds to decide. And if you *don't* decide, then we'll show you exactly what happens when someone wastes our fucking time. Do you understand me?'

Justin nodded hurriedly. 'Y-Yes. I'm sorry. I didn't mean to offend. I, er... I think we got off on the wrong foot.' He cleared his throat again and tugged at the collar of his shirt. 'My father owns this hotel, along with two others. I *was* to inherit them when he died. That was always the plan, but recently he told me he intends to change his will and cut me off.'

'Why?' Alex broke in.

Justin's pale cheeks flushed pink. 'He found out I owed a friend some money. Caught me trying to pay it back out of the business. It, well, it was a *lot* of money. A bet gone wrong. We'd been out at the casino, there had been a lot of champagne...' He sighed. 'I got a bit brave and it didn't pay off. My friend had to foot the bill.'

'Well, I can see why he would be annoyed, but it seems a bit of an escalation to jump from that to will changes and murder,' Alex replied. He frowned and leaned forward, lacing his fingers together.

'Yes, well. You don't know my father. Nothing is more important to him than his precious hotels,' Justin said bitterly. He looked towards the window for a few seconds, his eyes unfocused. 'I'm not prepared to lose a future I've more than earned because of the stubbornness of one bitter old man. I need him gone before he gets round to changing the will. He hasn't yet, but that's only because our solicitor is out of the country for a month. So I know it might sound mercenary, taking him out before he has the chance to screw me, but the stakes are too high to mess around.'

Alex looked at Antonio, who raised his eyebrows and blew out a long, slow breath, clearly on the same page. It was cold. Very cold. This was the man's *father* they were talking about. But business was business. They were in the business of solving dirty problems, and Justin had a dirty problem that needed solving. The only real question left to be answered was whether or not it was a job worth taking.

Antonio cleared his throat and sat forward. 'How exactly do you intend to pay us, if you're so deep in debt?'

'I'd pay you after you've completed the job of course. Like any other contractor.' Justin shrugged as though this was a ludicrous question.

'No,' Alex replied firmly. 'We'd expect at least fifty per cent of the payment prior to carrying out the job. The rest upon completion.'

Justin ran a hand back through his floppy rust-coloured hair. 'How much are we talking?'

'That depends,' Alex replied. 'We'd need to scope it out, work out how easy it would be to get to him.'

'It would be very easy,' Justin said hurriedly. 'I could get you into his house when he's alone. He lives by himself and I have a key. It's on the edge of a village, no other houses around it, so no one to see you.'

'It also depends on how we carry it out. Whether we make it look like a suicide or an accident, or a natural death. Whether or not we need to dispose of the body,' Antonio added.

'There are lots of things to consider. Not least the risk we would be taking ourselves,' Alex finished.

'I think suicide would be a good option,' Justin mused. 'He's been lonely since my mother passed, so it wouldn't be beyond the realms of imagination. Or maybe it would be best to make it look like a heart attack. Less chance of it looking suspicious, I imagine.'

'In that case, we'd need poison. A very strong and very specific type of poison that wouldn't show up in a toxicology report. Or that, if it did, could be passed off as nothing,' Alex replied. 'There's only one person in the UK who can get hold of that kind of poison at short notice.'

'Who's that? I don't really want the information I've shared with you being passed along to other people,' Justin said in a reluctant tone. 'The smaller the circle, the better.'

'We completely agree,' Antonio told him. 'We never tell the Viper what we need it for, and she never asks.'

'The Viper?' Justin cocked his eyebrow. 'And a woman. How interesting. I like meeting interesting people.'

'Trust me, you wouldn't want to meet this one,' Alex told him. 'No one, even in our circles, knows who she is. There are middlemen who carry out the exchanges, and no one gets past them. She's simply known for being able to produce poisons that aren't available anywhere else. We don't pry into her business; she don't pry into ours. That's the deal. So your secrets are safe. But she *is* expensive.'

Justin sighed, sounding bored. 'Fine. Whatever. What's the price?'

Alex bit his top and bottom lips together as he contemplated it for a moment. Out of the corner of his eye, he saw Antonio's hand stretch out on his leg then casually tap three of his fingers against it. The action was slight, unnoticeable to anyone else. But Alex knew what his brother was trying to share. Five and three. Eight. He wanted Alex to ask for eighty grand. That was too much money for a man who was, by his own admission, in considerable debt, to produce. Alex shifted his own flattened hand slightly sideways, conveying his disagreement. He heard Antonio sigh slightly.

'Where are the other two hotels?' Alex asked, an idea forming.

'Nearby,' Justin replied. 'You can find them online, under The Sinclair Group.'

Alex did so, a silence falling over the room as he scanned the details of the three luxurious-looking boutique hotels. 'How much money, realistically, can you get together as a down payment?' he eventually asked.

He could sense, rather than see, Antonio's frown. This was not a question they'd usually ask. They were always very firm on the terms of payment. But there was a unique opportunity to be taken here, and Alex was suddenly very interested in seeing whether it could be viable.

Justin made a sound of reluctance and pulled a pained expression. 'Maybe ten grand. But that would be at a push. Whatever your price is, though, I will give you the rest in *full*, the *second* I inherit.'

Alex nodded. They wouldn't usually even entertain such a low sum for something like this. He scratched the slowly appearing five o'clock shadow on his usually clean-shaven chin.

'If you choose to go ahead, we'll take the ten grand and carry out the job. Then when it's over, you'll sign thirty per cent of the hotel chain over to us as payment.'

'*What?*' Justin cried, his eyes bulging out of his sallow face. He let out a short, sharp laugh. 'You're not serious?' He moved his wide gaze back and forth between them both. 'You *are* serious. *Jesus Christ*. No. Absolutely not. That's preposterous. No. Name your *monetary* price and I'll pay it, but these hotels are mine. This is my *family business*.'

Alex had to hide a smile of amusement at the emphasis that this cold lizard of a man put on *family*. He wasn't so hung up on family when it came to his father.

'That's the price, Justin. You can take it or leave it. And once we have partial ownership, we'll take over a number of rooms – permanently. Let's call it owner residency.'

Justin's face was now turning an alarming shade of red, and his chest puffed out as he pulled himself upright and inhaled deeply. 'This hotel will not be owned by *anyone* other than me. Now, I'm serious. Name your *real* price.'

'This ain't a negotiation, Justin,' Alex reminded him, his expression cold as he held the other man's gaze. 'You want our services, that's the price. If it's too steep for you, that's fine.' He shrugged. 'We'll be off. We have other clients to see.'

He shifted forward in his seat, but Justin shot a hand out to stop him.

'No, wait!' He sighed and rubbed his forehead, looking deeply unhappy now. 'OK. OK, fine. But we'll have to talk about the rooms. The whole—'

'I don't think you understand,' Alex cut in, his voice as hard as steel and his brown eyes flashing with a warning. 'I've named our price, and when the job's complete, we *will* collect. Including the rooms. *You* need *us*. We don't need you. And if I were you, I'd make sure *now*, before we go any further, that you are absolutely OK with this arrangement. Because double-crossing the hit men you've hired to kill someone else would be a very, *very* bad idea.'

Justin's face paled to a pallid grey. He ran his tongue along his bottom lip and then nodded. 'I'll give you what you've asked for.'

Alex nodded. 'Ten grand upfront. Cash, unmarked notes, brown envelope, by tomorrow evening. We'll send someone here to collect. If the cash is here, we go ahead. If not, we'll assume you decided against using our services.' He stood up and buttoned his jacket.

Antonio stood up beside him. 'We'll also need the address and the key to the house. We'll need to do surveillance for at least a week before we can carry out the hit. Take this number.' He flicked a card out from his pocket and handed it over as Justin stood up to see them out. 'Buy a burner with no access to the internet and a no-trace SIM card, then drop call me so I have the number. We may need to contact you for more information.'

'Right, yes. G-Got it,' Justin stuttered as they walked out into the foyer.

'Before we go, is there anything else we need to know?' Alex asked, turning to meet the other man's eyes. 'Anything at all? Any possible complications, or anything you haven't told us about the situation?'

Justin looked away and shook his head. 'No. Nothing.'

'Alright then.' Alex stared at him for a moment longer, his dislike for the man intensifying. 'Let's go,' he said quietly to Antonio.

They walked out onto the street, and Alex rubbed his hands together as the frosty air nipped at his bare skin.

'What you thinking?' Antonio asked, walking round to the passenger side of the car. 'What's all that about the hotel rooms?'

Alex unlocked it then slipped into the driver's seat, turning on the engine as they both closed their doors against the cold.

'The funny money. It's getting too suss, everyone coming in and out of that warehouse. It's only a matter of time before we have to move it again.' Alex leaned back against the headrest and relaxed his elbow on the car door, looking back out to the front of the hotel. Their counterfeit money operation was doing well. So well they'd had to expand it. But expansion came with its own set of issues. 'People are starting to wonder why there's so much activity in what should just be a storage unit. But with a hotel, people come in and out all the time. There's natural traffic. Even the staff don't need to know. They're used to regulars and long-term clients at a place like this. No one would think anything of our guys coming and going, so long as they dress inconspicuously. The rooms are private. And *warm*. No risk of the plates getting too cold in the winter.'

Antonio squinted up at the building. 'How d'you think we're gonna get the machinery in? They ain't exactly made of fucking marshmallows.'

Alex tilted his head in acknowledgement. 'It'll be a ball-ache, but it's doable. There are ground-floor rooms.' He nodded towards the windows. 'Long as we cover them up while we're moving them so no one sees.'

'And you really trust this guy enough to keep this kind of secret?' Antonio asked sceptically.

'No. But I trust that he's smart enough to know that if we go down, we'd take him right down with us, and to know that he wouldn't last two fucking minutes in prison,' Alex replied. He pulled away from the kerb. 'And *that's* our insurance.'

* * *

As the brothers drove away from the hotel, neither of them noticed the black car with the tinted windows pull out behind them from a few spaces back. Neither of them saw the thickset bald man behind the wheel frowning darkly as he took down their number plate or were aware of the call he placed as they turned the corner.

'I'm following them now,' he said, his voice deep and guttural.

'Good. Stay on them,' came the reply through the car speakers. 'Get everything you can on them.'

'Oh, I will, boss,' the man replied darkly. 'You can count on that.'

EIGHT

After Greg had disappeared behind her front door, locking her and their daughter out of the only home Orla had ever known, Cat had slowly picked up the bags he'd dumped on the drive and placed them in the back of her car. At least he hadn't taken that. Well, he hadn't taken it *yet*. At some point, he was bound to realise that even her car was paid for through her father's company. *His*, she corrected mentally. According to the will he'd thrust in her hand, it was *his* now.

She'd driven around blindly for a while, not paying any attention to where she was going as she thought over her very limited options. Eventually she'd found herself back at the graveyard and had walked tiredly to the bench nearest her father's grave, slumping down heavily. She pulled out the will and read it over and over, trying to make sense of it all. But no matter how many times her eyes scanned the militant lines of black ink, she couldn't. It was crazy. Her father would *never* do this to her and Orla. It was fake. It had to be. No matter how good the forgery of his signature was. And it was good, she had to give Greg that.

Her eyes dropped to the witnesses' details. It was a man and a woman with the same last name. A couple she'd never heard of before. Who were they?

The one thing she was certain of was that they were real people. Greg knew the first thing she would do is contest this, so he wouldn't risk falling at the first hurdle with imaginary witnesses. He would put up a tough fight when she took him to court, and it was going to be expensive. But where on earth was she going to get the money for that? She barely had any money in her account right now. She couldn't even afford to put a roof over her head with what she had access to, so she certainly couldn't afford a lawyer. It would be pointless to try the company lawyer – she'd realised that already. If Greg had made sure she couldn't even access the building and her own house, there was no way he wouldn't already have made sure she was blackballed with their lawyers. Which meant she was on her own. She'd have to find and somehow fund her own legal team. Which meant she'd have to get a job and try to save up for the legal fees. But that, in itself, posed another problem.

She hadn't worked since before Orla was born, and before then, she'd worked for her father. But that was years ago, and considering everything else he'd done to her today, Cat somehow doubted Greg would let anyone write her a reference. He wanted her to suffer. But who would hire her with a huge gap and no references? And without a job, how could she afford lawyers? How was she even going to put a roof over Orla's head? How would she feed and clothe her?

'Oh *God*.' The words came out as a strangled cry, and she dropped her head into her hands as great, deep sobs suddenly bubbled up from her core.

She was still grieving her father, and now to have her whole life fall apart – to have it *ripped* from her like this – it was just too much to take. She felt the weight of it all bear down on her as she floundered in the darkness, with no idea where to turn.

'I don't know what to do,' she cried helplessly. 'Oh, Dad, I need you so much right now.' She looked up at his grave, barely able to see it through her tears. 'I don't know what to do. He's a *bastard*. He's taken everything and I don't know how to beat him. I need you back, Dad. I need you to tell me how to fix this. *Please...*' She trailed off, wishing she wasn't just talking to the thin air.

'The dead won't answer you here, love.' The voice came from somewhere behind her, and Cat turned to see a strikingly beautiful, smartly dressed woman standing beside a tree, a few yards away. 'You're better off talking to them at home, where they lived. Ain't nothing but death and decay around here.'

'*Huh!* Home...' Cat shook her head, dropping it back into her hands again as fresh tears stung. Usually she'd be too embarrassed to break down like this in front of a stranger – in front of *anyone* – but she no longer had the strength for embarrassment. 'That would be great if I still had a home to go to. But I don't. I don't have anything anymore. He took it all.'

* * *

Maria watched the other woman deflate, and her brow furrowed in a small frown. She pushed her hands down deeper into the pockets of her fitted winter coat and glanced over at the small mound of slightly raised earth that she'd been here to check up on. She should just walk away and leave this stranger to her demons, but something about her was tugging at Maria's curiosity.

'What do you mean?' she asked, almost reluctantly.

'Sorry?' The woman glanced back around at her with confused, red-rimmed eyes.

'What do you mean you don't have a home?'

Maria assessed her. She didn't look homeless. Her clothes looked subtly expensive, and her hair had been recently highlighted. She wore diamond studs in her ears, and her soft leather boots certainly weren't old.

The woman wiped her tears from her cheeks, looking – understandably – surprised by the question. 'Um, it's – it's my husband. He, er, he took the house. I tried throwing him out so he changed the locks and threw me out instead. Our daughter too.' Her voice cracked, and fresh tears glistened in her eyes. 'She's *three years old*, for God's sake.' She dropped her head back into her hands, her shoulders shaking as she silently sobbed.

Maria grimaced and looked around, letting out a long breath. She should go. She didn't have the time or capacity to take on someone else's problems. Especially someone she didn't even know. But the sheer desolation radiating from the woman had touched a nerve, and she couldn't seem to walk away. She took a step closer to the bench.

'So go hire your own locksmith,' she told her. 'Beat him at his own game. Take it back.'

The woman shook her head. 'I can't. Legally, I can't. He's got it all tied up.' She waved a set of papers in the air, and although Maria couldn't make out the words, she could see it was a will. 'It's a long story, but the punchline is that I'm out on my ear with my daughter, no home, no job, no one I can go to for help and no money. And I have no idea what to do now. Other than try and spin sleeping in the car as a bloody adventure, so she doesn't know the truth.' She let out a sound that could have been a laugh, were it not so pitiful. 'I'm sorry, this is not your problem. I don't even know why I'm telling you this.'

Maria tilted her head to the side with an expression of silent agreement, then stepped forward and sat down next to her on the bench. She rested back and crossed her legs, pushing her hands deeper into her pockets again, in a bid to warm them up. It was a bitterly cold day.

'Well, I did ask,' she replied.

They sat there in silence for a few moments, and Maria felt a pang of deep sympathy for the woman still trying to stifle her sobs beside her. In her line of work, Maria couldn't afford to be soft. Over the years, she'd built a skin so hard it made diamonds look as brittle as glass, but the way this woman had broken down at what her situation meant for her daughter had touched a nerve. Maria didn't have children of her own, but she could understand, to a degree, how she must feel. And no mother should ever be put in that sort of position. Especially by the father of the child in question. Maria looked up to the swollen grey skies with a grim expression. Some people had a lot to answer for.

'There's a B&B a few streets from here,' she said eventually. 'I know the woman who runs it. It's cheap and basic, but she keeps it clean and makes a decent breakfast. If I had a word, I'm sure she'd give you a bit of leeway on payment terms, just until you sort yourself out.'

And if she didn't sort herself out, it was cheap enough that Maria didn't mind footing the bill. Not that she'd mention this to the woman. She didn't look like the sort who'd be happy to feel like a charity case. But Maria couldn't, in good conscience, walk away after hearing that her little girl didn't have a bed to sleep in tonight.

The woman glanced sideways at her. 'That's kind of you, thank you,' she said, her tone unsure. 'But I have to be honest, I don't know when I'll be able to pay. I'll start looking for work today, but I've not worked for years and have no references. I'm not sure how long it will take me to find a job.'

Maria turned to meet her gaze then swept her eyes over her in assessment. Her mother's thunderous face as Antonio shut the door on her, earlier that day, sprang back to mind. It wasn't going to be easy finding someone so desperate for a house-keeping job that they'd put up with Sophia's fury over them being there. And it would be even harder to find someone whose silence they could command too. Because loyalty couldn't be bought. It had to be earned.

She pursed her lips together tightly, debating the idea that was forming in her mind. Under normal circumstances, they'd never invite someone who wasn't from their world into the family home where they conducted so much of their illegal businesses. But then, who from their world was going to be interested in a housekeeping job? Even if Sophia hadn't made it clear she was going to be as difficult as possible, no one worked their way into a position of trust with the Capellos to mop their floors and do the washing. Which meant they would have to consider taking someone on from outside of their normal parameters anyway. It wouldn't be too much of a risk, not really. So long as they didn't talk shop directly in front of whoever they hired. And besides, it was only temporary.

Maria made her decision and pushed away her residual doubts.

'Well, I might be able to help you out with that too,' she told her. 'What kind of work would you be willing to do?'

The woman frowned warily. 'It depends what you mean.'

'I need a housekeeper and cook for my mother's house, for a while,' Maria replied. 'And I need whoever I hire to be discreet about what they hear and see while in that house, as my brothers and I conduct highly sensitive business there.'

She'd have to vet her, of course. Make sure she wasn't some kind of undercover law enforcement or linked to any of their enemies. But that was easy enough. And besides, the chance nature of their meeting had already reduced the risk of either of those situations greatly.

The woman's expression cleared, and a small spark of hope flickered in her eyes. 'I can do that. I'd have to work around preschool hours, but I'd be incredibly grateful for the work, if you think I'm suitable.'

Maria nodded. They would have to start off on a trial, see if this would work. But it was certainly a step forward in solving the issue of help for her mother. 'Well, let's give it a try and see how we get on.' She held out her hand. 'I'm Maria.'

The other woman took the offered hand and shook it. 'Catriona. But please, call me Cat.'

NINE

The weekend passed in a hectic blur as Cat scoured the shops, looking for the things she and Orla needed at the cheapest prices. She was trying to spend as little as possible of the small amount of money she still had access to without depriving her daughter of the things she was used to, but it wasn't easy. The B&B Maria told her about had indeed had space for them. It was just a simple double room, but it was clean, had its own en-suite bathroom and a little area under the eaves that Cat had managed to fashion into a makeshift play area for Orla.

She'd explained to Maria that she wouldn't be able to start until Monday, when Orla was next due into pre-school, and the woman had accepted this without issue. Since then, with so many other things to think about and sort out, she hadn't given the job much thought. Her days had been spent trying to make their new nightmarish situation more bearable and distracting her bewildered young daughter. And each night, after Orla had fallen asleep, she'd cried silent, angry tears and tried, in vain, to figure out what on earth she was going to do.

The only local friends she still had contact with had been those she'd worked with at her father's company, years before.

But they still worked there and each message she'd sent out had been left either unopened or unanswered. One of them had eventually sent her a response, telling Cat she was so sorry that she couldn't meet up to talk, but that they'd all been told that there would be legal implications if they discussed anything regarding the company with Cat. Greg had also apparently threatened them with losing their jobs, if he found out they'd had contact with Cat at all. She'd risked enough simply telling her that, so Cat had thanked her, wished her well and then sobbed frustratedly into her pillow.

Greg had cut her off from everyone. He'd done it slowly over the years – she could see that with painful clarity now. He'd used emotional blackmail and distraction, every time she'd tried to see her friends, always coming up with what seemed like a valid excuse for her to cancel plans or spend more time at home. It had been even easier for him once Orla had come along, and eventually the distance between her and her friends had simply been too big. But at least she'd still had her dad, and she'd still been able to catch up with her old work friends, even after she'd left to have Orla. She'd still regularly visited the office and had managed to grab the odd coffee or lunch, here and there. But now he'd taken that too, and Cat had never felt so completely and utterly alone.

He'd sewn it up well. She had to give him that, as bitter a pill as it was to swallow. She had no family left, no friends and no money to try and fight him. He was set. She hadn't given him the satisfaction of contacting him since he'd thrown them out, three days before. And he hadn't bothered contacting her either. Not even to see if Orla was OK, or to find out where they were staying. For all he knew, she and his daughter could be sleeping rough under a bridge. He didn't even know about the money she was using to keep them going. Upon reading some sensible advice, years before, in a magazine, she'd stashed some money in an old account he didn't know about, as a backup fund in case of an unexpected emergency. She desperately wished she'd saved more in there now, but then again, she could never have predicted this situation in a million years. So she guessed she just needed to be grateful that she'd had the sense to do this much.

'Yay, my new lunchbox!' Orla cried gleefully, as Cat handed it to her at the pre-school gates on Monday morning.

It was so pitiful that she should find such joy in something so small, when her whole world was falling apart around her, that for a moment Cat had to blink away the threat of more tears. But that was the beauty of childish innocence. Orla didn't understand any of it and was quite happy to trust in the pretty little lies her mummy had spun to smooth over all the confusing happenings.

'Have a good day, sweetheart. I'll see you later,' Cat said, bending down to give her a squeeze and a kiss.

'You too, Mummy,' she replied, her sweet voice warming Cat's heart, the way it always did.

'Hello, Orla,' said her teacher, a sunny smile of welcome on her face as she approached.

'Hi, Miss Shannon,' Orla replied. 'Look, I got a Elsa lunchbox! And I been on holiday!'

'*Have* you?' Miss Shannon asked. 'Did you go away for the weekend?'

'Yes, me and Mummy,' Orla replied. 'We still *are* on holiday.'

'Are you now?'

Miss Shannon shot Cat a quizzical look, and Cat shook her head dismissively with a quick smile, as if to indicate it was just the random ramblings of a three-year-old. She didn't want to explain it all to the teacher just yet.

She walked away as Orla skipped inside and checked her watch. She was doing OK for time. She still had half an hour until she needed to be at the address Maria had given her. Her stomach growled, reminding her she hadn't had breakfast and she instinctively glanced up at the Starbucks across the street. But she couldn't afford to waste money on takeaway food right now. She had to save everything she had for Orla. Her own needs could wait.

Twenty minutes later, Cat drove through the gates and pulled up on the wide gravel drive of a large, beautiful house, and her eyebrows rose as she scanned the front of it. She'd grown up in a fairly big family home, and her own house was a decently sized detached four-bed, but this was next-level big. She wondered how many bedrooms it must have and how far back the building went. She could easily fit two, maybe even three, houses the size of her own inside this one.

'What do you people *do*?' she muttered under her breath.

Checking her watch again, she stepped out of the car and smoothed down her plain black jumper. She hadn't been sure what to wear, not having done this kind of work before. Was she expected to look smart? It was something she hadn't thought to ask. After much deliberation, she'd decided on black yoga trousers and a black jumper. Simple and inoffensive.

Cat rang the bell and waited. A few seconds later, it was opened by a tense-looking Maria, though she still managed a smile of greeting as she stepped aside to let her in.

'Cat, good to see you. Come on in and I'll show you around.'

'Thanks.' Cat looked around the spacious cream-and-gold entrance hall, and followed Maria as she walked through, pointing towards doorways.

'That's the formal lounge, the informal lounge and utility room, this side,' Maria told her. 'Then this side you have a bathroom and the office. It's more of a library really, but we use it as the main office. You remember I told you we work from here, my brothers and I?'

She glanced back at Cat, and Cat nodded.

'That room just needs a hoover and the bin emptying. Everything else in there, just leave it. Especially the desk – don't ever touch the desk.'

'Noted,' Cat replied. She glanced back at the door and wondered, once more, what these people did. Maria's last few words had felt more like a warning than guidance.

'At the back here is the kitchen and dining room, with the pantry off the back of the— Oh, Mum, there you are.' Maria stopped short, and her shoulders seemed to tense up a little further.

Cat moved sideways to see around her and tentatively smiled at the petite Italian woman sat at the breakfast bar, scowling at them.

'Yes, Maria, *here I am*. Here I am in *my* kitchen, in *my* home, that *I* designed and your father paid for, before *you* were even a mischievous glint in his eye,' came the sharp retort. 'And yet here *you* are, thinking you can tell *me* what I can and cannot do here!'

Maria sighed, walking over to the breakfast bar. Cat bit her bottom lip, unsure whether she should follow her closer to the woman who was now openly glowering at her, or whether she should wait where she was.

'Mum, we've talked about this,' Maria said tiredly. 'I'm not trying to tell you what to do; I'm trying to *help* you. You've bust your arm and your ankle, for God's sake! How do you expect to cook and clean? How do you expect to run around this kitchen or hold yourself up while you chop vegetables with your one good hand? How do you expect to run the hoover, or haul washing up and down the stairs? Eh? It's impossible!'

'I will *manage*,' the woman replied through gritted teeth. 'You think I haven't managed worse than this in my life? You wait till you have children, Maria. Then you'll know how quickly you learn to overcome the impossible. How quickly you learn that *nothing* is impossible.'

Maria rolled her eyes. 'OK. Look, this is Cat. Cat, this is my mother, Sophia.'

'Hello,' Cat ventured, moving a few steps closer to the two of them. 'Nice to meet you.'

The older woman stubbornly squeezed her lips closed, and her pencil-thin eyebrows rose high on her barely lined forehead as she pointedly looked away.

'*Mum*,' Maria prompted, her voice sharper now.

'No!' Sophia snapped hotly. 'I have one fall and you take over my house and my role here like I am some invalid old fool. Well, I am *not*! And I will *not* greet this *puttana* you bring into my home!'

There was an audible gasp from behind her, and Cat swung her head around to see the most handsome man she had ever set eyes on walk into the room. Trying not to let her jaw drop as he strode across to the breakfast bar, she quickly took in his appearance. He towered over all of them, and his crisp white shirt strained over his broad shoulders. His thick black hair had just the merest hint of a curl at its short ends and his thick, well-defined eyebrows did nothing to hide the mesmerising deep brown eyes underneath. Catching herself staring, Cat blinked and looked away, embarrassed.

'*Mum!* What's wrong with you, that you speak like this? Eh?' the man admonished. 'I'm shocked. You're better than that.'

He eyed her with a look that a parent might give an errant child, and to Cat's surprise, Sophia's expression softened. Her shoulders dropped, and she looked a tiny bit guilty, her eyes searching the man's face.

'You know how I feel about all of this, Alex,' she said, her tone devoid of the anger that had been there moments before.

'Still, that's no way to treat a guest in this house. *You* taught us that,' the man she'd called Alex replied.

He shook his head and tutted as though disappointed, then turned in a slow circle, shooting Cat a mischievous grin and a wink once his back was turned to Sophia. Cat bit her lip to stop herself from laughing. Alex must be one of Maria's brothers, she deduced. And it appeared that, unlike his sister, he had his mother wrapped around his finger. Which he was certainly using to his advantage right now. But she certainly wasn't complaining if it meant he could ease this transition. Because this was *not* what she'd been expecting to come into at all.

Sophia huffed and crossed her arms. Or, rather, she crossed one arm. The other she simply placed awkwardly over the top. 'Well, what do you expect from me?'

'I expect you to be big enough to accept the help Maria has arranged for you,' Alex replied. 'Or, OK, don't look at it as help. Look at it as a challenge. See if you can teach...' He looked at Cat and lifted his brow in question.

'Cat,' she told him.

'*Cat* all your skills and tricks. See if you can't make her almost as good as you are at all this. Eh?' he offered. 'Really, it would be *you* helping *her*.'

'Huh! *No one* could ever make my dishes as well as I do,' Sophia scoffed.

'Of course,' Alex replied smoothly. 'That's why I said *almost*.'

Sophia sniffed and glanced at Cat. 'Fine.' She scowled. 'But you'd best be able to keep up with me. I may look like I can't do much right now, but I assure you I am as sharp and nimble as a woman much younger than *you*.' She looked Cat up and down, then shuffled off her stool and, using a crutch with her one good hand, hobbled through to the pantry area.

'Sharp, yes,' Maria said quietly. 'Definitely not so nimble.'

She looked at Cat with a conspiratorial grin, and Cat couldn't help but return it.

'Well, she's certainly a very strong woman,' Cat replied.

'That she is,' Maria replied. 'This is my brother, Alex. You'll meet Antonio later.' She hesitated. 'Are you still happy to get started?'

She replied without hesitation. 'Of course.'

It didn't matter whether she was or wasn't. She needed the money. And this job paid very well, considering it was just cooking and cleaning, and the hours were flexible. Now she was beginning to understand *why* of course. But that made no difference.

'Nice to meet you, Cat,' Alex said, his voice as deep and richly toned as his eyes.

'And you,' Cat replied. She smiled, remembering his gasp as he'd entered the room. 'So, I'm guessing *puttana* isn't a flattering term then?'

He chuckled. 'No, I'm afraid not.'

Cat laughed. 'Oh well. What you can't understand can't harm you, I guess.'

'That's probably the best way of looking at it,' he replied.

'It's certainly *one* way,' Maria added wryly.

'So, Cat, you local?' Alex leaned against the large, square kitchen island. 'Maria hasn't told me much about you.'

His eyes moved from Cat's to his sister's and they shared a brief loaded look. Cat wondered what it meant.

'Kind of,' she replied. 'I'm not far from here now, but where I'm staying is a, er, temporary arrangement.'

'Huh.' His deep brown eyes searched her face, and she suddenly felt awkward. Like his gaze was somehow reading her at a much deeper level than just her skin. 'And when you say temporary...'

Just then Alex's phone rang, and as he looked at the screen

his smile vanished. He briefly closed his eyes and lifted his face to the heavens before answering.

'Yeah—' He fell silent as someone spoke on the other end. 'What state is she in? *What?* For fuck's sake... Yeah, I'm on my way.' He ended the call and slipped the phone back in his pocket.

'Bianca?' Maria queried.

'Yeah,' Alex confirmed heavily. 'I gotta go pick her up. Excuse me, Cat. It was good to meet you.'

'Likewise,' she replied.

He disappeared, and Maria sighed. 'Sorry about that. It's his wife, Bianca. She can be... a bit wild.'

'Oh.' Cat nodded, not sure how to reply to that. She turned her attention towards her new job instead. 'So, what shall I do first?' she asked.

'Right. Yes.' Maria opened her mouth to say more, but then her phone began to ring too. 'Sorry, one sec.' She answered the call and held it to her ear. 'What is it?' There was a short pause. 'Shit. OK. Give me ten minutes.' She ended the call and grimaced apologetically. 'I'm so sorry – I have to go. For now, just start with cleaning down here and see what Mum wants you to do. Follow her lead. She'll be frosty for a bit, but she'll thaw out soon enough. I'll be back to sort out the rest with you before you leave.'

'No problem – you go,' Cat urged with a winning smile. 'I've absolutely got this.'

'Thank you,' Maria called back, already heading towards the door. 'Good luck.'

Cat nodded and smiled, watching her leave, then she turned back to face the kitchen. She nearly jumped out of her skin when she saw Sophia had silently hobbled back into the room. The older woman was glaring at her sourly, all the softness Alex had coaxed out of her just minutes before gone. Cat's hopes faded, and she groaned internally.

I absolutely do not have this.

TEN

Alex pulled up outside of the casino and growled with annoyance as he saw his wife stumble out of the building. Jay, thankfully one of his more discreet men, walked out behind her. He tried to hold her arm to steady her, but she ripped it away, twisting back to swear at him. The action caused her to stumble again, but this time she lost her footing and went crashing down onto the pavement.

With an angry tut, Alex got out of the car and marched across the road to help peel his wife off the dirty concrete. Jay was already trying – and failing – to help her, cursing under his breath as she kicked out at his shin and let out a stream of offences.

He looked up at Alex with a stressed grimace. 'Boss, I'm sorry, she—'

'Don't apologise.' Alex held his hand up to halt the other man's apology. 'It ain't your fault.'

'Ain't his fault?' Bianca repeated with slurred incredulity. 'He fucking tripped me up!'

'No, he didn't,' Alex replied flatly, before turning his gaze back up to Jay. 'Go on, get off. I've got her.'

'He *did*,' Bianca insisted angrily.

Alex dragged her back up onto her feet. 'Come on – we're going home,' he told her, ignoring her comment.

'What? No!' She tried to pull away, but Alex had her in a tight-enough grip that she couldn't. 'What you doing? Gerroff me. I'm going back inside.'

'Just *get in the car*, Bianca,' Alex growled.

'No!' she declared hotly. 'I'm having fun; leave me alone.'

'Do you even know what fucking time it is?' Alex asked her, stopping to look at her properly.

She was a mess. Her leopard-print top was askew from the fall, her mascara had smudged all around her dark, vacant eyes and all that was left of her red lipstick was a dark ring of liner around the edge of her lips. A lock of her light brown hair fell forward, and she tried to blow it off.

'*I* dunno. Late?' she offered, her words slurring again.

'It's Monday fucking morning, Bianca,' Alex said quietly through gritted teeth. 'You've been here all night again.'

Bianca tutted and shrugged one shoulder. '*And what?*' she asked. 'Not my fault no one else can keep up.'

'*And* they wanted to shut the casino *hours* ago, except they had *you* mouthing off and threatening them with *me* if they didn't stay open for you. Which I don't appreciate, considering they're customers.'

Bianca tutted again and rolled her eyes dramatically. 'Even more reason why they shouldn't complain about my bloody custom then, innit?'

Alex shook his head and propelled her towards the car, clamping his jaw tightly shut before he said something he might regret.

'You're no fun anymore,' she grumbled. 'I miss the old Alex.'

'Yeah, well, I miss the old Bianca too,' he told her angrily, leaning her back against the car as he opened the passenger door. 'The one I used to be able to assume was at *home* just starting her day on a Monday morning instead of bladdered and falling out of a fucking casino!'

'Oh, you want me *home*, do ya?' Bianca shot back, her gaze and her tone suddenly sharpening. 'To do what exactly? Look after a husband who's never actually around? Sit there on me tod, twiddling my thumbs?'

Not bothering to answer her, knowing she was just after yet another fight, he slammed the door in her face and leaned on the roof of the car for a few moments. He stared out at the hazy grey horizon, ignoring the muffled curses below. As furious as he was with her, he knew he would bite his tongue and let this go, just like he had many times before. Because Bianca hadn't always been like this. And while he absolutely hated her on days like today, she was still his wife, and his responsibility as a husband was something he took seriously. The vows he'd taken hadn't been *through health and good times, for richer and easier only*. He'd promised to be there for her through it all. The good and the bad. And right now, he was certainly being tested on the latter.

They'd been together for eight years and married for seven. It had been fun at first. Each day an excuse for a new adventure. But while Alex had always had one foot firmly on the ground and one eye on all of his spinning plates, Bianca had never really tethered herself to anything in this world. Not even to him really. She didn't want to work, and that had always been fine with him. He made more than enough for them both. And with her unpredictability, he'd always been glad she'd shown no interest in joining the family business. But she didn't want to be a housewife either. She'd practically baulked at the thought of having children, accusing Alex of trying to tie her down when he'd raised the idea of having them.

Eventually, with no purpose in life and nothing to fill her time, Bianca had simply become a full-time party girl, going on benders with fair-weather friends, who served as a distraction from the emptiness of her life. She'd grown spoiled and sarcastic and self-serving – the total opposite of the woman he'd married. They'd stopped getting on, stopped being happy when they were together, and eventually Alex had found himself starting to avoid her. He knew, instinctively, that whatever it was that she needed, he could never give it to her. He doubted she even knew what she needed. But he also knew that he wouldn't leave her. Because despite it all, despite how lost she was, Bianca was loyal. She stuck by him and loved him, in her own way. And for that, he owed her the promises he'd made. Even if they did make him feel trapped.

With a heavy sigh, he walked around to the driver's side of the car and pushed these feelings aside. As he got in the car and glanced at his wife, now slumped against the window, snoring slightly, he suddenly wondered if either of them would ever find happiness again.

ELEVEN

Maria walked through the doors of the imposing, black-marble-fronted building she rented an office in and nodded politely at the security guard on her way to the lifts. She mentally sifted through the cases she had to work on as she rose to the top floor and shrugged off her long woollen coat. For the most part, her practice here was a money-laundering front. It was a bit on the nose, losing money illegally through the books of a law firm, but it was also why it was such an ingenious idea. No one would be looking in this direction, and even if they did, they'd have a hard time proving her books wrong with so many one-off clients. She kept her real cases to a minimum. There were enough to lend her legitimacy in the eyes of anyone looking, but not enough to take too much time away from her *real* business dealings.

Jen, her assistant, looked up from her computer as she entered the small lobby that preceded Maria's office and meeting room.

'Miss Capello.' Jen jumped up with a quick professional smile. 'Let me take that.'

Maria handed over her coat and fished her phone out of her

bag. 'Can you get me a coffee please, Jen? I've not had time to stop yet today.'

'Of course. Um...' Jen glanced at the closed door of the meeting room.

Maria's eyes followed hers. 'What is it?'

'Mr Capello is in to see you. He insisted on waiting so I put him in there.' Jen's cheeks warmed and her eyes dropped away from Maria's.

Maria frowned. 'Antonio?' she asked.

Jen nodded, and Maria sighed. 'Right.'

She glanced at the two comfortable chairs either side of the coffee table in their official waiting area. Maria knew Jen usually liked having the company of visitors, as it could sometimes be days between anyone other than the two of them coming in. But she clearly hadn't wanted Antonio's company today, which, knowing her brother as she did, most likely meant only one thing.

'Thank you. Two coffees,' she amended, before walking into the meeting room with a grim expression.

Antonio was stood in the far corner of the room, the other side of the long, dark wood table and its twelve matching chairs. He stared out across the city through the tinted glass wall, his hands clasped together behind his back. As Maria shut the door behind her, he turned to look at her. She didn't return his handsome smile; instead she raised an eyebrow with an icy look of accusation.

'What did you do to Jen?'

Antonio's face opened up in surprise, and he spread his arms out wide in a gesture of innocence. '*Me?* I didn't do anything! I was just chatting to her.' He took a step towards the table and reached out to spin a pen that had been left there. 'She's a nice girl.'

'Yeah, she is,' Maria agreed, her hard gaze not wavering. 'And she's my assistant, so leave her the fuck alone.'

'Whoa, bit hostile, ain't it?' Antonio looked aggrieved. 'Honestly, you pay a girl a compliment and the next thing you know, you're getting treated like you just robbed her fucking house!'

'What was the compliment?' Maria asked.

He shrugged. 'You know. Just a compliment. About how nice she looked.'

'Specifically?' Maria pushed.

He grinned with a groan of reluctance before answering. 'Alright, OK, it may have been something about how nicely her dress held the upper half of her torso.'

'Oh, for God's sake, Antonio,' Maria snapped, annoyed. He was chuckling now, like he was some naughty schoolboy trying to charm his way out of a prank. 'That ain't funny, and you ain't cute.' She pointed a finger at him across the room, her expression hard. 'You leave her alone, do you hear me? She's a bloody good assistant, and she knows how to keep her head down when she needs to, so I'm telling you now, you cost me Jen and I'll have your balls for earrings.'

He rolled his eyes but raised his arms in surrender. 'Alright, I'll leave her alone. Honestly, you women take things too seriously. I was just having a laugh with her.'

Maria's gaze cooled further. 'Say that in front of Alex – I dare you.'

Antonio sighed. 'Come on, Maria. I ain't here for a fight. And I didn't mean that to sound like it did, OK? Peace?' He arched an eyebrow.

There was a light knock at the door, and a second later it opened. Jen walked in with a pot of coffee, two mugs and a plate of biscuits on a tray. She placed it down on the table and turned to leave.

'Jen?' Antonio piped up. She paused and glanced back at him. 'I apologise if my earlier behaviour caused any offence. None was meant.'

She smiled tightly and nodded, then left the room, closing the door again behind her.

'OK?' This comment was aimed at Maria.

Choosing not to reply, she sat down and poured them each a cup of coffee. Antonio rounded the table and sat next to her, reaching over for one of the biscuits.

'So, what's up?' Maria asked, taking a sip of the hot coffee.

Antonio took a bite of his biscuit, munching quickly as he reached into his inside jacket pocket. He pulled out a thick brown envelope and chucked it onto the table in front of her.

Maria picked it up and ran a deep red nail under the flap. Peering in, she saw it contained two wadges of cash, bound by elastic bands. She nodded and sat back in her chair. 'OK, so he's in.'

'Looks like it,' Antonio confirmed.

She rubbed her chin absentmindedly as she thought the proposal over. 'This thirty per cent of the hotels – you know we can't put it in any of our names, don't you? It's too suss, directly after his dad's death. It will have to go through an account chain and end up in an offshore account. Make it look like it's an investing business, rather than someone collecting debt.'

Antonio nodded. 'Whatever you think best.'

'How are we framing it?' she asked.

Alex had told her what the client had asked for and what they'd agreed as payment, but he hadn't mentioned how he wanted to proceed.

'Alex wants to make it look like a heart attack. Sinclair junior can get us into his house and apparently it's pretty secluded, so no need for forced entry. He thinks it's easiest if it looks like natural causes,' Antonio relayed. He turned his coffee cup around on the saucer by the rim.

Maria watched the action absently. 'And how does he propose we do that?'

Antonio's hand paused, and his eyes met hers. 'We use the Viper.'

Maria's eyebrows rose. 'I hope you explained how much that'll cost.'

He nodded. 'We'll need something undetectable, something that won't show up on a tox screen.'

Maria conceded with a nod. 'The Viper it is then,' she agreed, staring out of the window across the smoky-grey tops of central London's smaller buildings. 'Do you trust this guy?'

'Not in the slightest,' Antonio answered immediately. 'But he hasn't got one vertebra in that back of his, and he wouldn't put himself in danger, so he's controllable.'

Maria screwed up her face into a grimace. 'I don't like the debt situation. If we're tied to these hotels, even through a business chain, it could cause a lot of problems for us. Do we really need that?'

Antonio thought it over. 'I think it could work to our advantage. If he's that terrible with money and needs bailing out again and again, we could potentially take the whole thing over eventually. Buy him out at pennies to the pound.'

'Potentially,' Maria agreed, though she wasn't convinced.

She was surprised Alex had taken the chance on this guy. From what she'd heard, he sounded secretive, weak and like he was going to end up being nothing but trouble. That certainly wasn't what *she* looked for in a business partner. And a job like this wasn't one they took on readily in the first place. Which meant Alex had to see a lot of worth in this deal somewhere. She wished she knew what he was thinking.

'Look, we'll get this done quickly, get this mate paid off and then have a sit-down with Sinclair and make it clear he has someone to answer to now,' Antonio said in an appeasing tone. 'It'll be fine.'

Maria sipped from her cup and said nothing. It sounded

logical enough, but she had a bad feeling about this client and she just couldn't shake it. Not that her worries mattered now. Alex had agreed to the job and the initial payment had changed hands, so the boat had sailed. And they were all aboard, whether they liked it or not.

TWELVE

Justin Sinclair had a penchant for fine wines that were way over his currently non-existent budget, but this didn't deter him from taking the hotel's private car to his favourite wine shop anyway. The driver pulled up on the double yellows outside, and Justin opened the door with an eager flourish.

'Oh...' He leaned back in and squinted at the driver. 'Just take this around the block a few times, will you? I'll be done in, say, half an hour or so. Good man.'

The driver muttered something unintelligible as Justin closed the door, but he didn't seem to notice. Instead, he puffed out his chest and pulled a deep, bracing breath in through his nose, then marched through the front door of the shop.

The little tinkle of the old-fashioned brass bell above the door caught the attention of the dough-faced man behind the counter, and he looked up with an expectant smile, but this morphed quickly to a look of surprise. His eyes darted around shiftily, then he stepped forward and ushered Justin further in.

'Well, this is a surprise. Come on in, please.'

'Thanks, old chap,' Justin replied with a smile. 'Think I will.'

'So, to what do I owe the pleasure?' the dough-faced man asked, his small brown eyes watching Justin curiously.

'Oh, Dalton, don't play coy with me,' Justin scoffed. 'I heard whispers about a certain Leroy that's come into your possession, and I simply had to get down here and buy it before Fenella does.'

He guffawed, amused by his own words. Fenella was an old school chum of theirs who delighted in having the best of the best of everything. He'd made a habit of trying to get in there first, when he could, just to disappoint her. Dalton tittered along dutifully but then quickly tailed off, looking awkward.

'The Leroy is a beauty, for sure,' Dalton confirmed. 'Richebourg Grand Cru 2001. But, well, Justin... it's a twelve-thousand-pound bottle of wine.'

'I'm well aware, my dear chap. Which is why I *have* to get to it before Fenella.' Justin laughed again. 'Just imagine her face when she finds out I've beaten her yet again.'

This time Dalton didn't laugh. He ran his hands lightly in opposite directions across the surface of the desk he now stood behind then looked away. 'Look, Justin, I know things have been a tad tough lately. You really don't need to put on a front with me.'

'A front?' Justin barked out a laugh to cover the sting Dalton's words had delivered. The sting immediately turned into a hot flare in his core, and he could feel his cheeks warming with a mixture of embarrassment and anger. He forced a grin. '*Please*... I'm good for the money, Dalton – there's no need to be crass.'

Dalton watched him for a moment, then his expression opened into one of frank honesty. 'No, Justin, you're not. And I get it, my friend. It's not you – it's your father. He's being an arse.'

Justin gritted his teeth as his temper flared, but he swallowed it down, and a steely glint appeared in his pale eyes.

'That may have been true for a while, but that little situation is about to be taken care of.'

Dalton's interest suddenly sharpened. 'You contacted the guy I told you about?' he asked.

'More than that,' Justin replied. 'I went through the whole chain right up to the problem solvers themselves. Very soon that miserly thorn in my side shall be obliterated, and I shall be free to spend what I want and rule my kingdom *exactly* as I see fit.'

'How?' Dalton whispered. 'What will they do?'

Justin raised his chin, looking down at Dalton haughtily. 'The details don't matter. But he'll be dead soon, and that will be that.'

Dalton nodded and reached under the counter, pulling out an ornate silver tray with a cut-crystal decanter and four matching glasses on it. He exhaled loudly, blowing the air through his cheeks. 'I think this calls for a drop of Remy.'

'It does indeed,' Justin agreed, accepting the drink Dalton handed him.

'What's it going to cost you?' Dalton asked, taking a sip from his own glass. 'I can't imagine something like that is going to be cheap.'

Justin swirled the honey-brown liquid around in his glass as he thought about his own plans. The plans he'd laid *after* his meeting with the Capellos. The plans nobody in the world knew except him. A small, cold smile crept over his face.

'Nothing actually,' he replied. 'In the end, it's going to cost me nothing at all.'

THIRTEEN

Bianca woke up and stared around the dark room with a frown, trying to piece together the night before. Or *day* perhaps. She wasn't really sure. This was her own bedroom, which was a relief, though for some reason she was facing the wrong way on her bed. Carefully she shifted herself up into a seated position and instantly regretted it as pain thumped through her fuzz-filled head. With a self-pitying groan, she slipped her legs off the side and took stock.

She was fully dressed, other than her shoes, and the bed was still made. Whoever had brought her home must have just dumped her on top and left. But who had that been? Her frown deepened as she tried to recall what had happened. Her last clear memory was of downing shots and throwing a small mortgage's worth of cash onto the roulette table. She knew, without needing to check, that she was alone in the house. The silence around her hung heavily in the air, and, even had it not been so stark, she knew Alex well enough not to assume he'd have stuck around after dropping her off. He'd have been too annoyed with her to stay until she woke.

The blue glow from the alarm clock on her bedside table drew her gaze and she stared at it for a moment with a frown. It was midnight. But she'd still been drinking and betting with her friends long *after* midnight, she remembered. Which must mean that she'd gone and lost a whole day again.

As if on cue, her stomach rumbled and she realised she was desperately hungry. Thirsty too. That was when she noticed the glass of water and the sheet of paracetamol next to the alarm clock. At least Alex had cared enough to leave her those before he'd run off again.

Standing up, she paused and closed her eyes for a moment, the movement jarring her aching head once more, then very slowly she picked up the water and began to drink.

The sound of a car and the lights moving across the bedroom wall drew her attention to the window, and she took the two steps over to it, peering out into the darkened street below. Two cars moved in convoy towards the house. She recognised them from the shape of the headlights as Alex's and Antonio's.

Alex pulled up on the drive, and her stomach did a small flip. She really didn't want to see her husband right now. She couldn't deal with his sanctimonious blathering about how she chose to live her life, while she felt so rough. And he *would* start, she knew it. And even if he didn't speak to her at first, she knew she'd see it in his face. All that quiet anger and lack of interest as she spoke to him. And she knew that the moment she saw that, things would escalate into a full-blown row again. She'd lash out, spewing her anger all over him and pushing him away from her like a wounded cat. It was what she did. It was all part of their dance. Their ever-spiralling circle of communication.

Alex got out of the car, and she waited for him to walk into the house, deciding she'd probably be better off pretending to be asleep, when he eventually came upstairs. But then he turned the other way, towards Antonio's car. Bianca watched, pushing a knotted tendril of her light brown hair back behind her ear. He hovered by Antonio's door for a few moments, talking too quietly for her to hear from inside the house, then he walked around to the passenger side and got in. A small sigh of relief escaped her lips as she realised she could relax and recover in peace. But this feeling was short-lived.

Across the road, the lights of a parked car suddenly switched on. The car slowly inched out and began to crawl down the road after her husband. Bianca's eyes widened and her hand flew to her throat. There had been no one in the street just now – she was sure of it. She'd have seen them get into the car. Which meant whoever was now driving it had already been in the car. Already there *waiting*. Who on earth would be sat waiting in a dark car at gone *midnight*?

The small mining operation inside her head forgotten, Bianca grabbed her handbag from the floor and quickly located her phone. Dialling Alex's number, she peered back out of the window worriedly.

'Come on, come *on*,' she muttered.

A dim light flashed up from inside Alex's car below, and her heart thumped painfully hard in her chest she realised he'd left his phone in there.

'*Shit!*'

She rang off and tried Antonio, but a second later another dim light appeared. They'd left *both* of their phones in his car. Which meant they were doing something that they *definitely* didn't want to be able to be tracked. And they were out alone tonight, with no men, which meant they were doing something covert that no one else probably had any clue about. They liked to keep the circle small, when they could, to protect themselves. Except tonight, that wasn't going to help them at all.

'*Shit!*' she yelled again, throwing her phone on the bed.

She gripped her hair in both her hands and sank down next to it. There was nothing she could do. Alex and Antonio were being followed by God only knew who, and Bianca had absolutely no way of warning them.

FOURTEEN

As the first weak rays of sunlight stretched their long fingers into the library office of the Capellos' family home, Maria stifled a yawn and rubbed her eyes. She poured more coffee into her empty cup and looked across to Bianca, who was agitatedly pacing the room.

'Want a top-up?' she asked, nodding to the other empty cup in front of her.

'Nah. I'm coffee'd out,' Bianca replied.

Maria cast her gaze back out through the window, her eyes trained on the entrance to the driveway. She was sat in her favourite spot, one of two wingback chairs, each side of a small, round wooden table in the window bay of the large office-cum-library. She quite often sat here in the mornings with a coffee when she couldn't sleep and came in early. She'd watch the sun creep over the line of trees that edged their front garden, boxing in the front of their home. But the sense of peace this usually came with wasn't present today.

They'd been here waiting for Alex and Antonio's return since around one in the morning, after Bianca had called and told her what she'd seen. Maria knew her brothers had gone to scope out Sinclair senior's house, but she had no idea where that was or how long they intended to be. She was as helpless as Bianca had been, with no way to warn them or cut them off. And so they'd come here, to where they hoped the brothers would return, once they'd finished their business.

'You must have *some* idea who it could be,' Bianca said, joining her at the window. She peered out at the drive nervously.

'I've already told you I don't,' Maria replied. 'It could be anyone.'

Bianca huffed and crossed her arms. 'It reeks of bacon to me.'

Maria rested her head back against the chair and watched a robin land on a low branch of one of the trees. 'I don't think it's Old Bill.'

'Why not?' Bianca asked.

'I just don't.' Maria fell silent, not adding anything more.

Bianca was part of their family, but she wasn't part of the firm. They didn't share details about their world with Bianca, and so she wasn't about to explain that she'd recently left the local chief of police with a hefty-enough warning to keep them off their backs for a while. He could have ignored this warning of course, but Maria doubted it. He wasn't the type.

Bianca sighed heavily and walked away, resuming her pacing at the other end of the room. She knew better than to push for anything more from Maria.

Just then, a shuffling sound came through from the hallway, and a second later the door to the library opened. Maria looked over to see her mother lean in with a confused frown. The frown immediately morphed into a smile when she saw her daughter.

'Maria! You're here early,' she exclaimed delightedly. 'Come – I'll make you some breakfast.'

'No, don't worry, I can't eat yet,' Maria replied.

'I could eat,' Bianca piped up.

Sophia's head whipped round, and her smile dropped when she saw her daughter-in-law was also there. 'Oh. Yes, you'll need something to soak up the alcohol, I imagine,' she replied drily. 'Well, you know where the kitchen is. Help yourself.'

Turning around more swiftly than Maria had imagined she could still move with her injuries, Sophia hobbled back out of the room, and the door closed behind her.

'Wow. How to say you hate someone without saying you hate someone,' Bianca said sarcastically.

'She doesn't hate you,' Maria replied, the lie falling smoothly off her tongue.

In truth, none of them really liked Bianca anymore. They used to, before she'd become such a nightmare. It was hard to like someone who caused Alex so much stress and unhappiness. But she was still his wife, so they hid their true feelings as best they could. Apart from Sophia of course. Their mother had never been very good at putting on a front.

'Well, why assume I've been drinking?' Bianca sounded annoyed now. 'It's just rude. I'm here trying to help the family out, for Christ's sake. I'm here *worrying* about my husband. Her *son!*'

Maria looked her over and pursed her lips. Bianca might be here for that reason now, but it was obvious that she'd been out on a bender prior to all of this. Her tired face had remnants of yesterday's smudged make-up – make-up far too heavy to be day wear. Her long, thick hair was falling out of the updo she'd styled, and her rumpled outfit wasn't exactly something she'd have put on for a supermarket run. Plus, Maria had noticed earlier that, up close, Bianca smelled a little stale.

'I really don't know why she feels the need to make such shitty comments to me,' Bianca continued, clearly getting riled up about it. 'It's fucking offensive.'

'Have you actually looked in a mirror lately, Bianca?' Maria asked, deciding to be honest. 'I know why you're here, but you can see why Mum jumped to that conclusion. The post-bender look isn't your best.' She pointedly gave her sister-in-law the once-over.

'Oh, that's just lovely, ain't it?' Bianca snapped. 'Not that it's any of your business, but yeah, I went out for a few drinks. And there ain't nothing *wrong* with that. I am entitled to a life. But after seeing someone follow my husband, I wasn't exactly thinking about sprucing myself up for your mother, to be honest.'

Maria tilted her head in acknowledgement and looked back out of the window. 'Fair enough.'

There was little point in explaining to Bianca that no one blamed her for *having a life*. That the reason Sophia was so prickly about Bianca's drinking was that they all knew what state she always ended up in, and that Alex was the one who had to deal with it. That they all knew how frequent these episodes had become. But Bianca wouldn't hear that. It would just cause another argument – and besides that, it wasn't Maria's place to explain that to her. It was Alex's, if he ever chose to do so.

'It's nearly eight, for fuck's sake,' Bianca muttered. 'Where *are* they?'

The worry in her voice was real now, and Maria bit her bottom lip, knowing exactly how she felt. She picked up her mobile and called Jay again, hoping they had news – *any* news – but knowing already that they didn't. Their closest men had been out all night searching for them. If any of them had heard anything, they'd have called her straightaway.

Jay picked up after just one ring. 'Nothing yet. I'm sorry – we're still out looking.'

'Forget it,' she ordered. 'Call them back. I want everyone here, ASAP. And tool up.'

'Boss?' he queried.

She stood up and scratched her forehead with her free hand. 'I don't know who or what we're dealing with, so until we do, I think we need to regroup and—'

'They're back!' Bianca cried.

Maria turned to the window, and, sure enough, Antonio's car was making its way up the drive. 'Forget that. Just head over here as you are. They've just pulled up.'

She heard the relief in his breath as he exhaled. 'Got it.'

Bianca was already in the hallway, and by the time Maria caught up, she was flinging open the door.

'Where the fuck have you been?' Bianca demanded, running down the front steps to confront her husband.

His expression opened up into a mixture of surprise and annoyance at seeing her there and hearing her words. He looked past her to Maria, his frown deepening. 'What's going on?' he asked, the question directed at her.

Maria descended the steps towards them with a grim expression. The relief she'd felt that her brothers were OK was now quickly being replaced by a cold trickle of dread. They looked surprised by this tense welcome, as if they had no idea anything was going on. As if they were even more in the dark about what was happening than she was. Her eyes met Antonio's then flicked back to meet Alex's.

'Actually,' she said heavily, 'that's what I was about to ask you.'

FIFTEEN

Antonio paced the floor in front of the wide bay window in the formal lounge, flicking the cap of his metal lighter open and closed, over and over. It was something he did whenever he was on edge. And today, like the rest of them, he had just cause to feel on edge. So Alex decided to ignore his sister's irritated glances at the lighter every time it clapped shut.

'And you're sure she didn't get the plate?' Antonio asked again.

'I've already told you she couldn't see from that angle. The car pulled out from directly across the road, and by the time it was far enough away for the plate to be visible, it was too dark to read it,' Maria replied. She rested back in one of the three matching plush cream sofas that surrounded the wide square coffee table and relaxed an arm along the back of it. 'Plus, I don't think she was in a particularly sharp state when it happened.'

She caught Alex's eye and saw the look of resigned confirmation on his face.

'What's your theory?' he asked her. 'You've had a few hours to think it through – where's your head at?'

Maria briefly lifted her eyebrows. 'That's the thing. I can't think of *anyone* who'd have reason to tag us right now. I mean, we've done a lot of things that people won't thank us for, but we've not crossed any firm big enough to want to take us on.' She pushed a hand back through her long, dark hair. 'There are no new players in town worth noting or that would be looking at us. I just can't see it.'

'Unless one of us has crossed someone the rest don't know about,' Alex said quietly.

He looked over to Antonio. Maria instinctively did the same, along with a couple of their men. The others kept their gazes firmly trained on the ground.

Antonio stopped pacing and frowned back at them from across the room. 'Why you all looking at *me*?' he asked, as if surprised.

Maria rolled her eyes.

Alex held his gaze levelly. 'Just asking the question. We need to find out what's going on – that means looking at all the angles. Is there anything we should know?'

'No, there fucking isn't,' Antonio shot back. 'What about you then, eh? Or *you*, Maria? Either of you poked any big fucking bears lately? Ain't my cup of tea that, to be honest. But thanks for checking,' he added sarcastically.

Alex sighed. 'Alright, so we're still on square one then.'

'Looks like it, don't it?' Antonio replied sharply.

'Oh, calm down, Antonio,' Maria said with a frown. 'This ain't about you; it's about all of us. It's about the fact we've found a bloody camper outside Alex's home. Not even here. His *home*.'

The reminder of the seriousness of the situation hit with the force she'd intended and the room fell silent, other than the incessant clicking of Antonio's lighter in his hand.

'That's a point. Has anyone checked around the block here?' he said suddenly. 'And around our gaffs?'

'I've done a couple of rounds and didn't find anything,' Jay piped up. 'I've left men outside both your places to keep watch for now. Just in case that changes.'

Alex nodded. 'Good. Keep someone outside the houses at night, and, Maria, keep someone with you in the day.'

'*What?*' She frowned. 'I can't do that – you know I can't. As far as most of the world outside this room knows, I ain't even part of this firm. I'm a civilian. I'm a lawyer, for God's sake. I can't start showing my real hand in broad daylight.'

'It don't have to be obvious. Have someone trail you from a distance,' Alex suggested.

Maria pursed her lips, annoyance flashing through her hazel eyes before she cast her gaze across all the men in the room. 'Fine. Danny, you're with me. But keep your distance.'

'Got it,' Danny replied, nodding to her.

Antonio's lighter-clicking paused, and he caught Maria's eye. 'You're sure this ain't Old Bill, after all that last week?'

'Pretty sure,' Maria replied. 'I could be wrong, but I doubt it. Besides, if it *was* them after all that, it would be you or me they'd tail. Not Alex.'

'True,' he conceded. 'So, to sum up, we're being watched and don't know who by, or why, or how big a threat this is?'

'Yeah,' Alex said heavily. 'We're completely in the dark on this one.'

'The worst place anyone can be in our game,' Maria reminded him.

'It certainly is,' he told her, forcing a smile.

But the smile didn't reach his eyes and nor did she return it. Because there was no belittling that statement. In their game, there were very few rules and no laws to be upheld. In their game, it was every man for himself and no place for the weak. And the blind were the weakest of them all.

SIXTEEN

Bianca turned on the tap and watched the cool, clear water gush into her glass. Her head was thudding horrifically now, begging her to nourish it with rest and food and water. She hadn't been able to take in much through the night other than coffee, her stomach churning in knots as she worried about what was happening. Because whilst she wasn't part of the firm, she knew exactly who her husband was and how closely her position in life was tied to his strength. Any threat to him was a threat to her, and this frightened her.

After taking a deep gulp of water and then another, and another, she paused to refill the glass before opening what she'd thought was the medicine cupboard. Inside was a neat selection of jars, advertising teabags and coffee and all that went with them.

'Fuck's sake,' she muttered. Sophia must have rearranged the kitchen again.

She tried another one and sighed loudly when she found herbs and spices.

'Can I help you?' came an unexpected voice from behind her.

Bianca swung round to see a slim, pale brunette hovering in the doorway, holding a full washing basket under one arm.

'Who the fuck are you?' Bianca asked, too tired at this point for niceties.

'Oh, um, I'm Cat,' the woman answered awkwardly. 'I started here yesterday. I'm the housekeeper.'

Bianca's eyebrows shot up, and she pulled her head back in complete shock. Unable to control it, she let out a sharp bark of amusement. 'Right, OK.' A ghost of a grin lingered on her face as she eyed Cat. 'Sophia has a housekeeper. And I thought hell would never freeze over. Shows what I know!'

The corner of Cat's mouth lifted briefly, and she tilted her head as if in agreement as she continued into the room. 'She *is* a very independent woman.'

Bianca watched her, unsure she was OK with this new development. The woman – here to look after the house and no doubt the people in it – was attractive and friendly. Warm even. She suddenly didn't like the idea of Alex seeing that every day at all.

Not returning the friendly smile as Cat approached, Bianca sniffed and turned back to the cupboards.

'What are you looking for?' Cat asked.

'Painkillers,' Bianca replied flatly.

'Here,' she said, placing the basket on the side and opening another cupboard Bianca hadn't tried yet. 'She had me move this all yesterday. All the medication's up here now.' She passed the packet to Bianca with another smile then turned back to pick up the basket again. 'I'd best get on. Hope you feel better.'

Bianca watched her retreat to the utility room, and just as she disappeared, Antonio walked in. He let out a long, low whistle as he caught sight of Cat and grinned with a look of interest.

'And *what* was *that* little piece I just saw go through there?

That Mum's new skivvy?' he asked, biting his bottom lip with a calculated look at the empty doorway. 'She's a sort.'

Bianca glared at him sourly. As if she wanted to hear *that* right now.

Antonio caught the look, and he rounded the kitchen island, leaning back against it and facing her. 'What's up, buttercup?' he asked, looking her over. 'You looked wrecked.'

'Yeah, so I keep hearing,' she replied moodily.

She didn't take much offence at his comment though. Unlike the others, she actually got along with Antonio. Probably because they were both accustomed to stays in the Capello family doghouse.

He pointed to the paracetamol packet in her hand. 'They ain't gonna do you much good.'

'Well, unless you've got some codeine up your sleeve, they're all I've got,' she replied.

Antonio glanced back over his shoulder. 'Codeine's for quitters,' he said quietly. ''Ere.' He fished a small bag of white powder out of his pocket and handed it to her. 'Treat yourself. Get back on top for a bit.'

For the first time that day, Bianca finally smiled. 'Thanks,' she said, tucking it into her bra. 'I could use a pick-me-up.'

'Mm,' Antonio murmured. 'Hey, the Drews have got an illegal boxing match on tonight. Fancy a flutter?'

'The *Drews*?' Bianca repeated, surprised.

They were the firm who'd taken out Alex's uncle and cousin the year before. She knew that side of the Capello family had run their own firm, unrelated to this one entirely, so that fight had not been theirs. And indeed, from what she'd heard, they'd asked for what they ended up getting. But they'd still been family, so she was surprised to hear Antonio so eager to go along to one of their killer's events.

'Yeah, they extended an invite, and I thought I'd take it up. No one else wants to go, but I thought it might be your bag.' He stood up and slipped his hands into his trouser pockets. 'I'll be heading out at eight – just let me know.'

Bianca thought about the cold, empty house she had to go back to. She'd not bothered to do a shop so there would be nothing there for dinner, and as she heard Alex's voice waft through from the lounge, she thought about how he'd no doubt be absent yet again this evening.

'Sod it, why not?' she replied, her spirits already lifting. Who wanted to be home and sober all night anyway?

SEVENTEEN

The following week passed in a blur for everyone. A drunken haze for Bianca, a stressful fog for the Capello firm and a daze of survival for Cat. Each of them was so tied up in their own issues that they barely noticed each other as they went about their days. The Sinclair job had been slowed down considerably after the encounter with the car outside of Alex's house, but as there hadn't been a sighting of any lurking cars since, they were slowly beginning to relax.

'Do you think she might have just made it up?' Antonio asked as they drove back out to Sinclair's country home.

Alex considered it as he turned down the road that would lead them the long, but ANPR-camera-free, way out to the house. 'No. What would she have to gain?'

'Your attention,' Antonio replied. 'Five minutes in the spotlight.'

Alex frowned. 'She wouldn't do that to me. She wouldn't put us through all this for attention – it ain't her style.'

'Yeah, sure. She's just a meek little wallflower that one,' Antonio said sarcastically.

'Oi, watch it,' Alex replied, shooting him a warning glance. 'Whatever she is or ain't, she's still my wife.'

Antonio held his hands up in surrender and turned to look out of his window at what little they could see of the countryside in the dark.

Alex suppressed a sigh. Bianca was sleeping off the latest of a string of wild nights, though thankfully he hadn't been called out to get her since the incident at the casino the week before. In fact, he'd barely seen her. If she wasn't out all night partying and gambling, she was shopping and spending obscene amounts of money. It had become a more regular pattern, and Alex knew he needed to do something about it before it got any worse. Rein her in somehow. But he just wasn't sure how.

As they pulled over on the dusty side of the road, where they'd left the car last time they'd scoped the place out, Alex pushed Bianca from his mind and focused on the job at hand. The location was ideal for what they planned to do. It was remote, the nearby village small and sleepy, and there were multiple routes away from the place, two of which were uninterrupted by cameras for miles.

Alex checked his watch. 'According to the schedule Justin gave us, Frank should be arriving home any minute.'

'Come on then – let's get out there,' Antonio said.

They got out of the car and trudged through the field that separated the road and the side of the house. As they neared the edge of the garden, they settled in behind a leafy bush and waited. They could see the front driveway from here and some of the inside of the house through the wide windows on the side. Just like the last time they'd been there, the lights were on and the curtains were open, as if the man who lived there had no concerns about his privacy this far out from the rest of civilisation.

A few minutes passed, and then the twin beams of a car's headlights washed over the gravel drive, the Bentley they belonged to swinging in and crunching along it a second later. The driver's door opened, and a man in his late sixties or early seventies got out with a grunt. He unfolded his bent body slowly, as though it pivoted on a stiff, rusted hinge, then walked into the house.

'Like clockwork,' Antonio commented.

'Mm,' Alex acknowledged. 'Soon as that stuff comes through from the Viper, we'll crack on. Get this over with. You got the AirTags?' He glanced sideways at his brother.

'Yeah, both in here.' Antonio tapped where the internal pocket was on his black, zipped-up jacket.

'Good. I'll set the nanny cam while you put one on his car, then we'll get out of here. It's too fucking cold for this old-school shit.' He rubbed his black-gloved hands together, the action doing nothing to help warm them up.

'Hold up,' Antonio whispered, tapping Alex's chest with the back of his hand. 'Who's this?'

Another set of lights swung up the drive, followed by a second car, and the brothers ducked down further. It pulled up next to the old man's, the bleached red paintwork and rusted rims a stark contrast to the gleaming black Bentley. The driver's door opened with a creak, and a thin young woman got out, wearing a tight minidress over bare legs. She had a big puffa jacket on, which she squeezed tightly to her with crossed arms as she trotted to the front door as quickly as she could in her high heels. The door opened, and she plastered on a wide smile as she stepped in and shrugged the jacket off. Frank took it and gestured for her to go through to the lounge, while he went to hang it up.

'Not quite as lonely as we thought then,' Antonio muttered. 'That could be a problem.'

'Nah, she's on the game, a temporary distraction,' Alex replied.

'Could still be a regular gig,' Antonio pointed out. 'Maybe

we should tag her car too. Last thing we need is a Tom turning up at the wrong time.'

Alex squinted and watched her through the window as she wandered into the lounge. Her eyes swept the room quickly, pausing on the electronics and the bowl of keys on the side table. She leaned over and pressed down on one of the sofas, as though testing it out, glancing back and straightening up as Frank walked into the room.

'Nah, she's not been here before,' Alex told him. 'She's sussing the place out. He might be a regular to the game, but she ain't a regular to him. Don't bother tagging her.'

Alex looked back into the darkness. Something about this place was giving him the chills. And for someone who wasn't afraid of much at all, that was saying something. He didn't spook easily, but for some reason, something was making the hairs of his neck stand up. Something out there, where he couldn't see. Something that felt threatening. That felt darker than the darkness it was hiding in.

He pulled in a deep breath and shook it off. He was being ridiculous. It was probably just the unusual quiet of the countryside at night. It was nothing like the ever-buzzing undertone of the city.

'Come on. Let's just get this done and get out of here.' Alex bent into a half crouch and moved quickly towards the house as Frank and the sex worker moved out of view.

Antonio disappeared to his left, in the direction of the car, and Alex ran to the tree he'd earmarked for the nanny cam. There was a small hollow where the first big branches split off that pointed directly at the front of the house – and it was far enough away from it, and tucked deep enough behind bushes, that he was confident Frank wouldn't have reason to go too close to it.

Alex took the small wireless device from his pocket, then pushed it into the hollow and covered it up with a handful of the dead leaves and small twigs within. He pulled out his phone and quickly checked it was working, then, satisfied that it was, hurried back to the car.

Antonio fell into step beside him as they reached the fence marking the edge of the grounds to the house, and Alex raised an eyebrow in question.

'It's done,' Antonio murmured. 'You?'

Alex nodded. 'All set.'

'OK. Let's get back. I've got a hot date to find,' Antonio replied.

'To find?' Alex queried.

'Yeah. Drop me at the strip club. I'm a hungry man, and I'm in the mood for fast food tonight. Something easy. Something to go.' He grinned through the darkness, and Alex sighed.

'Which one?' he asked.

Antonio seemed to consider it for a moment as they got in the car. 'Heaven Above. The Tylers' joint, in Soho.'

Alex's gaze whipped round to meet his brother's, a warning in his deep brown eyes. 'No. You've pissed off a lot of people lately, Antonio, but we *cannot* afford for you to piss off the Tylers.'

Antonio tutted. 'Oh, fuck off, will ya? I ain't planning on causing a scene. Besides, it ain't a *proper* Tyler joint – it belongs to Freddie's missus and her mate, don't it? Ain't like it's actually theirs.'

Alex stared at him in disbelief. 'You got a screw loose today or something?' He shook his head, anger creeping in. 'You mess about in there and Freddie Tyler would come down on you harder than if you'd punched him directly in the face. His missus means more to him than his entire empire, and you think I'd let you go in there, with all the shit *you've* been throwing out lately? Pull the other one.' He started the car and let it idle.

'*Let* me?' Antonio repeated.

'Yeah,' Alex confirmed. 'Let you. Up till now we've worked

as partners, you and me. But lately your antics have been off-the-charts reckless, and it's causing us some serious problems. Problems you don't seem to give a shit about. You've pissed off dealers, treated clients like shit, gone on drug-fuelled fucking killing sprees—'

'He deserved it!' Antonio exclaimed.

'No, he didn't,' Alex shot back. 'He deserved a warning. And even if he had deserved more, it should have been a joint decision between you, me and Maria. It should have been done carefully, with decent planning.' He rubbed his forehead, stressed. Antonio was becoming an increasingly dangerous liability, but no matter how they tried to reason with him, he just couldn't – or *wouldn't* – see it. 'So, yeah. For now, I'm calling the shots. Until you get your head together. Because I *will not* allow you to screw up anything else.'

'Huh!' Antonio let out a short laugh of disbelief and stared back at his brother for a moment, a cold half-smile on his face that didn't reach his eyes. 'Well, check out Lord Alex, taking charge of the kingdom.'

'It ain't like that and you know it,' Alex said in a strong voice, holding Antonio's gaze. 'Because, do you know what, if I was acting the way you have, I'd expect you to do the same. This is a dangerous fucking business we're in, and this firm needs protecting. Even from ourselves sometimes.'

Antonio regarded him silently for a few moments then turned to stare through the windscreen. 'Drop me home,' he said curtly.

'Yeah?' Alex checked, surprised at how easily that plan had changed. Antonio was well known for his stubbornness.

'Yeah. Maybe what I really need is a good night's sleep.'

Alex paused, noting that cold half-smile still on his brother's face, then silently he pulled out onto the road. What could he say to that? His brother was doing exactly what he'd hoped for. But why did his words elicit such a sense of deep foreboding?

* * *

As the brothers drove away, another car's engine sprang to life, a quarter mile down the road. The driver pulled out gently, keeping the headlights off, ensuring their presence remained hidden. He tapped the screen of the inbuilt console, and a ringing sound filled the car. The call was answered quickly, the receiver waiting silently on the other end.

'They've left,' said the driver.

'That was quick,' came the reply. For a few seconds, there was silence, and then the man on the other end of the line continued in a determined tone. 'Stay close to them and be ready. We move soon, in the next few days. This has gone on long enough. It's time to put a stop to it all, once and for all. It's time to put a stop to *them*.'

EIGHTEEN

Cat pulled up around the corner from pre-school, where she'd just dropped Orla, and parked under the gnarled, knotty, winter-stripped branches of an old oak tree. She turned off the ignition and sat motionless for a few seconds. Then suddenly she pulled her arms back and began hitting the steering wheel over and over in a brief, fevered fury.

'Fuck! Fuck, fuck, *fuck!*' she yelled to no one in particular. Tears began to stream down her face as she dropped her arms into her lap, and she quickly wiped them away with the sleeve of what was now her work jumper. '*Fuck you*, Greg Holden. Fuck *everything* about you. You don't *deserve* her.' Fresh tears sprang up, and her voice wobbled as she thought about what Orla's teacher had just said. 'And *she* deserves so much better than *you. Ugh!*'

She hit the steering wheel angrily one more time, but this time she accidentally hit the horn. A little old lady nearby on the pavement almost jumped out of her skin at the unexpected sound, and the small dog she was walking began barking at the car.

'Oh, I'm sorry!' Cat said, cringing as she mouthed the words through the window. 'I'm – I'm so sorry...'

She trailed off, her mortification swiftly dissipating when the old woman replied with a sneer and a middle finger.

'Wow. OK. Well...' She blew out a long breath through her cheeks and watched the old woman continue her slow walk down the road.

Leaning an elbow on the door, Cat dropped her head back against the seat and rested it sideways onto her hand. What little energy and hope she'd woken up with this morning had been beaten out of her already today, from one simple conversation at pre-school.

Is everything OK at home, Mrs Holden? Orla's teacher had asked. *Only, Orla seems very down this week, and we've had some behavioural incidents with some of the other children. She's been very withdrawn the last few days, and it just isn't like her.*

Cat closed her eyes and let the tears fall now, unchecked. She'd thought she could do this. She'd thought she could protect her from it all, shelter her from the ugly truth, but who was she kidding? Orla had lost too much. She'd lost her home, her sense of normality, her grandfather, her father – and however useless and uninvolved he was, he was still one of her parents. How on earth was a corner of a poky little room in a B&B and a few toys going to distract her from all of that?

And how was Cat supposed to drag them up out of that situation? Because she was failing at everything. There was no way out and no way up. At least not that she could see right now. But she'd kept going, every day, despite the fact her life was falling apart. Kept paddling and kicking. Because she had to – for Orla. But now she could see she was failing at motherhood too. No matter what she did, this was affecting her daughter more deeply than she'd had any idea of. And now she just felt entirely depleted. All she wanted to do was curl up under a duvet somewhere and hide from the world. Because nothing she did made any difference. Nothing she did helped Orla, and she wasn't any closer to getting the money together for a lawyer to fight Greg. And she knew she needed a damn good one, if she was to stand any chance of proving the will was a fake. So what was the point? Why even bother?

Because if you don't, you can't even afford your room rent, a voice whispered in her mind.

She sighed and closed her eyes for a moment, knowing this was true. Then, with the grim determination of someone with nowhere left to fall, she straightened up, wiped her tears and drove to work.

* * *

Sophia sat on one of the bar stools at the kitchen island nursing a coffee and staring moodily at the clock on the wall. It was eight fifty-three. That woman they'd brought into her house was due to start at nine and, so far, she'd not been late once, but there was a first time for everything. And the day she turned up late, Sophia would make sure she used that against her to the full.

It was petty, she knew. And historically Sophia was anything but petty. If anything, she was usually the most reasonable one in the family. The calm one. The one to help everyone else figure things out in a balanced way. But she'd also never been in this position before, and it had thrown her off completely. She'd always been needed. Always been useful. Always looked after everyone. But now here she was, broken and useless, and she just couldn't bear it. Was this what old age was going to be like? She didn't dare think about that yet. She was nowhere near having to worry about old age. She was still young – or young-*ish*, at least. And she was fit and healthy and strong. Or she had been before her fall.

The sound of the key in the door sounded, and Sophia

huffed, disappointed. The woman was on time again. Well, she'd just have to give her an extra-taxing list of things to do today. She'd tried all last week and the beginning of this one to overload her so much she'd quit, but so far everything Sophia had thrown at her had been taken with a smile and done, very annoyingly, to a decent standard. Not that she'd admit that of course.

Sophia pulled in a deep breath as the woman crossed the hallway to the kitchen and was about to reel off all the jobs she'd written down when the look on Cat's face made her pause. Her eyes were red-rimmed and puffy, and her morning smile was strained, as though she was struggling to put it on today.

'Good morning, Sophia,' Cat said dutifully. 'Is that today's list?' She pointed at the paper in Sophia's hand.

'What's the matter?' Sophia found herself asking.

To her surprise, the sight of Cat being upset bothered her. Just seconds before, she'd been looking for ways to break the woman, but now, seeing her like this, she felt nothing but concern.

'Oh, nothing. I'm fine,' Cat said with a dismissive wave of the hand.

'No, you're not,' Sophia replied bluntly. 'What's happened?'

'Really, it doesn't matter,' Cat replied. 'I just need to get on. I'll start in here and clean up from breakfast, then—'

'Oh, sod the dishes!' Sophia snapped, cutting her off. 'Now, sit down and tell me what's wrong, or I'll fire your bony backside before you can even repeat the word *fine*.'

Cat's mouth dropped open at the strong demand, then she shut it before taking a deep breath. 'OK, well.' Her bottom lip quivered, and she stopped for a moment to swallow and get it back under control. 'My husband threw me and my daughter, Orla, out a few days before I started working here. We're staying in a B&B until I can figure something more permanent out. And, er...' She blew out a long breath, looking away. 'Well, he took everything. And I tried to protect Orla from the worst, make it an adventure rather than a nightmare, but she's not coping as well as I'd thought. Her teacher said she's struggling and is not herself, and...' Cat's voice rose an octave and then trailed off as she began to cry. 'Oh God.' She quickly turned away from Sophia and wiped her tears on the backs of her hands.

At the sight of Cat's distress, Sophia's heart began to ache. She knew, all too well, how much pain a mother carries for her children. If your child hurts, then you hurt double. You carry their hurt with them, and then you hurt again because you can't take that pain away from them. It was one of nature's cruellest laws.

'I'm sorry,' Cat said. Her voice was steady again as she turned back round, but her gaze was cast down, as if ashamed of her outburst. 'I'm fine. It's fine.'

Sophia tutted. 'Stop saying you're *fine*. Of course you're not fine. No one would be, in your position.' She sighed heavily. 'Come. Sit down while I make you a coffee.'

'But—' Cat started.

'I said *sit down*.' Sophia's glare brooked no argument, and this time, sensibly, Cat listened.

Sophia slipped off the stool and used her crutch to hobble over to the stove. She picked up the Moka pot and filled it with fresh coffee grounds, before placing it on the stove and staring off into the distance.

'It's a thankless job,' Sophia said eventually, breaking the long silence that had fallen over the room.

'What is?' Cat asked.

'Motherhood.' Sophia turned and gifted her a small smile. 'Men think it's easy. They have no idea what goes into turning a baby into a well-rounded human being. Of course, even we only have limited power over that. But for those first eighteen years, it is *all* on us. It's on us to keep them alive and healthy. To protect them, physically and mentally. To teach them all they need to know, without scarring them for life.'

'Yeah,' Cat whispered, her eyes misting up. She quickly blinked the mist away.

'But the thing about kids is that they're more resilient than they look. And they understand more than we realise. How old is Orla?' Sophia asked.

Cat sniffed. 'She's three.'

'Mm.' Sophia nodded. 'Is she smart?'

'*Very*,' Cat replied proudly. 'All her pre-school teachers have said how bright she is. She's always been ahead.'

The Moka pot came to a boil, and Sophia took it off the hob, pouring the rich, dark coffee into a mug.

'Then why are you trying to pull the wool over her eyes?' Sophia asked.

The question was met with silence, and so she continued. 'If she's that smart, then she *knows* something bad is going on. She knows *you* better than you know yourself. She knows your moods and your mannerisms. It's the first thing a child learns to read. Imagine being her and knowing something is off with you at the same time you start staying somewhere else.' She picked up the mug and turned, balancing it carefully as she hobbled back to the island. She passed it to Cat, who took it with a murmured thanks.

'Perhaps being honest with her and letting her see you're telling her the truth would be better than trying to hide it. Because it's *you* that's her constant. Not her bed or her front door. Maybe seeing that she can trust in her constant, in her mother, is the best way to make her feel more secure right now.' She winced in pain as she shuffled back onto the stool. 'I don't know your daughter, and I may be wrong – that's up to you to decide. And you may not want my advice. But after raising three of my own children, that's my take on it.'

Cat was silent for a moment, sipping her coffee with a thoughtful expression. Then she put the cup down and nodded.

'Maybe you're right. Either way, it can't hurt to try at this point.'

'I'm not saying it will make things easy,' Sophia added. 'But at least she'll know she has someone she can trust, one hundred per cent. No matter what. And that counts for a lot.'

'Well, thank you for the advice.' Cat smiled. 'And for the coffee. It's really good by the way.'

'Yes. You won't get better coffee than that this side of Italy,' Sophia replied.

'I'd best get on. Shall I take the list?' Cat stood up and held her hand out.

Sophia glanced down at it, looking at all the things she'd added that didn't really need doing. 'No,' she said, sensing her feelings towards Cat shift. 'No, I think today we'll focus on some batch cooking. I'll teach you how to make some really good Italian food.'

'That sounds great,' Cat replied, looking both surprised and relieved in equal measure. She offered Sophia a smile. 'What shall I get out?'

'Eggs and flour first of all. We'll start simple,' Sophia replied.

And as Cat turned away, Sophia crumpled up the long list in her hand and threw it in the bin.

NINETEEN

Maria watched the man sitting on the opposite side of the long table in her meeting room, her red lips curling up in amusement as he smiled inanely back at her.

'So, what brings us together today, Miss Capello?' he asked, his pale blue eyes dropping down to her cleavage and lingering there for a moment before he dragged them back up to her face. 'I must say, it was a pleasant surprise to receive your meeting request.'

His puffy features were pallid, and his receding blond hair had thinned so much she could see his shiny red scalp through it. His bulbous nose drooped until it nearly touched his top lip, and his jaw seemed to melt into his thick neck, as though there was almost no distinctive join at all. Still, Maria preened under his gaze, flashing him a coy look as she pushed her dark hair back over her shoulder.

'I was rather hoping you might be able to do me a favour,' she replied in the smooth, sophisticated accent she adopted whenever speaking to clients or associates on this side of her world. At university she'd learned to hide the tell-tale signs of her roots, making sure that she could fake it well enough to never stand out in the higher circles of legal society.

'Oh, do you now?' the man chuckled, a twinkle in his eye. He leaned forward, staring at her with ill-concealed hunger. 'Well, what I like about giving favours is that it means that person owes you one back. And I'm sure we could come to some sort of suitable arrangement on that part. What is this favour you need?'

Maria smiled at him, genuinely this time, spun the file in front of her around and passed it across the table to him. 'There's a development that's just been passed for two hundred houses to be built on this land, which was green belt until recently. I'm actually amazed it got through, but somehow it did.'

He opened the file and nodded. 'Yes, I'm aware of this development. What about it?'

'I need you to quash it,' she replied.

He looked up at her with raised eyebrows. '*Quash* it?' He laughed. 'I can't do that. It's passed.'

Maria nodded. 'Yes, I thought you might say that. But I need it *un*passed. And I need it done quickly.'

He shut the file with a frown. 'It's just not possible. I'm sorry, Miss Capello. What's the issue with it anyway?'

Maria sighed. 'The issue is personal, and I'm not going to discuss it, but I need this done. Unfortunately, you're the only man who can do it, so, I'm sorry, but if you won't work with me willingly, I'm going to have to dirty my hands.'

She wrinkled her nose as if the idea of this didn't appeal to her, but this couldn't have been further from how she really felt. The man in front of her was a pest in more ways than one, and she was going to get great satisfaction from seeing him sweat.

'Dirty your hands...' he repeated slowly, his eyes narrowing as he began to realise that there was more to this than he'd initially thought. 'I think this meeting is over, Miss Capello.'

'Oh, I don't think it is,' she replied.

She picked up a small remote and clicked a button. A screen behind her lit up, showing camera footage of an empty office. The man opposite her paled.

'A little birdy told me that you have a tendency to cheat on your wife on a regular basis. Often with ladies you've paid for – two of whom have given me similar footage to what I'm about to show you, but this is my favourite tape of you. Because *this* one has footage of you rampantly fucking your regular bit on the side. The one you fuck because, well, because you *can*. And because for some reason she's happy to exchange information for time alone with you. Quite often, time alone in her husband's office.' She paused to glance at the screen, which was now showing the man and a petite, slightly older Indian lady entering the room.

The woman on screen locked the door and then turned straight into his arms, where they began feverishly kissing. The kissing swiftly turned to clothes being hurriedly removed, and they moved to the desk.

'I think we both know what comes next, and I'm sure you won't mind me pausing it here as it's not very pretty.' She hit the button just as he dropped his trousers, his large and blindingly white bottom now taking up the majority of the frozen screen. 'Now, I have no idea what she sees in you myself, nor am I particularly interested, but I'm sure that her husband, the Secretary of State, would be *very* interested. Wouldn't you say?'

Her guest's pale face turned ashen as he stared at his naked backside. 'This is a bit much just to stop a bloody building site. Why are you doing this?'

'I've told you – that's personal,' she replied.

Not that she'd ever tell someone like him, but this new development was over the fields next to one of their most well-hidden underground enterprises. The entrance was at the back of some old barns, through the doors of a container. It was sufficiently tucked away that under normal circumstances people would never find it. Any strays who happened upon it would be unlikely to notice anything amiss, but two hundred houses suddenly overlooking it would be a problem. She didn't need people seeing the men she had working on that project coming and going. It would ruin everything. And she'd worked far too hard and too long on that place to have to shut it down now.

'Maria, this would *ruin* me. I'd lose my job. My wife! This – this could put me in *jail*,' he stuttered.

'Yes, it could, couldn't it?' She glanced back at the still picture on the screen again. 'Of course, I could bury this. It could go somewhere it would never see the light of day again. I'd do you that *favour*, if you were to grant me mine.' She smiled at him coldly. 'That was what you said you liked about favours, right? That to grant one meant you were owed one in return. Well, there you have it. That will be my return.'

His cheeks flushed red as she cornered him completely. 'I want all copies destroyed. And proof of it,' he demanded.

'No,' she replied. 'No, I'll be keeping all copies of this in case I ever need any other favours. And you *will* put a stop to that development if you want me to keep it to myself. *That* is the deal. You are in no position to negotiate.'

The red in his cheeks glowed brighter and darker, and he glared at her with a mixture of alarm and fear and fury. But after several seconds he simply dropped his head into his hands and exhaled defeatedly.

'You're a *bitch*,' he spat.

'No. I'm just a businesswoman who's not afraid to get her hands dirty.' Maria stood up. 'You have a week to send confirmation, or I leak this to his office *and* the press.'

He stood up and made his way to the door, pausing for a moment, as if he wanted to say something, then leaving quickly as though not trusting himself to stay a moment longer.

Maria smiled and turned off the screen before walking

through to her reception area after him. The front door was just closing behind him, but Maria's gaze was drawn to the woman sitting in one of the chairs in the waiting area, an amused smile on her pale and flawlessly beautiful face.

'Anna Davis, what a pleasant surprise,' Maria said, trying to hide her shock at seeing her there. 'Please come through. Jen, can you hold my calls?'

Anna stood up, brushing down the tailored knee-length burgundy dress that hugged her slender figure. 'Thanks for seeing me,' she said politely, though they both knew that Maria would never dream of turning her away.

'Not at all. How are you? How is everyone?' Maria asked, guiding Anna through to her personal office.

'Well, thanks.' Anna looked around as Maria shut the door, then took a seat in the chair nearest the desk. She pushed her dark hair behind her ear and crossed her slim legs, before lacing her fingers together and resting them in her lap.

Maria sat down behind the desk, her mind whirling as she tried to work out why Anna Davis, underworld royalty by association to her long-term partner, Freddie Tyler, was here.

'I'll cut to the chase,' Anna said, just as Maria opened her mouth to ask, 'as I'm sure you're wondering why I'm here.' She reached down into the large handbag she'd brought with her and pulled out a pair of men's shoes. She placed them on the desk. 'Your brother left these in my establishment last night.'

Maria's stomach dropped, and she briefly closed her eyes, silently cursing Antonio and damning him to hell. Anna Davis wouldn't come all this way just to drop off a pair of shoes, which meant he'd done something. Something bad enough to put them on the Tyler firm's radar – and not in a good way.

Maria put her flattened hands together and touched them to her mouth. 'What did he do?' she asked, not sure she wanted to hear the answer.

Anna pursed her deep red lips and her grey-blue eyes met

Maria's. Her gaze was steely, but her expression was unreadable, and for a few long, tense seconds she remained silent. Eventually she pulled in a deep breath and exhaled slowly.

'Antonio visited Heaven Above late last night. He got a bit, er, let's call it *strong* with one of my girls.'

'Shit,' Maria muttered, horrified.

It was bad enough that he'd get *strong* with a woman anywhere, but on Tyler turf, with one of their own employees? Antonio was practically *asking* for a war with them. With the largest and most powerful firm in the city. With a firm they'd worked hard to become – and to stay – allies with.

'Out of respect for who he is, I simply had him removed and taken home,' Anna told her. 'Though he probably arrived back with a bruise or two,' she added.

Maria felt relief wash through her like a wave, at the tact and restraint Anna had shown. This could be salvaged.

'Thank you,' she said. 'I am so sorry for what happened. It will never happen again.'

'No. It won't,' Anna agreed, a hardness underlining her words. 'He's barred from my establishments. I haven't mentioned this to Freddie or anyone else, so his business with them is his own. But if this ever happens again on *my* premises, I won't be quite so discreet or accommodating.'

'Of course,' Maria said hurriedly. 'I completely understand. He'll be warned. And if there's any reparations to be made with your girl...'

'It's taken care of,' Anna replied. 'Just see to it that this remains a one-off. We have enough on our plate with our enemies. We don't need to deal with issues from our allies too.'

It was said softly enough, but Maria heard the warning loud and clear.

'That's not something you ever need to worry about. Our friendship with your firm is as important to us now as it was a year ago,' Maria said, holding Anna's gaze to press home her meaning.

A year before, their uncle Mani, who'd run a smaller firm to theirs in another part of the city, had gone up against one of the largest allies of the Tylers. The Tylers had got involved and spread the word that anyone helping Mani would be considered an enemy. When Mani had gone to them, seeking support in his pointless war against half of London, they'd turned him away. They'd held no love for their lying, cheating uncle, even before then. Nor for his predatory son, whose deep levels of depravity had just been discovered and made public. Their loyalty to the Tylers had been more than proven back then.

Anna nodded. 'Good. Let's hope it stays that way.' She smiled and stood up. 'Please pass on my regards to Alex and Sophia.'

'Of course.' Maria stood up and followed her out of the room. 'I would ask you to pass mine on to Freddie and Paul, but I think this time it's probably best that you don't.'

Anna smiled. 'Yes, probably. Goodbye, Maria.'

Maria smiled back. 'Bye, Anna.'

She watched her leave and then stared at the closed door, her heart racing as she thought about her errant younger brother.

'Miss Capello?' Jen asked tentatively. 'Is everything OK?'

But Maria didn't answer. Instead, she marched back into her office and grabbed her phone. She called Alex, who answered on the second ring.

'Alex, we need to do something about Antonio. I've just had Anna Davis in my office. He's gone too far this time.'

TWENTY

Cat paced up and down the long dining area adjacent to the kitchen in Sophia's home, and bit her thumbnail. It was a habit she'd forced herself out of years ago, but today she was so preoccupied with feelings of dread for what she was about to do that she didn't even notice herself doing it. Sophia had popped out for a bit with a friend, so she was alone in the house, and as she'd finished all her jobs for today, she really had no reason to put it off any further. However much she wished she could find one.

With a deep sigh and a grimace, Cat dialled the number and put the phone to her ear. Her stomach did a nauseous little flip when Greg answered the call.

'Yes?' he asked.

Cat unclenched her teeth with difficulty and fought the urge to say all the things she *really* wanted to say. 'We need to discuss Orla,' she told him in as flat a tone as she could manage.

He hesitated. 'Orla?' he repeated, sounding surprised.

'Yes, your *daughter*. Remember her?' Cat snapped, unable to stop herself.

'Obviously,' he replied icily. 'I'm just surprised that's what you're calling to discuss.'

Cat clenched her free fist and bit her bottom lip hard as her face contorted angrily. She made herself take a breath before answering. 'Well, *I'm* surprised you haven't yet asked to see her.'

She wasn't surprised. Not even slightly. Greg's lack of interest in his daughter was far from new, and he'd got all he wanted out of Cat, so he didn't even have reason to use Orla as a pawn against her. But at the very least her words should shame him. If he even had it in him to be shamed anymore.

'Oh. Right.'

His tone was reluctant, and it just fuelled Cat's hatred for him even more. But she closed her eyes and swallowed the hatred down, reminding herself that this wasn't about her. It wasn't about *him* either. She was doing this for Orla.

She'd taken Sophia's advice and had explained to her daughter, in simplified terms, that she and Greg were separating and that things would be changing. Orla had asked some questions and been a little subdued, but she'd seemed to be comforted, in the end, by Cat's honesty. The next morning, Cat had told the same version of events to her teacher, and the next evening Orla had asked when she could visit her daddy. Cat had promised to find out.

'Well?' she prompted as he fell silent. 'Don't you *want* to see her?'

'Of course I do. I just assumed you'd make that difficult, with all that's happened,' he replied.

'Oh, don't lie, Greg,' Cat snapped back in a low voice. 'You don't get to put your laziness as a father on *me*. If you'd wanted to see her, you'd have asked. But you didn't. And while I'd be quite happy never to see you again, *she* wants to see you. And I swear to God, whatever's going on with us, I'll be *damned* if you deprive her of this too.'

'Well, I'm busy tonight, but I could have her tomorrow,' he replied lazily, ignoring her anger.

Cat looked out of the French doors onto the manicured garden beyond and shook her head, wishing she could tell him where to go. Wishing she could protect her daughter from his lack of care for her but knowing that wasn't her decision to make.

'Fine.' She forced the word out. 'I'll drop her to the house at five with her overnight bag. You can drop her straight to pre-school in the morning.'

'Ooh, er, morning. Hmm. Not sure if—' He started making excuses, but she cut him off.

'You'll *take her* to *pre-school*,' she said sharply. 'And you can get used to that. Because whenever you have her going forward, you'll no longer have me there to pull your share of the weight. Oh, and you can start paying me that child maintenance you mentioned, too. You might have possession of my home and family business for now – and believe me, it *is* just for now, until I've got the means to fight you, Greg – but you can damn well start paying something towards your daughter. Not that you've even *asked* but we're currently sharing a room in a B&B. We don't even have a proper home right now.'

'Huh! Good luck with that. As for the maintenance, I'll have to work out what I can spare you. Maybe from next month,' he said with a mocking laugh that felt like a cheese grater on her nerves.

'*No*, Greg. You'll start sending something to help *now*, or I'll go through the CSA. And I doubt they'll care much for your excuses. I don't care much which way it goes, so I'll leave that up to you, but you have until the end of the week to decide.'

Unable to stand his voice for even a second more, she ended the call and let out a loud sound of frustration.

'Oh dear. Having baby-daddy problems, are we?'

The voice made Cat jump, and she turned around, a sinking feeling settling in the pit of her stomach.

* * *

Antonio leaned against the door frame and cast his eyes over the shocked-looking woman, enjoying what he saw. With her slim, elegant figure, rich chocolate brown hair and equally warm brown eyes in a pale, delicately shaped face, Cat was exactly his type. He'd watched her flitting around the house a few times this past week or so, smiling at him and wafting the scent of her perfume his way whenever she passed, and her presence had been driving him crazy. It was like she was a God-given gift, just for him. Placed here for him to enjoy at his leisure. But though he'd seen her a number of times, this was the first time he'd been here with her alone. The very thought of that sparked a bolt of excitement within him.

'Didn't mean to make you jump,' he said with a devilish grin.

'No, it's fine. I just didn't realise anyone was here or I'd have taken that call later,' she replied, pushing her loose hair back behind one ear and looking past him to the hallway. 'Sorry about that. I'm finished for the day anyway.'

'Well, how about that. Me too,' Antonio declared, walking over to her and stopping just a little too close. He watched her freeze, and his grin widened. He liked them like that. A little off-kilter. A little unsure. 'Two young, attractive people like us, both off work for the afternoon. Now, what should we do? I wonder. I can think of a couple of things.' He bit his lip and reached for her waist, looking down at her with intent.

She moved away much quicker than he'd thought she would, so he had no time to grab her properly before she nipped around him towards the hall.

'Sorry, I have to go,' Cat said in a rattled tone. 'My daughter's waiting. Sophia, um, your mum, she's due back any minute if it's her you're here for. Bye.'

She was out of the house faster than a bolt of lightning, and Antonio watched her leave with a mixture of shock, yearning and outrage. He'd wanted her. He'd wanted her for days, and now he finally had her alone she *ran off*? No. That wouldn't do. She couldn't tease him like that, running around here all the time, giving him those flirtatious little smiles, then leave him hanging. He exhaled heavily through his nose.

Clearly Cat was going to play hard to get, but that was OK. He had time, and he could gather some patience. He was the master of the long game. But one thing was for certain. He *would* have her. Whether she realised it yet or not. Because once Antonio Capello decided he wanted something, nothing in heaven or on earth could stop him from getting it.

TWENTY-ONE

Alex marched down the busy street lined with eclectic vintage shops and grabbed his brother by the jacket, swinging him round and shoving him into an alleyway between two buildings. He sidestepped the stream of dirty rainwater running down the middle into a small swamp above a blocked drain and pushed Antonio against the soot-blackened brick wall with a furious glare.

'What were you *thinking*?' he demanded.

Antonio assessed him for a moment. 'Yeah, you're going to have to be more specific.'

'Seriously?' Alex made a growl of frustration and shoved away from him, turning in a circle and running both hands down the back of his head. 'It's bad enough you pissing off our dealers and putting Maria on the line, but fucking with the *Tylers*? *Really*? Are you *trying* to destroy us?'

'Oh, that,' Antonio replied, stepping forward and scratching his nose with a sniff. 'Alright, admittedly that wasn't my best move.'

'Not your best move?' Alex rounded on him. 'It's fucking suicide! You're lucky Anna decided to deal with it the way she did – and God only knows why she did. You won't be so lucky again. I *told* you to stay away from them the other night. I *told* you to steer fucking clear.'

Antonio stepped forward until he was right in front of Alex, a hard glint in his eye. 'Yeah, you did, didn't you?' he asked, his casual tone not hiding the coldness beneath his words. 'But that's the thing, you see. I don't like being told what to do. Especially not by you.'

'What's that supposed to mean?' Alex asked.

'It means, I ain't some fucking puppy you can order round and expect to follow,' Antonio told him, his eyes narrowing as he pressed his face nearer. 'It *means* this firm is as much under *my* rule as it is yours, and you'd best not forget that. You don't have *no* right to tell *me* what to do.'

'Are you *serious* right now?' Alex exploded. 'Antonio, you're a fucking *mess*. You forfeited not being told what to do when you started putting us all in danger. Maria wants you *out* and, honestly, it's getting harder and harder to find reasons why you should be allowed to stay.'

'*Allowed?*' Antonio barked back with a humourless laugh. '*Allowed?* I built half this fucking business up without *either* of you lifting a damn finger! *I'm* the one who made the connections for the drugs. Dealt with negotiations, built up the dealer chains, carved out a section of this city's market to call our own. *Me*,' he growled. 'Not you, not Maria, *me*.'

Alex nodded, stepping back, away from his brother. 'Yeah, that was you. Same way other parts of the business were all of us. It don't matter who did what, Antonio – it's all under one firm. It's all for the good of this *family*. The same way me telling you *not* to piss off the royal fucking family of this city is for the good of this family. So whether you like it or not, you're going to have to step back and toe the line for a bit, if you don't want to cause complete carnage and either topple our businesses or get us all fucking killed. Do you understand me?'

Antonio glared at him for a few moments, and Alex glared right back, not willing to let it all go this time. He'd let Antonio run riot for far too long, and he shouldn't have. He should have reined him in a long time ago. Eventually, Antonio's lips curled up into a cold smirk, and he huffed out a silent laugh.

'Oh, I understand you loud and clear,' he replied. 'But if you're quite finished mouthing off on that soap box of yours, our current priority is not getting caught with a car full of hot cash. So, come on. We've got bills to clean, and we ain't got all day.' He turned and sauntered out of the alleyway, giving Alex no choice but to follow.

They walked together down the street in brooding silence, towards Antonio's car. Alex clamped his jaw tightly shut, not trusting himself to speak until he'd further calmed himself down. Antonio frustrated him beyond belief. As his brother, he loved him. But as his business partner, right now, he hated him. He was becoming more and more of a liability every day, and there was just no reasoning with him. If only Antonio showed some sign of understanding – of realisation about what he was doing to them all – he could have some faith in his brother turning things around. But all Antonio seemed to show was an ever-growing chip on his shoulder.

A couple walked past them, more engrossed in each other than where they were going, and they swerved into Antonio at the last second to avoid being run over by a bike. The man had a takeaway cup in his hand, and the flimsy cardboard crumpled between his and Antonio's torso, sending hot, milky coffee splashing out over both of them.

'What the—' Antonio exclaimed.

'Oh God, sorry, mate, I didn't—'

But the man didn't get to finish before Antonio grabbed the front of his shirt and lifted him up off the ground with the adrenaline-fuelled power of pure anger, and a deep, furious growl.

'Hey, hey, hey!' Alex turned to him in alarm.

They were in the middle of a busy street and – as Antonio had pointed out just seconds before – in possession of a lot of hot cash. The last thing they needed to do was draw attention to themselves.

'It was an accident. Come on, Antonio.' His eyes flashed in warning. '*Think*.'

Antonio made a sound of angry reluctance then threw the man to the side. His shoulder hit the wall of a shop, but he managed to stay upright, and his girlfriend, who looked terrified, quickly pulled him away.

'Pull it together, yeah?' Alex said quietly through gritted teeth.

Antonio looked down at his coffee-soaked jacket. 'Easy for you to say,' he muttered, disgruntled.

'Come on.' Alex propelled him forward, towards the car park they always used. 'We'll pop back to yours and get you cleaned up after the drops, OK?'

'It's fine. I've got something in the boot,' Antonio replied.

They reached Antonio's car, and Alex waited while Antonio changed his long, thick, woollen jacket for the more casual black bomber he still had in the boot from their escapades at Frank Sinclair's house. Out of habit, Alex cast his eye around the full car park, double-checking that they weren't being followed. He'd found, over the years, that it usually paid off to undertake their more routinely nefarious tasks, such as this, in plain sight. Somewhere busy enough to hide their actions among everyone else's but with enough space they wouldn't be watched too closely.

Antonio zipped the bomber up and closed the boot, walking around to the passenger side to get the money. Just as he reached for the handle, Alex called out to him in a low, urgent voice.

'Stop. Don't open the door.' He squeezed his gaze at the van that had just entered the car park at the other end. It had stopped still, just inside the entrance, not driving onwards in either direction. 'Keep walking like we're just passing these cars,' he ordered, carefully moving to do the same.

Antonio did as he'd asked. 'Who is it?' he asked without looking around.

Alex kept his head turned just enough to keep the van in his peripheral vision. 'I don't know,' he said slowly. 'But something ain't right.'

The van turned and began slowly making its way down one of the many rows of cars ahead of them. Maybe he'd been wrong, Alex reasoned. Maybe he was just jumpy after the spectacle in the street. Still, it didn't hurt to be careful. They were carrying a lot of money in that car, and it was just the two of them out here today. He was pretty sure the occupants of the van hadn't seen them with the boot open though, so even if they were a threat, they shouldn't know which car was theirs.

As the van drew closer, he tried to see who was driving, but the side windows had been tinted, blocking his view. Alex frowned. There weren't many reasons to black-out van windows, and certainly no good ones. He glanced ahead. They were walking in the direction of the high street, as though off to do some shopping. If they kept going at this pace, they would directly cross paths with the van, just ahead. He slowed to a pause and called out to Antonio in warning, but it seemed the people inside had seen the penny drop, and the van sped up to cut them off quicker. The side door opened, and four men in ski masks jumped out, leaping towards them.

'Antonio, run!' Alex yelled.

He turned to do the same but skidded to a stop just a second later at the sound of his brother's curses. Two of the men in masks had hold of Antonio and were dragging him back towards the van. The other two were running towards him.

'Hey! Get off him!' Alex bellowed, starting back towards the van, not caring who he had to fight to get there.

Antonio was putting up a good fight, wildly thrashing around, and as one of his arms came loose, he didn't waste any time in punching the man who was struggling to keep hold of him square in the face. The other yelled at one of the men running towards Alex to come help him, unable to hold Antonio alone, leaving just one for Alex to now get through.

Alex reached into his back pocket and pulled out a switchblade, flicking it up as the man neared. He swiped it through the air, narrowly missing the man's arm, then swiped again, this time nicking him across the bicep. With a cry, he retreated, unable to take Alex on alone and unarmed, but Alex remained hot on his heels.

'Give me back my brother,' he roared.

The three other men had managed, between them, to get Antonio into the van, and now one of them came back to help the other with Alex. For a second, the pair tried grabbing him, but all they managed to do was awkwardly circle him while keeping out of the vicious arcs Alex was making with his knife. It was a tense stand-off, but then suddenly someone called out a warning from the van. They made a last-ditch attempt at grabbing Alex, then as one of them took his attention, the other kicked him hard in the stomach.

Alex flew back against the side of a car and made a loud whooshing sound as all the air was knocked out of his lungs, but he still managed to keep hold of his blade, knowing it was the only thing giving him the edge in this two-on-one situation. Winded and sinking to the cold, wet tarmac, all he could do was watch as the two men jumped back inside the van with the others, closed the doors and screeched off with his brother.

He let out a helpless sound, fighting to get his breath back as he reached out at the fading tail lights, then, folding the blade away with hands still shaking from the adrenaline, he reached for his phone. It took a second for him to find the number and for the call to connect, then Maria's voice sounded on the other end of the phone.

'Maria,' he said breathlessly. 'They've taken, *ugh*, they've taken Antonio.'

'*What?*' she exclaimed. 'Who has?'

'I don't know,' he replied, closing his eyes and resting his head back against the car he'd slumped down beside. 'I have no fucking idea.'

TWENTY-TWO

Maria looked up at the tall, brick Soho building and smoothed her long, dark hair before reaching forward and rapping loudly on the discreet door. A few moments passed and then the door opened, a young, thin, blonde woman staring out suspiciously from the other side.

'Can I 'elp you?' she asked, not particularly friendlily.

'Is Anna or Tanya around?' Maria asked.

The girl sniffed. 'Not 'ere. Try Club Anya, round the corner. One of 'em's usually there, this time of day.'

'Thank...' Maria trailed off as the girl promptly shut the door.

She composed herself and turned towards Greek Street, where she knew the club to be. Orange-and-white plastic fences cordoned off an area where workers in hi-vis safety vests were doing something in a large hole in the road, and Maria crossed to the other side, so as to not get in the way. As she did, she heard an unmistakable voice shout out behind her.

'Oi! Watch where you leave those bloody tools! These coffees nearly ended up on your 'eads!'

One of the workers called out an apology, and Maria

watched the scowling woman resecure the cardboard tray in her hand. With her signature long red curls, bright red lipstick and curve-hugging knee-length dress, Tanya Smith was a strikingly beautiful woman. She was also Anna Davis's business partner. Pursing her lips determinedly, Maria hurried back across the road towards her, cutting her off just as she reached the front door of Club Anya.

'Tanya, hi.' She raised a hand in greeting with a tight smile.

Tanya gave a puzzled little frown as though trying to place her, then her expression opened up into a dawning smile. 'Hi. Maria, isn't it? Capello?'

'Yeah, that's me,' Maria answered, glancing at the club door. There was a closed sign clearly displayed through the glass. 'Can I come in? I, er, I need to discuss something with you.'

She hadn't wanted to believe it was the Tylers who had taken Antonio, but it was the only thing that made any sense. If Anna, or perhaps one of the others, had let slip that Antonio had treated her girls and her place of business with such disrespect, Freddie would be furious. He'd have had Antonio taken somewhere secure where he could deal with him privately. The very thought filled her with dread. What would Freddie do to him? What idiocy would come out of her brother's mouth in return? What did all of it mean for their professional relationship going forward? They couldn't afford to be frozen out by the Tylers. Because that would be the end of all of it. Of everything they'd built. These worries swirled around her head like a blizzard, but she forced herself to relax and smile politely.

''Course,' Tanya replied easily. 'Come on in. I'd offer you a coffee, but our bloody machine's broken and half of this lot's now on the pavement.'

'Oh, don't worry. I'm fine,' Maria rushed to assure her as Tanya led the way inside. 'I can't stay long. Is Anna here?'

'Yeah, she's in the back. Come on through.' Tanya walked briskly across the empty club towards a hallway at the back, her heels tapping out a sharp rhythm and echoing around the large, high-ceilinged room.

As Maria followed her into a small but cosy office, Anna looked up from a sea of papers covering the desk, her eyebrows shooting upwards in surprise.

'Maria, how are you?' She subtly turned the top piece of paper over to cover the rest, her gaze sliding questioningly towards Tanya.

'Maria wants to talk to us about something,' Tanya told her with a slight shrug.

'Please sit down,' Anna offered. 'What's up? Antonio lose his socks too?'

A hint of amusement lifted the corners of her mouth, but this didn't comfort Maria. Anna Davis was well known for her ability to keep up a cool mask, no matter what the situation. Maria took the seat opposite Anna and smiled back, working to keep her own expression as unreadable as Anna's.

'Maybe, but that's the least of his worries right now,' she replied carefully. 'Antonio's missing.'

'Missing?' Tanya repeated, sitting down on a small, comfortable-looking sofa at the side of the room.

'Yeah, he and Alex were in a car park when a van appeared and four blokes took him,' Maria told them.

'Just him?' Tanya queried.

Maria nodded. 'Alex tried to fight them off, to get to Antonio, but they knocked him back and scarpered. Quiet location, blacked-out van, ski masks... It was a well-planned set-up.'

Anna's grey-blue eyes held hers, the previous warmth in them gone. 'And you think it was us,' she stated quietly.

Maria drew in a deep breath, aware she was suddenly on rocky ground. 'I think the only people who'd have cause to want to string my brother up right now – and quite rightly so – would be you guys.'

Annoyance flashed across Anna's face, and her jaw tightened. 'I thought I'd made myself clear, Maria. The matter was dealt with and we moved on. The last thing I want to waste my time on is a feud with a friendly firm. I can't see the point there. Can you?' The question was laced with subtle warning, and Maria cringed internally.

Goddamn you, Antonio, she silently cursed.

'That's the last thing *any* of us wants of course,' Maria agreed. 'I just wondered whether perhaps Freddie might have caught wind somehow? You and I put the matter to bed, yes, but if he knew...'

'Then he'd raise hell to teach your brother a lesson,' Tanya finished, nodding slowly. She cast her gaze to meet Anna's. 'Who was there? Any chance it could have got back to him?'

Anna shook her head. 'No, definitely not. I was discreet. The only people who know wouldn't say a word. And even if someone had, he'd have been here raging to me first, checking the facts before he made a move. You know how careful he is. No.' Anna rested back in her chair. 'This is nothing to do with us.' She turned her attention to Maria. 'If we're all you can think of when it comes to who your brother's pissed off lately, then you need to dig a little deeper. Because I assure you, from what I've heard, we're just the tip of the iceberg.'

'Right.'

Maria felt a coldness sweep through her as she hit the dead end. Not that she'd wanted it to be the Tylers. Literally anyone else in their world would be a better adversary to face. But this had been the only solid lead she had. So if it hadn't been the Tylers who'd taken him, who the hell had?

TWENTY-THREE

Alex paced back and forth across the small, dimly lit lounge of the tenth-floor flat, biting his thumbnail as he worried about his brother. It had been hours since he'd been taken. Hours in which he could have been beaten or tortured, or worse. Antonio was a pain in the arse half the time, but he was still their brother, and Alex couldn't stand the thought of him being in a situation where he was outnumbered, and no doubt bound, surrounded by enemies. The outrage of it all built up in the centre of his chest like a molten ball, so hot it almost hurt.

'Where the fuck is he, Darren?' Alex growled.

'Alex, I *told* you, I don't know. I really don't,' came the earnest reply from the man sat in the middle of the room on one of his own dining chairs.

He wasn't tied up. Not yet, at least. Joe and Danny stood either side of him, keeping him in check, and Darren wasn't stupid enough to try and move, even had they not been there. Instead, he sat dutifully still, his hands in his lap as he looked up worriedly at his boss.

'Look, I get it. He pissed you off once too many times. Yeah?' Alex shrugged. 'He's fucked about with your supplies, messed up your chain by keeping hold of the goods himself here and there. Stuffing it up his own nose rather than sending it down the distribution line. It must have made you look proper unreliable. Not what any drug dealer needs.'

Darren let out a frustrated sign. 'Honestly, it *weren't me*. Alright, had he pissed me off? *Yeah.* 'Course he had. It ain't exactly cool having to tell my regulars I ain't had the delivery I was promised. Even worse having him waltz in here and take it back in *front* of them, after I'd started doling it out. I looked like a right twat.' Darren sniffed. 'But I ain't stupid, man. I don't bite the hand that feeds me. Even if it does nick back me dinner from time to time. Man's still gotta eat.'

Alex nodded, his anger and worry rising as each second ticked on. He believed Darren. He really did. But he had to be sure before he moved on. Rounding on the man, he suddenly bent down and grasped his neck, bellowing in his face.

'*Where. Fucking. Is he?* You wanna die, Darren? You wanna go slowly and painfully? Or do you want to save us all the fucking runaround and the grief of having to hide your fucking body, and just tell us?'

Darren's eyes bulged as Alex squeezed, but he still managed to shake his head vehemently from side to side as he squeaked out his reply. 'It wasn't me! It wasn't me! Alex, I swear to God!'

Alex let go of him and stepped back, staring down at the now gasping man with a cold, hard expression. 'It better not have been, Darren. 'Cause if I find out down the line it was, you're gonna wish I had just killed ya.'

Darren nodded, putting his hand up as if to signal a white flag. 'I hear you. I swear down, I know nothing. I didn't know he was gone till you arrived. But if I hear anything, I'll come straight to you. You are my boss after all. And I'm still loyal.'

His last few words had a hint of accusation in them, and Alex felt a small spear of guilt. Darren *had* been loyal. Even when Antonio messed things up for him time and time again.

But Alex didn't have time to pussyfoot around people. He needed to get to his brother before it was too late, and Darren was someone Alex *knew* Antonio had screwed over. He was someone with just cause, and even though it had seemed a little far-fetched, after Maria had discounted the Tylers, he was the next best bet they had.

Looking up at Joe and Danny, he tilted his head towards the door. They peeled off without a word, and Alex stood there for a moment, staring out of the window at the grey side of the next high-rise block.

'See to it that you do pass on anything you find out. It'll be rewarded,' he said gruffly.

'Yes, boss,' Darren replied quietly.

Alex sniffed and walked out into the hallway where his men were waiting.

'What now?' Joe asked as they walked together into the cold stairwell.

'I don't know,' Alex admitted. 'I can't think of anyone else he's pissed off lately who'd have the means to take him like that. Short of nicking a sniffer dog to track him d...' He trailed off, his eyes widening as something suddenly occurred to him.

'What?' Danny asked. 'What is it?'

'I think I know how to find him,' Alex breathed. He'd slowed to a stop, but now he darted forward, suddenly full of purpose. 'I think I can figure out *exactly* where he is.'

TWENTY-FOUR

Cat finished the last set of bedding in the last spare room and fiddled around with the corners of the duvet until it was so perfectly straight a hospital matron would have been proud. Casting her eye over it one more time, she felt almost disappointed that there was nothing more to do to improve it then turned with a sigh back to the hallway.

Sophia came out of her bedroom, still hobbling slowly and awkwardly on her crutch. She blinked, looking surprised when she saw Cat. 'What are you still doing here?'

'I said I could stay late today, remember?' Cat replied. 'Get some of the bigger jobs done that I don't usually have time for.'

In truth, there was nothing big that *needed* doing. Sophia had kept the place spotlessly clean, so her job was really just to maintain things, but in a house this large there were always tasks that could be found.

Sophia checked her watch. 'Yes, but it's nearly seven. I didn't mean to keep you *this* late.'

'Oh, it's fine. Really,' Cat insisted. 'I like to get ahead of myself, you know?'

'But what about your daughter?' Sophia asked, looking concerned. 'Orla, isn't it?'

'Yeah, she, er...' Cat bit her lip, trying to quell the sting that pulsated in her stomach as she thought about Orla right now. 'I don't have her tonight.'

Sophia studied her for a moment, her piercing gaze seeming to see right past Cat's attempt at a blasé response and right into the very core of her mind. Cat fought the urge to look away, knowing it wouldn't help. The woman was too sharp for that to put her off.

'She with her dad?' Sophia asked.

Cat just nodded, not trusting herself to speak without opening the floodgates of bitter hate and deep worry. Sophia didn't need the ins and outs of her personal dramas.

'Well.' Sophia looked around her immaculate hall. 'You're on the right track, keeping busy, but you're not going to find much more to keep yourself distracted around here. Why don't you go home and run yourself a nice hot bath, pour a glass of wine and relax, eh? Give yourself a break.'

Cat let out a short laugh, and a corner of her mouth lifted in a wry smile. 'I would if the B&B actually had a bath. But even then...' She trailed off with a sigh. 'I don't want to sit there all night without Orla. It feels too weird. I know I'll get used to it eventually, but...' She shrugged. 'I don't know. I can't face it yet.'

Sophia's expression softened slightly in a look that could have been sympathy. Cat wasn't sure though. She was still learning to read the older woman. Sophia was as sharp as a sushi knife and as hard as nails when she wanted to be. But she'd thawed out over the last few days, ever since Cat had walked in upset, and Cat felt like she was now getting to know a whole different person again.

Sophia hobbled over to her and gestured down the hallway behind her. 'Then you stay here. But not to clean. I'm going out for dinner and I won't be home until late. These four walls are driving me insane.' She rolled her eyes dramatically. 'And no one else is due here tonight. Maria mentioned earlier not to expect any of them. So you'll have the house to yourself for a few hours.'

'Oh, I—' Cat started to protest, but Sophia cut her off.

'No, you will not turn me down. I *insist*,' she said firmly. 'Go and have a hot bath, read a book, listen to music, whatever, I don't care. But *relax*. Give yourself a break – you deserve it.'

Cat shifted her weight from one foot to the other, feeling awkward. 'You're sure you don't mind? I mean, leaving me here alone?' She suddenly felt a pang of anxiety, thinking about all the things that could go wrong.

Sophia laughed, amused. 'Why not? You're here all day, aren't you? What are you going to do – burn my house down? Steal from me?' She laughed again at the look of horror on Cat's face. 'Oh, darling, if any of us thought you'd do either, you wouldn't be here at all. Even if you were a thief, which I know you are not, you're far too smart to ever consider stealing from *this* family.' She gave Cat a knowing look, the smile still playing on her lips.

'I – um...' Cat glanced behind her towards the bathroom. The lure of a hot bath to take her mind off things really was inviting. But this conversation was making her feel incredibly off-kilter.

'Catriona?' Sophia called her attention back with her full name. 'Stop overthinking it. Stay. Have a bath. Use the nice bubbles and help yourself to some wine. There's a bottle in the fridge. When you return home, you'll sleep better, then tomorrow Orla will be back and all will be well again.'

'OK. Alright, I will.' Cat watched Sophia make her slow way down the stairs, knowing better than to offer help after several previous failed attempts. 'Thank you, Sophia.'

'It's nothing,' Sophia called back to her. 'I'll see you in the morning.'

As her employer disappeared around the foot of the stairs, Cat's gaze moved to the bathroom. A little pinch of hope rose in her chest, and a slight smile warmed her face. She still missed Orla and felt sick with worry about how she was coping with Greg, without her. But for the first time since she'd left her home, Cat allowed herself a moment to think about herself. And it felt nice. It felt more than nice.

Walking first to the airing cupboard, she took out a freshly washed, thick, warm bath towel and carried it through to the bathroom. Then, as her smile spread wide across her face, she shut the door and set about running herself a bath.

TWENTY-FIVE

'They're in there,' Alex murmured, peering through the dense row of trees bordering the small, half-abandoned industrial estate below.

He stepped back to the path where Maria stood with one arm crossed tightly over her middle, taking a deep pull of smoke from the cigarette in her other hand. She only smoked when she was stressed, and, right now, all of them were incredibly stressed.

'You're sure?' she asked in a low, urgent tone. 'You're absolutely certain? This is *that* accurate?' She gestured towards his phone with her cigarette as she blew out the smoke.

'It's that accurate,' Alex confirmed. 'They'll have taken his phone off him in the van, probably thrown it en route, but they won't know about this.'

It had suddenly hit him, as he'd departed Darren's flat, that his brother had been carrying their spare AirTag in the inner pocket of his bomber jacket. The bomber jacket he'd changed into when the coffee had been knocked all over his suit jacket. The first tag had been left on the underside of Frank Sinclair's car in order to track his movements. They hadn't used the second, meaning it would still be in Antonio's pocket, and Alex had access to the tracking.

They'd had to wait to gather their men together and to make sure they had enough weapons to go in there. They had no idea how many men would be inside or whether they'd be packing heat. They still didn't even know who they were dealing with. All they knew was that Antonio was inside one of the buildings below.

Alex's phone buzzed, and he glanced at the screen. 'They're nearly here. Keep a lookout up here and warn me if anyone else arrives.'

Maria nodded and sat back against the hood of her car with a strained expression as she stared down at the dimly lit, square grey buildings.

Alex jogged a little way down the road and then through the trees, down the sharp slope, to the service road below. Several darkly hooded figures ran over to meet him at the corner of the building next to the one they needed to enter, and they stopped for a moment just out of sight.

One of the men slipped his hood down and looked at Alex with a hard expression. 'What's the plan?'

Alex scratched his forehead, eyeing the collection of pipes, bats and blades they each held. 'We don't know how many are in there, so it's hard to make a plan. All we can do is try and sneak up, pray the element of surprise helps and do whatever's necessary to get him out.'

The men exchanged a few grim glances, but all of them nodded their agreement. No one liked this. Least of all Alex. It was a badly laid plan – if it could even be *called* a plan – and he knew he was asking a lot of them. It was putting every one of them in danger, and that was something he didn't do lightly. But on this occasion, there were no other options to consider.

'Split off after we've got him out. Get alibis, stay low, check in with me tomorrow. Got it?'

Alex raised an eyebrow and was met with a return chorus of *Yes, boss*.

'Right. Let's go. You three with me at the front, you four round the back,' Alex ordered. 'Be ready to go in just after we do.'

Praying he wasn't walking into something they couldn't handle, he led his half of the group on towards the front of the small, square building. It wasn't very big, the corrugated metal walls not broken up with windows. Most likely, it was supposed to have been used as a storage unit. There was one small door at the front and a much bigger roller door at the back, but other than that it was plain, with no markings or signs. No clue to tell him who the place belonged to.

It surprised Alex that there were no guards outside. They were either far too confident in the secrecy of this place, or he was walking into a very big trap. He felt the heaviness of unease settle on his chest but pushed on, trying to ignore it. If it was a trap, then he'd deal with whatever was coming to him. No matter the cost, he couldn't just leave Antonio there. Blood was thicker than water after all. And in their world, blood was thicker than anything.

They reached the door, and Alex paused, straining his ears, trying to hear anything that could give them some clue as to what they were about to face. He could just detect a couple of muffled voices. One with a questioning lilt to its tone and the other with a louder, more aggressive, mocking tone.

'Well, he's alive at least,' whispered Danny, who also had his ear to the door.

He cracked a half-hearted grin, which Alex returned. They'd all know the sound of Antonio's scathing sarcasm anywhere. Still, just because he was alive, it didn't mean he wasn't badly hurt. Antonio would give as good as he got until his last dying breath.

Praying he wasn't dragging them all to bloody premature

deaths, Alex lifted his hand and counted down with his fingers from three. As he dropped the first finger, Danny gently pressed the door handle down. As he dropped the second, he cracked it open just the first couple of millimetres. As he dropped the third, Danny swung it open, and the four of them ran in, holding their weapons up high or outstretched.

Alex paused just inside, as the rest of them fanned out, and bellowed loudly, making sure his voice travelled through to the back. '*Right, you cunts!* I want my *fucking brother back!*'

Six men surrounded Antonio, who sat tied to a chair with rope, his face bloodied and his nose clearly broken. As the men around him jumped to action, moving together and hesitating in alarm, Antonio began to cackle in loud, manic amusement. Blood was caked all over his face, and the way it framed each of his teeth made him look almost rabid.

The rest of Alex's men stormed in through the back, and the men around Antonio began shouting threats back as they huddled in a small circle of defence. Two had knives but none of them had guns, Alex noted with relief.

The fight broke out almost immediately with a resounding war cry from both sides. Within seconds, everyone was punching and kicking, the clatter of knives being knocked to the ground, and the sickening crunch of pipes against bones the only sounds to puncture the ongoing roar of accusations and curses.

Alex went straight for the largest – clearly the highest-ranking of the six by the way he'd ordered the others into action – and they started to dance around each other. Alex eyed the knife his opponent held and watched how nervously he turned it. How easily it turned in his sweat-slicked hand.

'You made a big mistake here,' Alex growled. 'What did you want with him?'

The other man grinned coldly, his eyes nervously twitching

to the fights around him as his men were slowly but surely overpowered.

'Ain't my place to say,' he replied, his tone gravelly and hard.

Alex felt his anger intensify. 'It damn well *is* your place,' he shot back. 'You'd better start talking, if you know what's good for you.'

The man's leathery face twitched in tired amusement. 'Oh, I know what's good for me, mate. It's you who's in the dark.'

Realising he wasn't going to get any further, Alex launched himself forward, catching the man by surprise as he punched him square in the face with all his considerable strength. The man flew back and landed awkwardly on his side. The knife flew out of his hand, and he scrambled to get to it, but Alex was quicker, kicking it out of the way before laying into the man with all the power and fury of a raging bull.

'If you ain't gonna tell me,' he growled between punches, 'there ain't no point in talking, is there?'

He hit out again and again, but the other man was stronger than he'd thought, and he suddenly flipped Alex over, catching him by surprise. He managed to land a hard, painful punch to Alex's stomach before Alex regained control, the pain setting free whatever anger Alex had been holding back. He let out an almighty roar and flipped him back, pinning the other man down and slamming his fists into his face again and again in swift, merciless succession.

'You think you can take my brother and then beat *me*?' he yelled. 'Eh? *Do ya?*'

'Hey, *hey*. Boss?'

Someone tugged at his arm, and he almost swiped them away before realising it was one of his own men. He pulled back and looked down at the mess of blood beneath his hands. At the mess of blood covering the man coughing and spluttering beneath him. He'd stopped fighting back, clearly conceding defeat.

Alex stood up and looked over towards Antonio. Two of his men were untying him, the others making sure the rest of his beaten captors stayed put at the side of the room where they were now licking their wounds.

'Get him up. Let's go,' Alex ordered.

'It won't change anything, you know,' croaked the man on the floor.

Alex looked down at him. He wasn't smiling, the tone not mocking him. 'What won't?'

'Taking him back. You're wanted men. We're just a courier service. There'll be others.' He coughed, groaning in pain.

Alex dropped down, squatting on his haunches. 'Who sent you?' There was a short silence.

'The Raven,' Antonio called over. 'Some cunt they call The Raven.'

Alex frowned and stood up as Antonio was helped to his feet. 'Who?'

'No idea. Guess that's what we need to work out,' Antonio replied, touching his nose gingerly.

Alex turned to find Danny. 'Hey, take him home and call the doctor. Get him cleaned up.'

'Where *you* going?' Antonio asked.

Alex was walking towards the front door. 'To update Maria.'

His phone started buzzing, and he pulled it out. It was her. He answered and stopped walking, his eyes widening as he listened to her urgent words. '*Shit.*' He swivelled round and yelled out the warning. 'Get out, everyone. *Now*. Old Bill's coming in hot. It's a *fucking* raid.'

Everyone immediately sprang to action, picking each other up and running towards the exits together, no longer caring who was running up against who. Because when it came to getting away from this most dreaded of common enemies, the men who'd just been fighting each other were now instantly allies.

'I've got him,' Danny yelled as he hurried Antonio out through the back.

Satisfied his brother would be OK, Alex bolted through the front and across the front of the buildings towards the thick protection of the trees. He just made it, skirting around the end of the service road as three police cars flew in past him. Looking back at the building as a cold fist of anxiety gripped his stomach, he pushed on, knowing he had to keep moving. Maria was still on the road above, waiting for him.

He turned to climb the steep wall of earth and trees to the road, but he only made it one step before unsettling a loose rock. It sent him stumbling backward into full view of the road then skittered across the hard tarmac. Exposed, Alex turned towards the police cars, and his eyes locked with the last officer getting out of the car, across the wide, empty space between them. He froze, and for a second the pair of them remained still, as all the other officers disappeared into the building, but in that second Alex saw it all. He saw the surprise on the officer's face. The shock as he registered the blood all over Alex's clothes. And then the recognition.

'Hey!' the officer called out. 'Don't move!'

Alex turned and ran back under the cover of the trees, pushing forward and up the hill, grasping branches and whatever else he could in the darkness as he scrambled desperately to safety.

'Hey!' The sound of pounding shoes on tarmac grew closer. 'Hey! I see you, Capello!'

'*Shit*,' he cursed.

Two more steps. Then one. Then his feet finally reached flat ground.

'Officer Brady requesting assistance on the southside of the perimeter,' he heard the officer shout breathlessly somewhere below him. 'In pursuit of...'

But Alex didn't pause to hear the rest. He pelted down the road faster than he'd ever run before, until Maria's car came into view. She reached over and pushed open the passenger door, and he jumped in, slamming it behind him.

'Go! Quickly!' he ordered.

Not that he'd needed to voice this. She'd screeched away down the road the second his backside had made purchase with the seat. The back of her car kicked out as she rounded the first corner, and she expertly drifted before reigning it back in and racing away from the scene behind them.

'What happened?' she demanded. 'Where's Antonio?'

'Safe,' he replied. 'He's OK. He's with Danny. They got out the back in good time. And no one will be looking that way now. Not now they've seen me.'

His expression clouded, and he glared out of the window, furious with himself. Sick with apprehension.

'What do you mean, *seen*?' Maria asked, glancing at him.

'I mean seen. Recognised,' he said heavily. He pinched the bridge of his nose and closed his eyes. 'One saw me as I was getting out. He recognised me from the questionings on the Benny King hit two years ago.'

'Are you sure?' Maria asked. 'Maybe you're being paranoid?'

'Nah, he used my name, Maria. He knows.'

The sound of sirens in the distance began to blare out from somewhere behind them, and Alex turned to look out of the back window. 'Shit.'

'Don't worry – I'll lose them before they come into sight,' Maria promised, her voice calm as she sped up. 'But you can't go home.'

'Well, I can't go with *you*. You can't be my lawyer if they think you're involved,' Alex pointed out.

Maria was silent for a moment as she thought it through. 'I'll drop you to Mum. They won't be far behind us, but you'll be OK there. She'll buy you time while you change, and she'll give you an alibi.'

Alex nodded, and they fell into a tense silence as they raced against the sound of the sirens, both praying the cars belonging to them didn't catch up before they had time to cover their tracks.

TWENTY-SIX

Cat lay back in the deep, hot bath and let the creamy lavender-scented bubbles caress her aching shoulders. *God*, she'd missed this. She hadn't realised quite how much she'd missed the simple luxury of a relaxing bath, with everything else she'd had going on. She'd been in here nearly an hour, and her fingers and toes were now lined with the oversoaked patterns of Christmas trees. But she didn't care. She was enjoying herself too much to get out just yet. Lifting her foot from the water, she nudged the hot tap with her big toe and then rested it back again as heat flooded the bath once more.

Glancing at her now empty glass, she wondered if she could chance a second one. It had been a little on the full side when she'd poured the crisp, chilled Chardonnay earlier. Probably more like a glass and a half, if she was being honest with herself. And it had gone down oh so easily, the cold liquid slipping down her throat and soothing her from the inside out too. But she had her car with her. She wouldn't be able to drive home if she had any more. She wrinkled her nose in a small expression of annoyance, then relaxed her face again as she played with a small peak of bubbles.

She *could* leave her car here and walk home of course. It wasn't far. She could walk back in the morning for work. It would probably do her good. The only reason she drove here each day was because of the round trips she had to do, with Orla's pre-school, but Greg was dropping Orla straight there tomorrow. The reminder sent a fresh surge of unhappiness through Cat, and she sat up.

'Sod it,' she muttered.

Stepping out of the now-steaming bath, she turned the hot tap off and wrapped the big fluffy bath towel around herself. Then she picked up the glass and padded out of the bathroom, through the hallway and down the stairs to the kitchen. She was just opening the fridge when the sound of a key in the door made her nearly jump out of her skin. She froze and looked down at her towel and the wet strands of hair clinging to her collarbones with wide eyes.

Shit.

Who was coming in? Sophia had told her the house would be empty all evening!

The door opened and shut, and she half turned one way then the other, panicking as she tried to figure out what to do.

'Mum? *Mum*. Where are you?' It was Alex.

His voice was loud and sounded urgent, so she imagined she had about three seconds before he strode into the kitchen looking for Sophia. That was going to be embarrassing, but at least it wasn't his brother, Cat thought with relief.

Sure enough, Alex marched right in and then stopped with a frown as he saw her standing there, dripping all over the kitchen floor, the empty wine glass still in her hand. Cat opened her mouth to explain but then faltered as she realised the state he was in.

Alex's black jacket was open, the white T-shirt beneath covered in deep red stains that could only be blood. It continued in spatters up his neck onto his jaw and covered his hands. Dirt streaked his face and caked his knees and palms, as though he'd been crawling around in the mud, and his usually neat jet-black hair was all mussed up. White-cold fear zapped through her as she wondered what on earth he'd done, and her heart raced as she tried to work out what to say.

The sound of a police siren began wailing in the distance, and this seemed to break Alex out of the frozen trance they were both trapped in. 'My mother. Where is she?' he asked urgently.

'She's out,' Cat replied. 'She's—'

'*Shit*,' he cursed, a flicker of fear flashing across his face.

It was the briefest of moments, but the vulnerability Cat saw there seemed to imprint itself into the walls of her mind. He needed help. She glanced behind him into the hallway and then made a snap decision.

'They're coming for you?' she asked.

He looked at her warily, clearly unwilling to answer, but that was an answer itself.

Cat nodded. 'OK. Take your clothes off.'

'What?' he asked, his frown deepening.

'Take your clothes off,' she repeated, placing the wine glass down on the side. 'Come *on* – you don't have time. Give them to me. I'll hide them. Go upstairs and get in the bath. Get all that off you – make it look like we're having a lovers' night in. I'll call you down when they ask if you're here. Go on. *Quickly.*'

He hesitated only a moment more then did as she'd asked. She turned away to give him privacy then took the bundle of clothes he placed on the side into her arms as he ran up the stairs. It crossed her mind that her DNA would now be on his clothes too, and that in doing this she was making herself an accessory to whatever it was that he'd done. This frightened her, but she swallowed the feeling down quickly. It was too late to turn back now.

Cat took a black bag from the roll under the sink and

dumped everything into it, making it as small as possible. Her heart thudded, the feeling vibrating all the way up to her throat, as the sound of sirens grew closer. Her hands shook slightly as she tied the bag up, then she fell to her knees and opened the bottom cupboard in the corner of the room. There was an empty space that was impossible to see and hard to get to. She shoved the bag around and pushed it as far in as possible, ensuring no part of the bag was visible.

They were outside now. She could hear them getting out of the car. Her heart leaped as a door slammed, and she glanced upwards, silently begging God to give her the nerve to pull this off. She suddenly wasn't feeling so brave and was realising, swiftly, what a terrible, *terrible* idea this had all been.

Taking a deep breath, Cat pulled out a second wine glass and then the wine from the fridge, and quickly began to pour.

She nearly dropped the bottle when the knock came and had to close her eyes for a second and grip the side, to steady herself. 'Come on, Cat,' she muttered. 'Pull yourself together.'

Securing her towel a little tighter, Cat picked up both glasses and walked through to the hallway, carefully smoothing her expression. She had to look natural. This was important.

As the second, more impatient, knock sounded, she was already halfway to the door.

'Yes, I'm coming. Just a minute,' she called. She turned the hall light on and placed the glasses down on the side table in view of the door, then finally opened it with a carefully expectant expression. 'Oh. Hello.'

She tried to sound surprised, her eyes moving from one officer to another. There were two on the doorstep, and another car was now pulling up just behind. The officers in front of her were watching her sternly.

'Hi. Is Mr Capello in, Miss...?' The officer speaking eyed her questioningly.

'I'm Cat, the housekeeper. Sorry, what is this about?' she replied.

'We need to speak to Mr Capello. Is he in?' The other officer leaned halfway in the doorway, looking around behind her as he spoke.

Cat was careful not to move, not to open the door enough to give them entry. She licked her lips. 'Um. Which Mr Capello was it that you're after? There are two.'

'Mr *Alex* Capello,' the first one answered. 'We need to speak to him about an urgent matter. Is he in?'

'Oh. Yes, he is,' Cat replied, forcing a smile. 'It's not a very good time right now though.'

'Yeah, I'd imagine it's not,' said the second officer in a hard tone. 'But like we said, it's urgent. So if you could step aside please, miss, we need to come in for a little chat.'

'What's this?' came a deep voice from behind her, and Cat sagged a little in relief.

Alex gripped the door frame and widened it to reveal himself to the officers, looping his other arm casually across her shoulders. Cat tried to act natural, like this was normal. Like they really were lovers instead of barely more than acquaintances. Alex's hair and hard muscular torso were now wet, the blood and mud washed away and a towel that matched hers neatly tied around his waist.

The first officer's eyes swept across the two of them, his eyes resting on Cat's face with an unreadable expression. The second officer's expression widened in surprise before this was quickly veiled.

'Officers?' Alex questioned.

Sneaking a quick glance, Cat could see he looked annoyed, his stare challenging. He was good at this. Very good. She suddenly wondered how much practice he'd had.

'Can you give us a run-down of your whereabouts this evening, Capello?' the first officer asked.

Alex looked pointedly down at his dripping-wet body and then at Cat. 'I've been here, with Cat, since about half six. Was running some errands with my brother before that. We're, um...' He scratched his head, looking awkward. 'Well. I'd prefer this stay private, to be honest, officers. My wife, she, er...' He grimaced. 'Well, this is just private. That's all.'

'Yeah, I'll bet,' the first officer said drily.

He began to turn, seeming bored of this conversation now that Alex had a plausible alibi, but the second officer didn't seem so convinced.

'Sorry, so you've been here all night?' he queried.

'Like I said, Officer Brady,' Alex repeated, a note of irritation seeping through as he eyed the man.

'Where's your car?' the man he'd called Officer Brady asked.

'Home. Cat picked me up so I didn't have to drive home. It is illegal to drink and drive, you know, Officer,' he replied mockingly.

Cat reached back and picked up one of the glasses, passing it to him, to highlight his point. She picked up the second glass and simply held it, unable to force herself to take even a sip. Her muscles were so tense that if someone were to so much as tap her right now, she was sure she'd shatter.

The second officer seemed to pick up on this and narrowed his eyes. 'You look worried, Cat. Everything alright? Anything you want to tell us? We can talk on our own if you like.'

Alex barked out a laugh. 'Christ on a bike. *What* is going on? What is it that you like me for, eh? Whatever it is, I can tell you now, you're barking up the wrong tree. And I'm starting to get pissed off.'

'What's the matter, Capello? Scared she'll actually answer?' the officer shot back. He looked back at Cat. 'Why don't you tell me what's really going on?'

Cat forced a laugh. 'Really?' she asked, as if she was amazed by this question. 'Of course I look worried, Officer. I *am* worried.' She felt Alex's arm tense across her shoulders. 'You can clearly see what's going on here. Up until *you* arrived, Alex and I were enjoying some very nice alone time in the bath. I'd just come down to top up our glasses when you arrived, and now here we are at the front door for anyone driving down the road to see. Here *I* am with a married man. A married man with a wife who, quite honestly, *terrifies* me.' She saw the officers exchange a look of acknowledgement and realised they probably knew Bianca too. 'If she finds out, I don't know what she'll do to me, OK? So *yes*, I *am* worried. And quite frankly I'd quite like to get back inside, out of sight of the road.'

'Me too. And unless you've got a warrant for something, which I'm sure you haven't, you lot can get the fuck off my mum's drive,' Alex said strongly.

And with that, he pulled Cat backward and slammed the door.

He kept his arm around Cat as they turned away, murmuring a warning not to move away from him too quickly, and for a moment they lingered in the hallway. After a few more seconds, they heard the sounds of the officers moving away, and slowly they both relaxed.

As Alex released her, Cat felt a wave of relief wash over her. It was over.

'Thank you,' he said, his deep voice sincere.

Cat looked up at his face and saw the sincerity there, his gaze darting between her eyes as if searching for something. She looked away, feeling suddenly awkward and realising, now the adrenaline was wearing off, that she was still soaked and freezing cold.

'It's fine,' she found herself saying, despite the fact that this was all anything *but* fine.

'It's not,' he replied, as if able to read her thoughts. 'But you did it anyway. Seriously, thank you.'

Cat looked up. 'What happened? Why were they here? What *was* all that...?'

She trailed off as she looked back at where the blood had been the most concentrated, not wanting to finish her question. Not sure she even wanted an answer to it.

Alex pulled in a deep breath and exhaled heavily, his penetrating gaze suddenly dark and heavy. 'Come. Let's sit down. I think it's time we talked.'

TWENTY-SEVEN

The following day had passed in a blur for Alex as he and Maria tried to track down The Raven. It hadn't been as easy as they'd hoped, but his sister had finally informed him, at nearly midnight, that she'd found a lead, so all he could do now was wait. Waiting seemed to be all he could do on a few fronts at this particular point in time. After hearing Antonio was safe and had been sorted out by the doctor they used to patch them up after incidents like this one, Alex had given him some space. But as Saturday morning had come around, he'd decided it was time to go and check on Antonio in person.

He'd let himself into his brother's spacious two-bedroomed flat, expecting to find Antonio resting still, in bed. Instead, all he'd found was evidence of yet another party, the glass coffee table covered in a layer of fine white dust along with three discarded rolled-up fifties, a bright red thong on the sofa and no sign of his brother – there or in either of the bedrooms. So Alex had sat on the chair closest to the wall of windows and settled in for the wait, his eyes resting on the horizon over the tops of all the smaller buildings below.

But his mind wasn't on Antonio, the way it should have

been, today. It was still firmly stuck on Cat. On the way she'd protected him, without question, two nights before. It had been unexpected – an unexpected godsend. He could still see the look of terror in her eyes when he'd first walked in. And he could understand her reaction. He'd been covered in blood and dirt, police sirens wailing in the background, and this wasn't her life. This wasn't something she was used to. Hell, it wasn't something *he* was exactly used to either. But at least for him, it was a risk he knowingly took.

Still, she'd barely even hesitated. She'd dived right in, taking charge and giving him the alibi he so desperately needed. A good one too. She'd been so strong, putting on a convincing show for the officers and not once betraying how alarming the series of events must have been for her. He admired her for that. She had guts. Their following conversation echoed through his mind.

So, what happened? she'd asked.

It's complicated, he'd told her.

I still want to know. If I'm protecting you, I at least deserve to know why.

And she *had* deserved to know why. She'd earned it. So he'd chosen his next words carefully.

You've been here a couple of weeks now. Seen us come and go. You're a smart girl. You've probably gathered by now that our business is a little... unusual.

She'd given him a slight nod, her pale face not giving anything more away.

Someone took my brother and hurt him. We don't know why yet, but I did figure out where they took him. So tonight I went and got him back. Some people got in my way, and I did what I had to do to move them out of my way. The police arrived at an unfortunate moment, and one caught a glimpse of me from a distance, hence the visit.

Did you kill them? she'd asked, her voice level.

No, he'd replied truthfully.

But you hurt people. It had been a statement rather than a question, but he'd confirmed it nonetheless, holding her clear gaze in his.

Sometimes.

What is your business? What is it you actually do?

He'd taken a moment before responding to that, warring with himself over how much he should tell her. She needed to be told *something*. Despite the fact she clearly wasn't familiar with their world, Maria had brought her into their mother's house, into their family hub. She was going to see and hear things. And she'd proven herself trustworthy enough.

Mainly, we solve problems. If someone has an issue they can't resolve using more traditional routes, they come to us. And that can mean anything. That's what we're known for. Finding solutions for things that other people can't.

She'd nodded and had seemed to think it over for a while, her expression still carefully neutral. He'd watched her, transfixed by how calm she seemed. She'd proven calmer and more in control than many of the people who'd willingly chosen this life would have in the same situation.

A noise in the bathroom pulled his attention sharply back to the present, and, with cat-like reflexes, he was up and out of the chair in a flash. It had been a shuffling sound, nothing like the random clanging of pipes or gurgle of water one might expect to come from an empty bathroom. But *was* it empty? He paused, realising he hadn't actually checked it when he came in. He'd seen the partially open door and darkness beyond and had just assumed it was empty.

He walked over, pushed open the door and reached for the switch. As the light flicked on, he peered inside, and as he found the source of the sound, his mouth dropped open. The shower curtain ring that had previously been attached to the ceiling above the roll-top bath had been half pulled out, now only partially clinging on to the plaster, the rest leaning at a perilous angle as it threatened to fall completely. The curtain that had until recently hung from it had been ripped off and was now being clutched to his brother's chest like a favoured blanket as he slept soundly in the bath in nothing but his underwear and what appeared to be a woman's phone number written across his side, in red lipstick.

For a moment, Alex just stood there, speechless, amusement and annoyance fighting for top spot in his emotions.

'Christ alive,' he muttered. 'It must have been some party.' Shaking his head with a sigh, Alex turned on the tap in the sink and splashed cold water over Antonio's face. 'Hey. Wake up. Come on.'

'Wha— *Whoa*! What the— What you *doing*?' Antonio spluttered, half sitting up and looking around in dazed confusion. 'What happened?' He glanced up through bruises, puffy eyes at the curtain rail and frowned.

'Yeah, I dunno. Get up. Come on.' Alex leaned over to help his brother out of the bathtub.

'I'm OK,' Antonio protested, but he leaned on Alex just the same.

Alex walked out to the living room and pinched the bridge of his nose. Antonio was supposed to be resting. He'd had his nose broken, an eye socket fractured and was covered in bruises. And yet here he was, barely two days later, coming out the other side of yet another bender.

'Have a good time with Chantelle, did ya?' Alex asked flatly as Antonio stumbled out after him.

'Yeah, Trixie too,' Antonio replied, scratching the back of his head as he surveyed the room. 'How'd you know about Chantelle?' He turned back to Alex expectantly.

Alex pointed at the lipstick on Antonio's side. Antonio twisted to get a look at it and then grunted an acknowledgement.

'What *are* you fucking doing?' Alex asked, holding his arms out questioningly before dropping them, as if giving up.

'Living my life, mate. You should try it sometime,' Antonio replied, sounding bored.

'This ain't living, Antonio. This is shoving all our gear up your fucking nose and whoring your way through the city like you're on some desperate search for the clap,' Alex returned.

'Hey,' Antonio chimed. 'They were both very nice girls, I'll have you know.'

'I didn't say they weren't, but this is getting out of hand. It's all the time,' Alex said helplessly. 'I pulled you out of that warehouse just two days ago. You could barely stand, you've broken bones. You're *supposed* to be on bed rest.'

'*Some* of it was in bed,' Antonio quipped.

Alex gave him a scathing look, and Antonio smirked before looking away. The smirk eventually faded, and he walked over to the kitchen.

'Want a coffee?'

'Go on then,' Alex replied, following him in.

'Danny said you got followed out. What happened?' Antonio pulled out two cups and flicked on the kettle.

'It was fine. Maria dropped me at Mum's. Mum was out, but Cat was in – she gave me an alibi,' Alex told him.

'Oh?' Antonio stopped dead and turned to look at Alex, an odd expression on his face. 'What kind of alibi?'

Alex grinned. 'One you'll find amusing actually. But don't tell Bianca, whatever you do.'

'Go on,' Antonio urged.

Alex relayed the whole story, laughing a little now that he retold it, seeing how amusing it must be from an outside perspective. But Antonio didn't laugh along with him. He simply listened and continued making the coffees, then handed a steaming cup to Alex with a tight expression.

'Hey, you alright?' Alex asked. 'You seem, I don't know... *off.*'

''Course,' Antonio replied. 'Just glad things worked out for you.' He cracked a strained smile. 'Wouldn't want to see you pulled in just for saving me from that bunch of dickheads.'

'Well, yeah. I wasn't exactly relishing the thought either,' Alex agreed.

Antonio walked through to the lounge, hunching his shoulders the way he always did when he was angry. Alex frowned and followed him over to the window, glancing sideways at his brother, whose expression was stony.

'Seriously, what's wrong with you?' he asked.

'Me?' Antonio turned to look at him with an exaggerated air of surprise. 'Nothing! Honestly. I'm good, mate. So. *Cat.*' He pulled a suggestive expression. 'She try giving you the good stuff, eh? She *accidentally* drop the towel, did she?'

'Nah, it weren't like that.' Alex frowned and pulled back with a shake of the head. 'She did me a solid.'

'I bet she did,' Antonio said.

Alex shot him a disapproving look. 'She just helped me out of a tight spot, that's all. Neither of us were thinking about anything other than getting those pork chops off the doorstep.'

'Yeah, whatever,' Antonio replied dismissively.

'She surprised me actually,' Alex continued. 'She's trustworthy. And strong. That's worth keeping around. We should probably start paying her more to keep her in the fold.'

'You don't mean in the *firm?*' Antonio asked, sounding astonished. 'She's just a cleaner, for fuck's sake. What do we need *her* for?'

Alex frowned at him. 'What's got into you? I don't care what she does. She's proven she can be trusted in a tight spot and can hold her own. That's worth its weight. And no, I ain't saying we take her on like that. I just mean we should show her she's valued. Make sure she stays on at Mum's.'

Antonio turned and fixed him with a long, hard stare, his expression intense. Alex stared back, utterly confused, trying to work out what his issue was. Eventually Antonio broke away and he nodded, turning back to sit on the couch.

'Whatever you say, brother,' he called back over his shoulder.

Alex watched him for a few seconds and was about to question him again when his phone buzzed. It was a text from Maria.

Found bird. My place. M

She'd found The Raven. Alex glanced at the back of Antonio's head, and he bit the side of his bottom lip. Under usual circumstances he'd involve his brother, but today he felt Antonio was better off left out of things. He needed to rest, and the rest of them didn't need to deal with a half-broken Antonio on a hungover comedown.

'I've gotta go,' he said, slipping his phone back into his pocket. 'I just came to check in on you. Look after yourself today, yeah?'

'Sure,' came the answer.

Alex tapped him on the shoulder as he passed then, after dropping his mug back in the kitchen, quickly exited the flat before Antonio could question him about where he was running off to.

As he marched down the hallway, Alex buttoned up his jacket and set his mind to the task ahead. He hoped the information Maria had was good. He hoped it led them right to this Raven person. Because whoever they were and whatever they thought they had against the Capellos, he didn't care. He was going to pay them back for what they'd done to his brother then put a stop to their antics, once and for all.

TWENTY-EIGHT

Cat sat on the bed with Orla in front of her and brushed her silky brown hair, smiling at the gentle curls at the ends. They were her baby curls. Cat knew at some point she'd have to cut them off – Orla could very nearly sit on her hair, it was that long now – but not yet. Her little girl was growing so fast, she just couldn't bear to speed it up.

Orla had been exhausted when Cat had finally got her home the night before. She'd picked her daughter up from nursery, finally feeling like she could breathe again, like she was whole again, as she'd pulled her into a huge bear hug. Then, all too soon, they'd had to rush off to one of her little friends' birthday parties at a nearby jungle gym. Orla had fallen asleep on the way back to the B&B, full of sugar and happy memories, and Cat had gently lifted her and carried her to bed, leaving her that way. She'd snuggled up to her in their shared double bed and had swiftly fallen asleep herself, content in that moment just to be there and have Orla in her arms. It was all that mattered. Everything else – Greg, her living situation, all that had happened with Alex and the police – it all faded away.

Now, finally, the weekend had arrived, and she and Orla

could spend the whole day together. They'd already been downstairs and had their eggs and toast with Mrs Marsh, the B&B owner. They'd helped wash up and had showers and done their washing for the week, and now Cat was getting ready to take Orla out for some fun at the park.

'So, did you have a nice time with Daddy?' Cat asked. 'What did you guys do? Anything fun?'

She tried to keep her tone light, tried to hide her anxiety. She hadn't had a chance to question Orla until now, and though she didn't want it to feel like an interrogation, she needed to know that Orla had been OK. That she'd felt happy and safe with Greg, without her there.

'It was OK,' Orla replied, her tone betraying neither excitement or sadness.

Cat frowned and continued brushing her hair. 'Only OK? Did you do anything fun together?'

'Well...' The little girl tilted her head to the side, thinking about it. 'We *did* have ice cream. And I got to sleep in my old bed. I like my old bed.'

Cat felt a surge of guilt rise up and pierce through her heart. She closed her eyes for a moment, pushing it back down. It wasn't her fault Orla didn't have her own bed. It was Greg's. The lying, cheating, soulless bastard that he was.

'I know, baby,' she said softly.

'And Jeanie read me a new bedtime story. But she said I had to leave it there. But I didn't want to leave it there; I wanted to bring it back here,' Orla continued.

'What?' Cat's hand stopped, the brush still halfway down Orla's hair. 'Jeanie? As in Jeanie who worked with Grandad?'

'Yeah. Jeanie,' Orla replied.

Cat put the brush down and turned her around, searching her daughter's clear blue eyes. 'So Jeanie was there with you and Daddy in the house?'

'Yeah. She put me to bed and made me dippy eggs for

breakfast.' Orla's little face suddenly clouded over, and she sucked in her bottom lip, looking worried. 'Daddy said I shouldn't tell you, but I forgot.'

Something cold and hard hit Cat in the centre of her chest. 'No, no, you did the right thing telling me, my love. You must always tell Mummy everything, OK? There are no secrets between us – that was wrong of Daddy to tell you to hide something.'

What on earth was Jeanie doing there?

Cat thought back to the day she'd last gone to the offices, the way her father's executive assistant had run after her in the car park. What she'd said about the will.

It has to be a fake, Cat had said.

I wish I could agree with you, Jeanie had replied. *But I know your dad's signature better than anyone. I'm so sorry. It looks legit. However it came about, your dad made this new will.*

Cat had believed her. Had taken her word without question because Jeanie had been with her father such a long time. Because she'd been close to him – close to them *all*. Cat had trusted her, but clearly that had been a mistake.

Cat forced a smile at Orla. 'Turn back around, princess; I'll finish your hair.'

Her mind reeled as she forced herself to act calmly for Orla's sake. How long had it been going on? Had Greg and Jeanie planned this together? Had they somehow blackmailed her father, or had they faked his signature together in private? They'd certainly had enough time to put it all into place, as the cancer had slowly eaten away at his bones and sapped the life out of him. Tears blurred her vision. Had that been what they were doing, while she'd been looking after him? While she'd been at her father's bedside, trying to make his last days as comfortable as possible? Had they really been plotting ways to take her family business and her home away from her, while she'd been distracted by all the grief and pain?

Careful not to make a sound that would betray her emotions, Cat wiped away the brimming tears, and as she did so a new feeling took hold. A hot, bubbling feeling that formed a ball in the pit of her stomach and grew bigger and bigger until it radiated through her entire body. And as it seeped into the very last few pores, something inside her snapped.

She was *done* taking this shit. She was done simply surviving while people stole everything from her and her daughter. And she was done playing by the rules. No one else was playing by them, so why should she? She was going to get back what was hers if it was the last thing she did. No matter what it took.

TWENTY-NINE

Maria looked around the small East End street at the various cans littering the ground, the bright graffiti covering the old brick walls and the myriad of small shops crammed together with their tiny neon-lit fronts. Old-school hip-hop boomed out from somewhere, and two homeless men sat together at the entrance of an alleyway, staring out at her with suspicion. She felt a surge of pity as she saw how young and thin they were. A little way down the alley, a makeshift tent made of cardboard was strung up over a large pallet and two dirty sleeping bags. They must stay there, she realised.

As a cold gust of wind blew through, she sighed, then reached into her pocket and peeled two notes off the roll of cash she always kept on her. Then she walked across to the homeless men – or boys really, as they couldn't have been older than eighteen – and dropped them into the cardboard box in front of them, before turning swiftly away towards Alex, who was stepping out of his car.

Three other men followed him, one of whom opened his jacket to show her he was carrying a gun. She nodded her approval, and he nodded back in respect.

Alex eyed the boys behind her with a small frown. 'What you doing?' he asked.

'They're just kids. They shouldn't be living rough in this.' She gestured to the grey, swirling skies.

Alex conceded her point with a grudging tilt of the head. 'No, they shouldn't. But you can't save 'em all.'

'Forty quid ain't going to save anyone, Alex, but it might just help them survive the day,' she said in a clipped tone. 'Anyway.' She marched on down the road, her black patent heels cracking out a sharp rhythm on the concrete pavement slabs. 'There don't seem to be any watchers outside the pub. Probably will be inside. You speak to the Drews?' She glanced at her brother as he fell into step beside her.

He nodded. 'Yeah. This place falls just out of their jurisdiction, so they've got no issue. It's actually in no man's land, so we're good to go.'

'Oh, perfect.'

The Drews ran a large portion of the East End, and Maria had initially assumed this pub fell under their protection. The fact that it wasn't on their, or in fact *anyone's*, turf was the best news she'd had today. It meant they could do whatever they needed to without having to hold back. It meant that they could go and surprise The Raven, as he sipped his Saturday afternoon pint, and demand answers. It meant they weren't going to be stepping on anyone's toes when they paid him back for what he'd had done to Antonio. And this was something Maria was greatly looking forward to. She wasn't a particularly bloodthirsty woman, and Antonio was *far* from her favourite person right now. But he was her brother. He was family. And *no one* was allowed to touch her family.

The pub looked as worn down as the rest of the place, half of the dark-green-and-black tiles on the outside walls smashed or missing entirely. One window was boarded up, and the others were so filthy it was impossible to see through, but there was an A-board outside, advertising a deal on a jug of Coronas and letting people know there was karaoke every second Thursday. This, at least, told them it was open.

As they headed for the front door, Alex moved a little closer to her, and Danny suddenly appeared on Maria's other side. Two of the men went ahead, and the last man fell in behind them, everyone now on high alert. Everyone looked at Alex expectantly, and he gave the nod to go in.

Maria saw Danny rest his hand on his gun as they walked into the dark, dank pub, but just as the stale smell of old beer and body odour hit them, she realised that this wasn't going to help them at all. Because as the door closed behind them, two other guns were already pointed at their heads.

'Hands where I can see 'em, thank you,' came a hard, guttural voice.

Danny dropped his hand away from his gun with a curse.

Maria looked over to the man who'd spoken and deduced that this must be who they were looking for. Of average height and stocky, with a skinhead and deep lines etched into his forehead above a heavy brow, he looked every inch the thug she'd heard so much about. He looked around sixty with serious blue eyes and a blurry tattoo of a swallow on his neck, partially covered by a thick gold chain.

He was stood at the bar, casually resting against a bar stool, as though their presence here was not a surprise in the slightest. And as Maria saw the boy dart out through the back door, she realised why. She sighed silently then let it go. It wasn't personal, after all. They were just doing what they needed to do to make a bit of extra cash. She should have left someone to keep an eye on the pair as they'd approached this place. But it was too late now.

'So, you're The Raven,' she stated, stepping forward with a hard, icy look and ignoring the guns.

They wouldn't use them. Their guns were for show and as a

deterrent for any potential violence. They were most likely not even loaded, but that wasn't a chance they could take. Which meant all she had planned for the next hour was now firmly out of the window. *This* annoyed her, but there wasn't much she could do about it.

'And you are?' he asked, cocking one heavy eyebrow. 'I don't believe I've yet had the pleasure.'

'*Pleasure.*' Maria laughed under her breath. 'Oh, it's going to be anything but that for you. But you can have my name. It's Maria Capello.'

There was a flicker of surprise in his eyes, and then he nodded, looking over to Alex. 'Which must make you *Alex* Capello.'

'It does indeed,' Alex replied menacingly.

The Raven nodded again, then rubbed his hand back and forth over his chin as he appeared to be thinking over his next move. The atmosphere had shifted, and Maria felt confused. It was as though he hadn't known who they were, hadn't been expecting their visit, but that couldn't be right. Surely he'd have been expecting *some* comeback after taking Antonio.

'Would you like a drink?' he eventually asked. 'Come on – what's your tipple?' He directed the question at Maria. 'I'm guessing a white wine spritzer? Or a G&T perhaps?'

'Scotch. Top shelf,' Maria shot back coldly.

Alex held up two fingers to the barman to indicate he'd have the same. No one asked the other men what they wanted, nor did they offer their choices. This meeting was between the Capellos and The Raven only.

The Raven pushed off the bar stool and turned to walk around the bar, through a door to the side. He gestured for them to follow.

'Leave your muscle here,' he ordered.

Maria clamped her jaw shut as she shared a grim look with

Alex, but Alex held his hand up to indicate the man should stay behind, just the same. What else could he do?

They followed The Raven through to the other side of the dank pub, to a smaller room that housed a pool table and a smaller round table set back in an alcove, at the back. Two men were playing pool, but when they saw who'd walked in, they immediately stopped. The Raven nodded back towards the main bar, and they placed their cues on the table, despite being mid-game, and filed through the door silently.

They all sat at the little round table, and Maria noted that two of The Raven's henchmen had followed them in and were now standing either side of the door like second-rate bouncers. One had a swastika tattoo on his hand, and the other was missing one of his front teeth. *Hardly the army of dreams*, she thought sarcastically.

'What's your actual name?' Maria asked, turning her attention back to The Raven.

He cracked a small smile. 'You can call me Silas.'

Maria narrowed her eyes. 'That wasn't what I asked.'

'But that's the answer you're getting, Miss Capello,' he replied with finality.

Alex had been quiet as they'd walked through, probably trying to rethink what they were going to do here today, Maria guessed. But now he spoke, his anger contained but still crystal clear in every syllable.

'Why did you have our brother taken? Why did you try and take me?'

Silas – or whatever his real name was – had the good grace to look a little embarrassed. 'I had good reason to do so but, admittedly, if I had realised who you were, I would have handled things differently.'

Maria frowned. 'What do you mean?'

Silas sighed. 'Do you know what kind of business I run?'

'You're a pimp and a loan shark, right?' Maria replied.

'Pretty much,' he replied. 'Though I prefer to put it in more palatable terms to clients.'

'So?' Alex prompted. 'What's that got to do with the price of eggs?'

'I'm getting there,' Silas replied, a little too shirtily for Maria's liking. 'Hold your horses.'

'You'd best get there *faster*, Silas,' Maria snapped. 'Because our patience is wearing a bit *thin*.'

His expression immediately changed, and his eyes glinted darkly as he turned his gaze on her. 'Oh yeah? And what you gonna do about it, eh? This is *my* gaff, remember? And it's *my* men at the door.'

'Yours, is it, this place?' she queried, not ruffled in the least. She looked around as if assessing the run-down dump then levelly met his gaze. 'What I'm gonna *do* about it won't happen now. I think even you can work that one out. Your upper hand is very fucking temporary. And if you don't start talking or you get on my wick any further tonight, I might just have to come back and petrol bomb this shithole. Do the local council a favour.'

Silas leaned forward, narrowing his gaze. 'Big words for a bird who hasn't been let out of here yet,' he growled.

Maria leaned in too. 'Keep us in here, or harm us in any way, and see what fucking happens next.'

It was enough to shut him up, as she'd known it would be. He knew who they were. He also knew he wasn't a big-enough player to even consider taking them on. His glare held hers for a few seconds longer, and then he sat back, gesturing to the two men who'd stepped closer to back off.

'Now *talk*,' she demanded through gritted teeth.

Silas tore his gaze from hers and sat back as the barman walked over with their drinks. 'I have a client who's borrowed a lot of money recently. More than I'd usually shell out in one go, to one person, but I knew he was good for it. Or *thought* he was.

He's worth a fortune, just ain't got quick access to his money.' He shrugged. 'Perfect cash cow for someone like me. He's borrowed before, always paid on time and eventually in full. But he hadn't borrowed *this* much before.'

'And?' Alex asked.

'Well, his first payday came around, and for the first time he didn't have what he owed me. Said he was having some trouble accessing *anything*. It's unlike him, so I gave him a few more days. Gave him a warning. But when that was up, he still didn't have anything to give me. And we ain't talking pennies here; I'm talking *thousands*. A hundred thousand, to be exact.'

Alex whistled, but Maria simply watched Silas more closely. He was angry at this client, but she also detected something else in his eyes. Tension or worry. No, it was fear, she realised.

'Whose money is it?' she asked bluntly.

Silas bristled. 'That's *my* business,' he told her.

Maria squinted and looked around again at the peeling paint and threadbare carpet. 'You don't have the money to front a hundred-grand loan.' Her mind began working the situation through. 'You use other people's money. People you then *answer* to, right?'

He didn't answer, but the look on his face told her that she was bang on the money.

'Answer the question,' Alex demanded.

Silas's gaze flickered over to the men at the door, and he lowered his voice slightly. 'I have various business partners. People with money who want more out of it than they could get in normal investments. People who are happy to do deals under the table for quicker, bigger profits. So I can't exactly tell them their money ain't coming back or that their profits are going to be late now, can I?'

'Who's the client?' Alex asked, turning the glass of Scotch around slowly on the table.

'Now *that's* what I was trying to get to,' Silas replied. 'That client is Justin Sinclair.'

Maria and Alex exchanged a look. That was the last thing they'd been expecting.

'I sent two men over recently to have a little chat with him,' Silas continued, 'only to hear that he already had company. Company whose presence wasn't exactly in my best interests.'

'Hang on, that doesn't make sense,' Alex said with a frown. 'If you're talking about us, you said you didn't know who we were when you took Antonio.'

'I didn't.' Silas rubbed his forehead, looking stressed. 'The men I had watching the place saw you go in and followed a few minutes later. They didn't know who you were. Figured you were just checking into the hotel or something. But then they heard you talking in the lounge. Talking about taking me out. So I had you followed to find out where you lived and to figure out a good time to take you. Get in there first, before you got me.'

'What? No...' Alex shook his head with a loud sigh. 'That wasn't what they heard. *Fuck's sake.*' He let out a low growl of annoyance. 'We were discussing a hit, yes. But it wasn't *you* he wanted taken out. He never mentioned you at all actually.'

He turned to Maria, and she stared back at him grimly. This complicated things. Significantly. Justin had admitted to a bit of debt and a penchant for the gambling tables, but owing a hundred grand to a loan shark was a whole other level. They'd never have touched the job if they'd known about this.

'So, your men,' Maria said, looking back at Silas, 'they just assumed it must be you they were discussing,' she deduced, angry now. 'They didn't stop to *think*. Didn't stop to consider the possibilities. And then neither did you. You all just dived right in like a bunch of fucking idiots, stalking and kidnapping my brother without a second's fucking thought.'

'I actually don't know whether to laugh or kill you right here,' Alex added.

'I mean, I'd rather the former,' Silas replied with a forced laugh.

'No one cares for your opinion,' Maria replied coldly.

'Look, we fucked up. I'm not denying it,' he said. 'And I want to put it right. I have no beef with you.'

'No, it's *us* who has beef with *you*,' Alex pointed out.

'Like I said, I want to put it right. I messed up, and I owe you a debt. A big one,' Silas pressed.

Alex shook his head. 'You can't *repay* what you've done. You honestly think you can have one of us – a *Capello* – kidnapped and beaten, and just *owe us a favour?*' He made a sound of derision. 'We're done here.'

Maria stood up and turned to the door, barely keeping a lid on her anger as she stalked past the two men either side of it and back through to the main bar. Alex followed her through, ignoring the pleas of the man behind him to wait. They were well past waiting.

'Let's go,' Maria growled, as she reached their men, not stopping to check they were following as she exited the miserable, dilapidated building.

There were two types of enemies in her opinion. The ones you hated and respected, and the ones you hated and didn't. And she couldn't stand the ones they didn't. At least an enemy with a clear goal and the balls to shoot for it made sense. But idiocy like this made her very bones itch with the need to unleash hell upon the fool who'd dared to waste her time. And the fact that she was here, faced with him, unable to touch him with his goons surrounding him, fuelled her frustration even more. She dug her nails into her palms and gritted her teeth as she silently strode back towards her car.

Alex fell into step beside her, and she knew, without needing to look at or ask him, that he felt exactly the same way she did.

'We'll balance the scales, Maria,' he said quietly. 'Don't worry.'

'Oh, I know we will,' she replied, her voice as hard as her furious expression. '*No one* gets to do what they did and walk away from it. *No one*. He'll pay his dues. And I'll be the one to collect them.'

THIRTY

Cat drove through the streets surrounding her old house in random circles as Orla sang all her favourite nursery rhymes at the top of her lungs in the back seat. Eventually, as Cat had known she would, Orla quietened down and drifted off, one chubby, cherubic cheek smooshed against the side of her car seat, her lips puckered into a perfect little O. Cat stared at her daughter in the mirror, double-checking she was fully asleep before turning her car around and heading for their old home.

She'd not been able to get it out of her mind – the revelation from the day before that Greg and Jeanie were together. And they *had* to be together. There was no other logical reason for Jeanie to have been there both to put Orla to bed *and* cook her breakfast in the morning. And if she *was* correct, then Jeanie was most likely still there today. There in *her* house, her *home*, with her husband. Not that Cat was bothered by the latter. Jeanie could have that rat of a man. But she sure as hell couldn't have the rest.

Pulling up on the drive, as she had so many times before, Cat switched off the engine and got out of the car, shutting the door quietly behind her so as not to wake her sleeping daughter.

She walked up her front path then knocked on her own front door, the anger she felt at having to do this bubbling almost painfully in the pit of her stomach. A few seconds later, the door opened, and when Jeanie saw who was there, she froze and her eyes widened. She quickly tried to shut it again, but Cat was quicker, and she jammed her foot in between the door and the frame.

'Oh no you don't,' she said in a low, angry voice. 'You're going to speak to me and tell me what the *hell* is going on.'

Jeanie let go of the door with a huff of annoyance and glanced behind her as if looking for something. 'Look, you need to speak to Greg, not me. He's popped out, but—'

'*No.* I need to speak to *you*, Jeanie,' Cat said determinedly.

'I don't know what you want me to say, Cat,' Jeanie replied, crossing her arms defensively. 'It just happened. I'm sorry if us being together hurts you—'

'*Hurts* me?' Cat cut her off again and let out a snort of amusement. 'Jeanie, I couldn't give two shits that you're together. You want to be with that snake and play second fiddle to the teenage piece he's *also* in a relationship with, that's fine by me. I was done with it a *long time* ago.'

'What?' Jeanie asked, blinking in shock.

'Oh, you didn't know?' Cat smiled. 'Yes. He's been with her for a while, and that's still going strong by all accounts.'

'You're lying,' Jeanie accused, the shock still written on her face.

'Really?' Cat asked, arching an eyebrow. 'You actually trust that the man who had an affair with *you* wouldn't be cheating on you with someone else? Or is it that he's cheating on her with you? I guess it depends which affair started up first, doesn't it? I'll leave you to work that one out. But *no*, Jeanie. I am *not* bothered in the slightest by you shagging my shitbag of an ex,' Cat said strongly. She took a step forward, forcing Jeanie back.

'What I *am* bothered by is him defrauding me out of my family business and my home.'

Jeanie crossed her arms. 'It's not yours anymore, Cat. In fact, it never was. Legally speaking, it's passed straight from your dad to Greg. And you're just going to need to get used to that.'

Cat shook her head, the fight suddenly leaving her as the weight of it all bore down on her once more.

'Jeanie, that will is a fake,' she said tiredly. She wiped her hand down her face, stressed. 'You know Dad would never have written that. You *know*. You were by his side for years; you've known *all* of us for years. And whatever's going on with you and Greg, I don't care. If you're happy, then I wish you the best. But surely you can see how wrong the rest of it is? I've got Orla living in a B&B, for crying out loud, sharing my bed because I can't afford more than one poky little room.'

Jeanie looked away uncomfortably, and Cat took a half step closer, reading the action as a chink in the other woman's armour.

'Please, Jeanie. Help me?' she asked. 'For Orla's sake, if no one else's, I need to prove he's faked that will. I need your help.'

Jeanie sighed irritably. 'He didn't fake the will.'

'Jeanie, he *did*,' Cat argued.

'No, Cat. He didn't. He'd never set eyes on it until it came out after your dad's death. And that's the truth,' Jeanie replied.

Cat shook her head in denial. 'No. You're wrong. I just need you to—'

'For fuck's *sake*, Cat, what aren't you getting?' Jeanie snapped, cutting her off. Her eyes held Cat's, her gaze sharp and cold even as the hint of a smile played at the edges of her mouth. '*Greg* didn't fake the will.'

Cat blinked and stepped backward, something twisting in her stomach as Jeanie's meaning hit home. 'You – *you* did it,' she breathed, the words a statement rather than a question.

Jeanie smirked now, all her former pretence done with. 'Do you know how many late nights I stayed behind in that office while your dad was alive? How many plans I cancelled because something urgent came up that he just couldn't sort out without me?'

'That was part of your *job*, Jeanie. You were his PA; it came with the territory – not to mention the hefty salary,' Cat said in disbelief.

Jeanie shrugged. 'Sure, I'm paid well. But do you know what really got to me over the years? *You*. Princess Catriona,' she mocked. 'Waltzing around the office when you felt like playing accountant, despite the fact you hadn't earned the position – despite the fact you hadn't earned *anything*, then waltzing off again when you felt like having a kid.'

Cat's jaw dropped, and she stared at Jeanie in stunned silence.

'But it didn't stop there, did it? *Oh no*. You stopped working to have Orla, so Daddy bought you a *house*! Outright!' Jeanie barked out a sharp laugh. 'And of course you'd got Daddy to hire your husband too, by that point. So when you suddenly didn't feel like working anymore, Daddy just upped Greg's pay, so that you didn't have to feel the pinch like any normal person.'

'You're seriously angry that I had a *child*?' Cat asked incredulously.

'No, I'm angry you had it all passed to you on a fucking plate,' Jeanie spat. 'And *then* I realised he was going to pass the entire company to you too. To *you*, the pampered little princess who has no idea how it all works, who hasn't even fannied about with the accounts in years. Huh!' She snorted, as if the idea was thoroughly absurd.

Cat felt herself start to shake with fury. 'So you thought you'd just take it from me. Gift it to my gormless husband to get back at me for, well, what? *Existing*?' She ran a hand back through her hair, reeling. 'He really doesn't know?' she queried, remembering Jeanie's earlier words.

'Not a damn clue,' Jeanie confirmed. 'It was my way in, you see. We've been seeing each other for months, and everyone knew he only stuck with you because you were the key to the kingdom.' She looked Cat up and down, no longer masking her sneering dislike. 'So I changed the will, forged the signature, paid off a couple of witnesses. I was waiting till your dad had passed, knowing that Greg would ditch you the moment he realised he didn't need you, and that then we'd be free to run the company together. I have the knowledge, and he has the ownership to make sure I'm given full reign – and the kind of salary I *really* deserve. It's a match made in heaven. And you actually made the whole thing easier by ditching him first.' She laughed. 'So thanks for that.'

'You evil bitch,' Cat seethed. 'You won't get away with this.'

'I already have,' Jeanie shot back. 'Or haven't you been paying attention? Look around, Cat. You've got nothing. The best you can do is try and take me to court, but we both know you don't have the money for that. Lawyers are expensive, and even if you do scrape enough together for a cheap one, they won't be a match for the *company* lawyers. I can make sure it's dragged on and on until you've run out of money to fight me and have no choice but to give up. And let's be honest, even if you made it to court, it's a bit of a far-fetched story, isn't it? We have paperwork and witnesses – and don't forget, Greg would have *me* in his corner to vouch for this. Me, a long-standing employee who worked closely with your dad and knew his wishes better than anyone.'

'How could you do this?' Cat asked, still stunned by all the revelations now swimming chaotically round in her head. 'This is insane, Jeanie. And I'm not standing for it. I'll tell Greg what you've done, and—'

'Go ahead!' Jeanie exclaimed. 'Like he'd believe you! I'll just tell him you're crazy and desperate and saying anything you can because you don't like the cards you've been dealt. It will hardly take much convincing.'

Her fury spilling over, Cat took a determined step forward. 'If you honestly think I'm just going to roll over and take this, you're sorely mistaken. This is my *life* you're messing with. My *daughter's* life. My dad's legacy.' She leaned further towards her, sparks almost flying from her eyes. 'I will fight you with everything I have, and I will make your life a fucking misery. Here, at the office, at your house. I will not leave you alone until you are so sick of me, you'll be *begging* me to take it back.'

Jeanie drew herself up to full height, a stubborn glint in her eye. 'No, you won't actually. Because if you don't quietly crawl back under whatever pathetic little rock you now sleep under, I might have to put a call in to social services.' She gave Cat a nasty smirk. 'I am *very* concerned about Orla right now.'

'What are you talking about?' Cat spat, alarmed by Jeanie's words but trying not to show it.

'Well, as you said yourself, she's sharing a bed with you in some squalid B&B. Who knows how clean it is or who else lives there?' Jeanie wrinkled her nose. 'That nice teacher of hers also sounded worried when I asked how she was doing too. What was her name? Miss Shannon, wasn't it? I'm sure social services would agree – what with how unsettled poor little Orla is – that placing her back in her own home, with a devoted father who can financially provide, and a caring stepmother who's very willing to help out, would be much better than leaving her with a mother who can barely put a roof over her head. Don't you think?'

'You fucking *cunt*.' Cat lunged forward, seeing red, but Jeanie ducked back and held the door in front of her like a shield.

'Now, now, Cat,' she taunted. 'You probably don't need an assault charge on your file, if social services are going to be taking a closer look at you, do you? Especially not with Orla right there in the car. Maybe I should add that to my report too. How concerned I am at how unravelled you've become.'

Cat bit back a sob as she turned and checked Orla was still asleep. She was, thank God.

'You think you've got away with this, but you haven't, Jeanie,' she said in a hard, shaky voice. 'I will get everything back if it's the last thing I do. And I will get *you* back for this.'

Cat turned and stalked back to the car, knowing she had to leave now before all sense left her completely and she beat Jeanie to death. She'd never been a violent person before this. Then again, no one had ever threatened to use her child as a pawn against her before this.

'That's right, off you go,' Jeanie called after her. 'But you can keep your threats to yourself. Because I'm not bluffing, Cat. You come for me and I'll have Orla off you faster than you can shout the word "fraud".'

The anger rose like a tide, and Cat spun round ready to launch at Jeanie once more, but she swiftly shut the door.

'I'll make you pay for that threat, Jeanie Barker,' she growled under her breath. 'And I'll beat you at this game, if it's the last goddamn thing I do.'

THIRTY-ONE

Antonio mopped up the last of the egg on his breakfast plate with a slice of toast and took a large bite as he watched his mother hobble over to the sink with the frying pan she'd just cooked his breakfast in. He dusted the crumbs off his fingers onto the plate and took a sip of his orange juice.

'That was blindin'. Thanks, Mum.'

She made a dismissive sound, the way she always did when someone tried to compliment her on the things she felt were her job.

Antonio eyed the clock on the wall. 'Cat coming in today?'

'Yes, she'll be here soon,' Sophia replied.

'You'll be able to get rid of her soon, won't you?' Antonio asked. 'You're moving around much easier now.'

Sophia frowned. 'Not yet. A bit of breakfast I can manage, but the rest of the house is too much with only one good arm and leg. Besides,' she added, 'it's been quite nice having her around. She's a good girl.'

It was Antonio's turn to frown. When Cat had first started there, Sophia had been adamantly trying to get rid of her, furious that they'd brought someone else into her domain.

'You've changed your tune,' he commented.

Sophia didn't answer, simply shooting him a stern look as she hobbled back out of the room.

Antonio smirked. His mother didn't like being wrong about anything. Still, he was surprised she'd warmed to Cat so quickly. But perhaps it *wasn't* that surprising. Sophia wasn't the only one who was gravitating towards her. He couldn't get her out of his mind. It was maddening. He wasn't used to being turned down by a woman. Much less one who he'd made it very clear he wanted. What was wrong with her? And there had to be something wrong. She was just some nobody, for God's sake. A part-time cleaner with another man's kid in tow. Hardly anything special. And *he* was a Capello. A powerful man. An attractive man with status and money and the ability to show her a very good time. And yet she'd shunned him, run away like she'd been scalded by his touch. It just wasn't on.

She should have been grateful that someone like him had shown her attention. She should have been thrilled to be offered the chance to sleep with him. For as long as he could remember, there had never been a woman he'd wanted who'd turned him down. He'd always been spoiled for choice, women fawning over him, competing for his attention. This new reaction, this rejection, just wasn't on. He didn't like it. No, he *detested* it. And these new feelings it had evoked had angered him deeply.

Standing up, Antonio swigged the last of his orange juice and glanced at the clock again. She'd be here any second now. He'd tried to forget about her, tried to move on, but the more he'd tried, the more maddening the situation had felt. Eventually he realised he'd just have to change her mind. Because Antonio didn't lose. Even if it took a bit of time to get there, he *would* fuck her. He would use her, screw her all night long, over and over, until he was spent and she was out of his system once and for all. *No one* turned down Antonio Capello. And he wasn't about to let one little bitch like Cat change that.

Right on time, he heard the sounds of Cat's arrival. She walked through to the kitchen and paused behind him. Antonio hid a sly smile before turning around to face her.

'Alright, Cat?' he asked in his most charming voice.

'Oh, hi,' she said in a reluctant tone. 'Is your mum around?' She glanced over to the utility room hopefully.

'Nah, she's just gone to get dressed I think.' He eyed her hungrily. Even dressed in those drab black clothes she couldn't hide her slender, well-proportioned body from him. She probably wasn't even trying to, he reasoned. She was probably *trying* to be a prick tease. 'Good weekend?'

'Yeah, fine thanks,' she replied, walking past him to the sink. She squeezed some washing-up liquid into it and turned on the taps.

'What did you get up to?' Antonio asked. 'Anything fun?'

'Er, nothing much really. I mainly spent time with my daughter,' she replied, not looking round. 'You?'

'Oh, come on now,' Antonio scolded. 'That ain't *all* you got up to, is it?'

He walked over to her and saw her shoulders tense as he drew close. It annoyed him. She'd been more than happy to play around with his brother in nothing but a towel, but here, now, fully dressed as they both were, she didn't want him near her? What a joke. He purposely stepped a little too close and ran a finger from her shoulder down her upper arm.

'I hear you and my brother enjoyed a nice bubble bath,' he continued, the playful tone of his low voice unable to cover the underlying tautness.

Cat's cheeks burned as she shoved her hands in the hot, soapy water and began to clean the plates. 'That's not what happened,' she replied quickly. 'It was just a lie for the police so he didn't get in trouble for helping you. It didn't actually happen. Christ, your brother's a married man!' Cat forced a laugh, but it sounded strained.

Antonio narrowed his gaze as a stab of jealousy zapped through him. 'Oh. I see it now. He's a married man, but you wish he wasn't, don't you?'

'What? No! Not at all,' Cat protested with a frown. 'I don't see your brother like that. And even if I did, it wouldn't matter. He's married, and...' She paused, a strange look flitting across her features. 'Well, I just don't like cheaters.'

'Yeah, 'course you wouldn't,' Antonio crooned. 'Besides, that's the wrong brother anyway. Alex is no fun. All work and no play that one.' He leaned into Cat's ear, mistaking her silence for subservience. '*Me* though. I'm a lot of fun. And I'm single. No wife for you to worry your pretty little head about.'

'Look, I'm sorry but I'm just not looking for anything right now.' Cat took a half step back and reached for the towel, but he grabbed her wrist and held her there. She leaned away as he tried to pull her closer. 'Antonio, please, can you let go of my hand?'

Her voice was calm, but there was an underlying quiver that stirred something inside him. He yanked her to him, pressing her body to his and slipping his free arm around her waist, grabbing her backside.

'What are you *doing*?' She sounded scared now, and he liked that.

'Playing hard to get ain't as cute as you girls think it is, you know,' he told her in a low, breathy voice.

He sniffed her hair. The sweet violet scent of her shampoo and the subtle musky spice of her perfume mixed into a concoction that felt like his own personal drug. He wanted *more*. He wanted to taste her. He wanted to consume her. He wanted her more than he'd ever wanted anyone before, and he knew, without doubt, that this need wasn't going to fade until he'd had her.

Antonio wasn't sure why he got like this over things he wanted. He'd always been this way, since he was a child. Never over a woman before, but then he'd never been met with resistance until now. It was just the way he was though. If there was something he wanted that wasn't his, he *had* to have it, no matter what it took. He couldn't rest, couldn't sleep, couldn't cope until it was his. Toys, cars, businesses... And now, for some inexplicable reason, Cat.

'I'm not playing *anything*,' Cat argued, the panic in her voice obvious now. 'Please, Antonio, you need to let go of me. This *isn't* OK.'

'Oh, come on, Cat,' he murmured. 'You know you want it.'

'*No*, I *don't*,' she shot back. '*Please*, Antonio!'

She started fighting to get away with more force now, but this just excited him more. He was close to getting what he wanted, and she knew it.

But then, all too soon, the moment was taken from him.

'What the *hell* is going on?' Alex's voice boomed around the small space, and Antonio had no choice but to let Cat go.

He sighed, reluctantly releasing her. 'Well, nothing now *you're* here, you big buzzkill.'

Cat jumped away from him as quick as a flash, and Antonio clenched his teeth.

'What are you *doing*?' Alex's glare was dark and angry, but it softened to a look of concern as he turned his gaze to Cat. 'Are you OK?'

'Not really,' Cat replied, her voice hotly indignant now Alex was here.

Gone was the scared little mouse of moments before, and Antonio's eyes narrowed slightly as he smirked at her. 'Oh, come on, Cat. We were only having a bit of fun, weren't we?'

'It didn't look like she was having much fun from where I was standing,' Alex responded.

'Well, maybe you were standing in the wrong *place*,' Antonio told him with a hard, icy tone.

He turned until he was square on to his brother and held his gaze with a challenge in his own. Alex needed to back off. Disappear and keep his nose out of it. And he *would* if he knew what was good for him. And, of course, he *should* know that by now. After a lifetime of siblingship. Alex might be the older brother, but they both knew that if Antonio wanted something, Alex would eventually have to defer. It was better for everyone that way, in the end. But something in Alex's eyes suddenly changed, and a small muscle by his jaw twitched.

'No. I don't think I am.' Alex took a step towards Antonio, his broad shoulders hunched up as he leaned in close to his brother's face. 'You leave her alone. She said no; she *means* no. And she's under the protection of this firm. Even if that means protecting her from one of our own. Do you understand?'

Antonio glared back at his brother, the bubbling ball of anger he'd been feeling bursting into a raging tornado of fire that swept through his entire body. Who the hell did his brother think he was speaking to? Who the hell did he think he *was*? Was this a joke? Was Alex really choosing some stupid woman over his own kin? Because that's what this was. A choice. A side picked. And the woman whose side he'd so firmly placed himself on wasn't even his own wife.

At this thought, Antonio's gaze slid down to the glittering gold wedding band on Alex's finger, and a terrible and wonderful idea suddenly came to him. He smirked and scratched his chin to hide the seething rage that would otherwise have contorted his features into a dark and ugly expression, and then he shrugged.

'I understand you perfectly, big brother,' he said, his low tone laced with sarcasm.

Looking Cat pointedly up and down, his smile cold, Antonio walked out of the room. He grabbed his car keys from the sideboard as he passed and left the house, and after slamming the door shut behind him, he pulled out his phone. Cat was going to regret playing hard to get. And *he* was going to be the one to set all the nasty little wheels in motion to see that she got her comeuppance.

'Bianca,' he said merrily, as a beep signalled that he'd reached her voicemail. 'When you next free for a drink? I've got some information I think you might like to hear.'

THIRTY-TWO

Cat placed the last glass in the kitchen cupboard and let out a heavy yawn, glad to be finished for the day. She heard Sophia shuffle into the room behind her and felt her heart drop a little. She knew the older woman was hoping she'd stay for a coffee before she left. It was something she'd started doing most days, since Sophia had warmed to her, and it was something she genuinely enjoyed. This time at the end of the day doing nothing, enjoying a moment of simple peace and adult company before picking up Orla. But she couldn't do it today. She couldn't look Sophia in the eye and pretend that she was OK. And she couldn't lie about why she wasn't.

'Are you all done?' Sophia asked hopefully. 'I have some new coffee in, sent over from my cousin in Italy. I think you'll like it.'

'Thank you, but I really can't today,' Cat told her, turning round with as big a smile as she could force. 'I have to get to Orla's pre-school early. Something to do with the nativity and outfits or something, I don't know...' She trailed off and waved her hand, hoping the lie wasn't too obvious.

'Ahh, I miss those days,' Sophia sighed, shuffling past Cat to where she kept the coffee. 'I had to make a penguin outfit once. A *penguin*,' she repeated incredulously. 'For a *nativity*. Can you imagine?'

Cat had to smile at that. 'No, not really. I'm not sure there were that many penguins in Bethlehem back in the day.'

'There were *none*,' Sophia agreed. 'But apparently that year, when the teacher told the kids they were going to be doing the story of Christmas, my Antonio got it into his head that they meant the North Pole. When they asked him to be a shepherd, he almost lost his mind. He was only six, but he was a very determined boy, even then.'

Cat's smile faded as she listened, glad Sophia was facing away from her and couldn't see her expression.

'He tantrummed about it for days. Refused to go to school until they allowed him to play the part he wanted, which, as it turned out, was a penguin. In the end, they gave in. It was the only way to get him through the school gates.' Sophia chuckled fondly at the memory. 'That's the thing about Antonio. Once he decides on something going his way, that's it. He'll stop at nothing to make it happen. It had me pulling out my hair when he was a child, but as a man it's served him well. Helped him build all that he has today.'

Cat felt sick and had to turn away quickly as Sophia moved to face her. She busied herself with pulling on her coat and picking up her bag, not daring to look up at her employer. Sophia sounded so proud of her younger son, and, as a mother, Cat could understand that. But clearly Sophia didn't know – or perhaps refused to see – how toxic a trait that had turned out to be.

Because Cat suddenly felt a lot like that penguin suit. She'd made herself very clear, the first time Antonio had tried it on, that she wasn't interested. He'd not liked it at the time, but she'd expected him to take the hint and move on. It was obvious from what had happened this morning, however, that Antonio didn't care whether she wanted him or not. He wanted her, and therefore he was now trying to find a way to force it.

It had put her in a very worrying predicament. She needed this job right now and couldn't afford to leave. But she also didn't relish the idea of being here each day, under Antonio's nose, like a goldfish in a bowl waiting to be caught. For a moment, she felt a stab of resentment towards Sophia. Maybe if she'd spent more time telling her son *no* as a child, he wouldn't be such a worryingly entitled adult. But then her anger swiftly faded. What right did she have to judge another mother? She hadn't been around to see these episodes, so she couldn't know how hard it was, or wasn't, for Sophia.

'I must head off,' she said, shooting the other woman a quick smile. 'See you tomorrow.'

'Oh, yes. OK. See you,' Sophia said, sounding a touch surprised by the abrupt goodbye.

Cat rushed outside and instantly felt some of the tension lift as the cool winter breeze lifted her hair from her neck. She raised her face to the sky, briefly enjoying the fresh feeling on her skin. Out here, in the sunlight, things suddenly didn't seem quite so dismal. *Maybe*, she reasoned, she was overthinking this too much. It wasn't OK, what Antonio had done today, but when Alex had come in, he'd made it very clear that it wasn't to happen again. That she was protected. Antonio was unlikely to go against his older brother on something like this, wasn't he? After all, he probably had his pick of women. Much as Antonio wasn't *her* type, he was a good-looking man, and he did have a lot going for him.

She got in her car and bit her bottom lip, thinking it all over. Was she worrying too much or too little about all of this? Either way, she really didn't need the added drama right now. Not with everything else she had going on. She still needed to deal with Greg and the will. That was her main priority. But exactly how she was going to do that she still had no idea. The conversation she'd had with Alex the other night, after the police had left, slipped back into her mind.

What is your business? What is it you actually do? she'd asked him.

Mainly, we solve problems, he'd replied, his words careful and his expression guarded. *If someone has an issue they can't resolve using more traditional routes, they come to us. And that can mean anything. That's what we're known for. Finding solutions for things that other people can't.*

Cat had understood what he'd meant. Not to what extent, but she knew it meant they worked on the wrong side of the law. She knew it meant that they were well versed in that way of life – and that they were successful at what they did too, based on their mother's home and what she'd seen of their lifestyles. She knew that it meant, put simply, that they were skilled and experienced criminals. The funny thing was, had she discovered this a few months ago, she'd probably have been horrified. She certainly wouldn't have ever considered lying to the police to protect one of them.

But the person she'd been a few months ago – before her dad had died, before she'd learned about Greg's affairs, before he'd scammed her out of everything she had – didn't exist anymore. She'd become someone completely different since then. And apparently *this* version of her had no problem offering herself up as a fake alibi to the police, to protect criminals. Which begged the question: how far would *this* Cat go to get back what was hers?

She backed out of the drive, lost in thought, and set off down the road. So *deeply* lost in thought that she didn't notice when the black car parked across the road, a few houses down, pulled out to follow her.

THIRTY-THREE

Alex stood in the shadows of the trees surrounding Frank Sinclair's property and stared up at the dark house. Already dressed all in black, he pulled out the black leather gloves from his pocket and slipped them on.

'You're sure you want to do this?' Maria asked quietly from a couple of steps behind.

He nodded, knowing she'd be able to make out his silhouette from where she stood. 'We need to see this through. And it's the best way, all round. You're sure you want to come in on this? You've been getting very close lately. You're starting to get noticed.'

He heard the small sigh escape her lips, and there was a short silence before she answered. 'Times are changing. There's been a shift lately. I think we've all felt it. Antonio can't be counted on the way he used to be.'

'But that doesn't mean we can't still keep your presence in the firm on the quiet,' Alex reasoned. 'The last thing we need is for you to lose your credibility on the legal side of things. That won't do *anyone* any favours.'

It had always been him and Antonio, as the front men, with

Maria running things with them behind closed doors. People in their world knew she was there. The people they trusted and their equals within other firms. It wasn't the best-kept secret in the world. But she rarely joined them publicly. This protected her image, kept her above board with the legal circles she moved in. As far as they were concerned, she was a well-respected and savvy lawyer who had great contacts and was a friend to all. If one of them got wind of who she *really* was, word would get around fast, and her credibility would be lost. Even worse than that, all the leverage she held over the people she'd blackmailed and manipulated over the years, for their gain, would instantly be lost. And those people would be all too happy to dig deeper and turn her in for anything they found in return. The risk she took, showing her face in their world, was much higher than theirs.

'I think we're past me hiding in the shadows, Alex,' Maria said with calm resolve. 'I know the risks better than anyone, but this has become the safer option now. What's the alternative? You keep Antonio by your side, coked up and unpredictable? Much as I love him, we're going to have to make some changes in the general structure of things going forward. And you can't run this firm alone. I mean, you technically *could*. But it would only be a matter of time before someone decides you're an easy target and tries to take you down. And what if they succeed? *No.*' He heard rather than saw Maria shake her head. 'We're all much safer having two of us up front and, right now, that needs to be you and I.'

Alex bit his top lip as she spoke, knowing she was right but not liking it all the same. And it wasn't the fact things were changing. He enjoyed working with Maria. She was as sharp and as hard as they came when it came down to business. More so than any man he'd ever met. But he didn't relish the thought of his brother's reaction to the news that he needed to take a back seat. That was going to go down like a lead balloon. But they'd deal with that later.

'Well, we're here now. So let's get this over with,' he said quietly.

They moved through the dark garden around to the back of the large house, where they paused momentarily for Alex to pick the lock of the kitchen door. It swung open silently, and they crept through the house and up the stairs towards the bedroom at the back, where they knew Frank would be sleeping.

Maria raised her hand, and Alex stopped still while she pressed her ear to the crack of the door. After a second, she nodded and pulled out the gun from the waistband of her black tracksuit, then gently swung the door open. Alex braced himself for a creak but none came, and he mentally thanked Frank for being so on top of oiling all his door hinges. It was certainly making their lives easier.

They stepped into the room, and Alex could see the outline of the older man under the covers, tufts of his salt-and-pepper hair sticking up above his pillow. He slept soundly, not aware in the slightest that two strangers who'd been paid to kill him were currently in his bedroom, watching him. Maria walked over to the armchair in the corner of the room and took a seat, and Alex made his way across the room, sitting down carefully on the bed beside Frank's sleeping form. Frank was facing away from him, curled up on his side. Slipping a knife out of his pocket, Alex held it close to his neck, not quite touching the skin, then gave Maria a nod.

Maria reached over to the lamp on the side table and switched it on, resting her gun on her lap, her eyes on Frank. It took a second or two, then Frank's low snores suddenly doubled into a snorting grunt, and he blinked open his bleary eyes. His forehead creased in a frown of confusion, the action slow, as sleep still clung to him, then suddenly he seemed to register that Maria was there and he tried to sit up.

Alex pressed the knife to his throat, and Frank let out a frightened yelp, his eyes darting from one to the other, back and forth as he sank back down in the bed.

'Hello, Frank,' Maria said calmly.

'Wh-Who— Wh-What's going on? Who are you? Please, take whatever you want. Just don't harm me. *Please*,' Frank begged.

'We're not here to rob you,' Maria replied. 'Are we, Alex?'

'No,' Alex confirmed. 'Not at all. We don't want any of your nice things. We've just been sent here to kill ya.'

'What? *No!* Oh, *please*,' Frank's face contorted into a look of real fear, and his voice rose an octave. 'Please don't! Oh God. Oh *God!*'

'He won't help you, mate,' Alex replied.

'*Please*, I'll give you *anything*,' Frank sobbed. He was shaking now, frozen in terror under the blade, his eyes glued to Maria's gun.

'Aren't you curious as to why?' Maria asked him, tilting her head to the side.

Frank let out a sound that might have been laughter, were he not so seriously terrified. 'OK. Tell me then. *Why?*'

'Your son, Justin. He hired us to kill you,' she told him.

For a moment, Frank stopped shaking, the shock overriding everything else. '*Justin?* No. He wouldn't do that to me. You've got it wrong – he must have meant someone else. *Something* else.'

'No, he was very clear actually,' Maria replied. 'We thought you deserved to know.'

Alex moved the knife away from Frank's throat and shuffled down the bed a bit, allowing the older man some space. He sat up and shifted back against the headrest, eyeing Alex warily.

'It was the decent thing to do, to be honest with you,' Alex added. 'A son betraying a father like that...' He let out a low whistle and shook his head with a disappointed look. 'It's pretty brutal.'

Frank wetted his lips, his eyes still darting between the two strangers in his room. 'Look, there has to have been a mistake, or – or perhaps he did this in anger and doesn't really mean it. You have to give me a chance to speak to him. *Please*. Just give me a day – or call him over here. A phone call. *Anything*.'

Maria held up a small vial with a clear, slightly greenish liquid inside. 'Do you know what this is?' she asked.

Frank shook his head.

'It's a neurotoxin derived from the hemlock plant. Ingest even a small-enough amount of the plant and it can kill you, though it's a messy process. Lots of vomiting, pain, all your muscles seize up, then eventual respiratory failure. Nasty stuff.' Maria grimaced. 'No antidote either. You'd think they'd have found one by now, considering how common it is to mistake for wild parsley. *This* though. This is a special concentrated variation of it, designed to kill quickly. Less pain and suffering.'

'So you expect me to take that?' Frank spat, shaking again now as the tears began to flow down his face.

'That was the plan,' Maria replied. 'It's what your son chose for you. And it's expensive stuff too. He could have just had you shot or stabbed or buried alive somewhere – though, admittedly, that one tends to only be picked for people who are *really* hated.'

'Yeah, he's spared no expense on your death,' Alex added.

'Which is nice, really, when you think about it,' Maria offered. 'He cared that you weren't going to suffer.'

'Well, not exactly,' Alex corrected, looking over to her. 'It was actually to make sure it looked like he died of natural causes, so it didn't affect the life insurance.'

'Oh, that's right,' Maria said, clicking her fingers with a nod. 'I forgot that bit.'

'Are you really trying to hurt me *more* before you kill me?' Frank asked incredulously. 'What the fuck is wrong with you people? How can you enjoy torturing someone like this?' He suddenly looked angry, and as his face reddened, he sat up straighter. 'Come on then. If you're going to kill me, just fucking kill me. But be warned, I will fight you to the bitter end. Because I don't intend on making this easy for any of you.' His breathing grew quicker, and he bunched his fists up, determination seeping through the fear still written all over his face.

Alex smiled. 'So, you're a fighter. Good. I was rather hoping you were.'

'*What?*' Frank asked, confused.

Maria slipped the poison back into her inside jacket pocket with a smile. 'There'll be no need for that, Mr Sinclair. Nobody's dying today.'

'You just told me you're here to kill me,' Frank replied, his fists still raised, distrust in his eyes.

'No, we didn't,' Maria corrected him. 'We told you we were *hired* to kill you. And we told you *how*.'

'Thing is, Frank,' Alex took over as Maria busied herself with putting her gun away, 'we only work with people we can trust. People we vet through a chain of other people before they even get to us. So it's not very often someone we *can't* trust slips through the net, but your son apparently managed it.'

'What does that mean?' Frank asked.

'He lied to us, and he hid things from us that caused us considerable problems,' Alex explained. 'And we won't work with someone like that.'

'So...' Frank exhaled with a deep frown of confusion. 'If you're not here to kill me, why *are* you here?'

'Well, we also can't just walk away from someone we don't trust, after revealing who we are,' Alex told him. 'Nor can we allow the problems he's caused us to go unrectified.'

'*You* can't let this go either,' Maria pointed out. 'He'd only find someone else to kill you, and they'd probably just go ahead with it. So that's something you need to deal with. Plus, there's the matter of the hundred grand owed to loan sharks against the promise of the hotel inheritance. *That's* certainly not going to go away on its own.'

'*What?*' Frank blurted, in shock.

'No, I didn't think you'd know about that,' Alex mused. He leaned in closer to Frank. 'The reason we're here, Frank, is that we're going to offer you a deal. One that, if you're on board, could be a solution to all our problems, yours and ours, once and for all.'

'And if I'm not on board?' he asked.

Alex and Maria exchanged a look.

'Well, see that ain't really an option,' Alex replied. 'Because if you aren't on board, then you're *also* a loose end. Which means we'll be left with no choice but to take you both out of the equation altogether.'

There was a short silence, and then Frank sighed defeatedly. 'Alright. I'm listening.'

THIRTY-FOUR

Maria pulled up outside Alex's house and yawned as he got out of her car.

'You sure you don't want to just crash here?' Alex asked, looking back at her as he got out. It was nearly four in the morning. 'You know we've got plenty of room.'

'No. Thank you, but I just need to get home to my own bed.' She smiled tiredly. 'Go on in – it's freezing out here. I'll see you later.'

'Alright. Drive safe.' He tapped the roof of the car and watched her drive off down the road.

They both knew why she really hadn't taken him up on his offer. It was nothing to do with the beds. It was that she didn't want to have to sit and make polite small talk with Bianca in the morning. He sighed and turned to walk up the path. *He* didn't even want to have to sit and make small talk with his wife in the morning, but unlike Maria, he had no choice. Things had become more and more strained between them recently, and he knew that a lot of it was his fault. But it was just so hard to be around her when everything she said or did was designed to be a barb and aimed directly at him.

He opened the door as quietly as he could and slipped off his shoes. As he shrugged off his jacket, a light in the lounge flicked on, and he turned, surprised to find Bianca sitting on the sofa fully dressed and glaring at him.

'Another four a.m. finish I see,' she said, her voice laced with bitterness.

'What are you doing up?' Alex asked, frowning in concern. 'What's happened?'

'Ha!' She barked out a laugh. '*What's happened?* Well, whatever's *happened* hasn't happened *here*, Alex, has it? Not *here* with your *wife*.'

'What are you on about?' he asked, already annoyed. Already knowing whatever this was, Bianca was gearing up for an argument.

'You tell me!' she shot back. 'Was it at *her* place, or did you splurge on a nice hotel? Eh?'

Alex's mouth dropped open in genuine surprise. 'What on earth are you talking about, woman?'

'Your little fucking *skank* on the side, Alex,' Bianca yelled, all pretence of calm shattering as she leaped up out of her seat. 'That skinny slag your mum's been dangling in front of you, at her house, the last few weeks.'

'*What?*' Alex's eyebrows rose and his jaw dropped again as her words spewed out. 'Are you kidding me? She's just Mum's cleaner, for fuck's sake!'

Bianca strode forward until she was right in front of him, fire dancing in her eyes as she yelled in his face. 'Yeah? Get in the fucking bath with *all* the family employees, do ya?'

Alex took a step back, and confirmation registered on Bianca's face. He realised a split second too late that his reaction had given her the answer she was looking for. But that answer wasn't what she thought it was.

'Bianca, that wasn't what happened,' he told her, holding his hands up as he tried to appease her.

'Yes, it was,' she screamed back, angry tears filling her eyes. 'I can see it in your *fucking face*, Alex.'

'*No*, it *wasn't*. Bianca, seriously, listen to me. I was running from the police, and I went there to find my mum, to get an alibi. But she was out,' he explained as she made sounds of disbelief. 'Cat was there – she'd just got out the bath...'

'Why would she be in the *bath* at your mother's house?' Bianca asked, her expression showing exactly how little she believed that.

Alex flung his hands up in the air, trying to find an answer and failing. 'I – I don't *know*! She just *was*! Maybe she had problems with her water at home, I don't know, but she was just *there*. I didn't even have time to explain before the sirens started wailing down the street. She took one look at the blood all over me, put two and two together and offered me an out. Told me to get in the bath and make it look like we were up there together. It was the only option I had, and it was a good alibi, so I took it.'

Another tear fell down Bianca's angry face. 'You really expect me to believe that?'

'Yes, Bianca, I do,' Alex replied hotly. His anger was beginning to rise now. He was sick and tired of these hysterics every time Bianca felt like a row. 'I've *never* cheated on you. I wouldn't. You're my wife, and we might not always like each other very much, but I take my vows seriously. And you *know* that. Or you *should* know it.'

Christ, she should know it, he thought angrily. He'd certainly put up with enough over the years that it should prove his loyalty. And yet here he was, still having to defend himself against accusations of cheating. Was Cat attractive? Sure! He could see that she was – he wasn't blind. But he *was* loyal, and that Bianca was calling his loyalty into the ring – now, after everything he'd put up with from her – pissed him off beyond belief.

'Yeah?' Bianca spat. 'Then why do you stare at her whenever she's around, at your mum's, eh? I've seen ya. Smiling and chatting whenever she walks past, like some dog on fucking heat, and I ain't the only one who's noticed. I ought to go knock her fucking *teeth* out!'

'*Dog on heat?*' Alex repeated angrily. 'Who the fuck do you think you're talking about? I've been polite and friendly to Cat, same way I would anyone *else* working at my mum's. That's all. There's nothing more to it than that, and I don't want to hear another word about it. What is the matter with you, Bianca?'

'What's the *matter* with me?' Bianca shot back. '*She's* what's the matter. And don't fob me off with that bullshit, Alex. I *know* there's something going on.'

'That's *enough!*' Alex roared, his temper finally getting the better of him. 'I've told you there's nothing going on, and there *isn't*. That's the *end* of it. Oh, and you ain't going round knocking *anyone*'s teeth out, and *yes*, that is a *fucking order*, Bianca. Because I am *not* having you start up trouble with good people for no reason. Not again. Do you hear me?'

'Oh, I fucking hear you, *oh lord and master*,' Bianca retorted sarcastically. 'I guess all us *bad* people need to just toe the line, right?'

'That is not what I meant and you know it,' Alex replied with a heavy sigh. He ran a hand down his face, done with this now. 'I'm going to bed. It's four in the fucking morning, I've been working all night and the last thing I need is more shit from you.' He turned and walked away. 'Come to bed, don't come to bed, I don't care. But you leave that girl alone, Bianca,' he warned. 'I mean it.'

'Yeah, well, we'll see about that,' she muttered as he walked away.

He reached the hallway and glanced back at her once more, the warning clear in his eyes. But as he turned away and began to climb the stairs, he had to suppress a small shiver that ran up his spine. Because the look in her eyes wasn't one he'd ever seen before. And he suddenly wasn't sure his warnings were going to be enough to save Cat from her wrath after all.

THIRTY-FIVE

Over the next few days, Cat slowly began to relax in the Capello household again. Antonio had only popped in twice, and both times it had been to discuss business with his siblings in the large library room hey used as an office. He'd shot Cat a smirk when they'd passed in the hall, then he'd left her alone, which she was thankful for. She hadn't found herself alone again with him, and she wasn't sure whether this was lucky coincidence or because Alex had made sure of it, but it didn't really matter. All she wanted was to come to work each day, do her job and get back to Orla, and that was what she was doing now.

She'd stewed over the predicament she now found herself in with Jeanie, night after night, the angry spiralling thoughts keeping her awake. She lay in the dark staring up at the cracks in the ceiling, going over and over her limited options and returning, every time, to the same frustrating conclusion. Jeanie was right. She held all the cards. Cat couldn't afford a good-enough lawyer to take this to court, and even if she did, Jeanie could easily do what she'd threatened. She'd drag it out long enough for Cat to run out of money, then it would be dropped.

Cat had gone to Greg, told him everything and begged him to believe her, but he hadn't been interested. He'd shut her down and walked away – as, deep down, she'd known he would. And so what options were really left to her? Every fibre of her wanted to become Jeanie's worst nightmare, be on top of her constantly, until she slipped up or gave in, but Jeanie had been one step ahead of that thought too, threatening her with losing Orla. The thought of that woman messing with Orla's life made her insides curl and twist with fury, and hot, silent tears had rolled down her face into the pillows.

So what was she going to do about it? She couldn't just do nothing. The only way out, it seemed, was to drag herself up and out of this situation slowly. She needed to get a better job, earn more money, sort out their living situation. Then she could think about saving up to get a lawyer. But the thought of how long that would take filled her with despair, and who would even hire her anyway?

Back before Orla, Cat had worked for her father. She'd done a basic college course in business finance then had worked his accounts. She wasn't officially an accountant, having never seen the need to complete the formal qualifications, only to step back into the job she already had. And it wasn't like she'd ever planned to move to another company. Why would she, with a perfectly good family business on her doorstep? Only, now here she was. No recent experience, no references, no family business to rely on. She didn't even have the funds to pay for the courses she'd need to prove her abilities.

But something occurred to her as she pondered the issue of Jeanie and the lack of opportunity to use her skillset, night after night. There could be one way that she might just be able to solve both problems, if she was willing to take a risk. It was a risk she'd never have entertained before, but things had changed. Her priorities were different now. They had to be. And as the idea took root in her mind, she closed her exhausted eyes in the early hours of Friday morning, filled with a new sense of hope, and drifted into a much calmer and more optimistic sleep.

'Mumma?' The croaky little voice sounded wrong, Cat realised, as it entered her dreams and began to wake her up. 'Mu- *Mumma.*' It came again, scared this time.

This reached her inbuilt protectiveness, and she forced open her eyes, feeling for Orla in the bed. She wrapped her arms around her instinctively. *What was that smell?*

'Mm? What is it?' Cat asked groggily.

Her throat burned, and her head felt thick and heavy. She blinked, trying to clear the sleepy mist from her vision, but it didn't go. *Why did she feel so lethargic?*

It hit her all of a sudden, and she bolted upright in the bed, instantly regretting it as the smoke she inhaled sent her lungs into a spasm. There was a fire. She pulled Orla to her, trying to stem the coughing.

'It's alright,' she told her petrified daughter, unable to keep the alarm out of her tone. 'Pull your nightie up over your mouth and nose. Come on – that's it, baby.' She coughed again, pulling her own nightwear up.

The fire wasn't in their room, but thick black smoke was pouring in through the cracks around the door. There were noises outside in the hallway now, people panicking as they tried to get out. They needed to move, she realised. *Fast.*

Hauling Orla up onto her hip, she got out of bed and opened the door. The smoke was thicker there, and while she couldn't yet see the flames, there was heat. Too much heat. Everything in her body told her to turn around and barricade themselves in, but she knew that would be a death sentence. Their window looked out across the narrowest of alleys onto the brick wall of the next building. There would be no one to see them and no space for a fire crew to winch someone up to save them. They *had* to escape down the stairs. And they had to go before the fire took over the hallway.

Orla was howling now, her little body shaking as she clung on to her mother for dear life. She was terrified.

Closing the door momentarily, Cat looked around. She slipped her feet into the nearest pair of shoes and grabbed both their coats.

'OK, Orla? Listen to me.' She slipped her arms into her own coat, pulling it around them both. 'You're going to close your eyes, OK? I'm going to put your coat over you and over your head to keep you safe, alright?' Orla continued crying, but Cat felt her nod into her shoulder. 'Good girl.' Her voice wobbled, and her heart leaped as a terrible crashing sound reverberated through the door, followed by a loud scream. 'It's fine. We're going to be fine. OK?'

Fighting back her own terror, she reopened the door, and this time she had to stifle a gasp. The flickering orange glow of flames was now showing at the other end of the hall, horrifyingly close to the top of the stairs. There was no time for anything else. There was no time to build up the courage to run towards the flames. She just had to do it.

Cat took the first step and then the second, forcing her feet forward, one heart-lurching pace at a time. The heat was almost too much to bear on her skin as she moved closer, and she pulled Orla's coat up further to protect her. The smoke was too thick to see much, and as a waft of it blocked her vision, she reached out and gripped the stair rail, pulling herself towards the top of the stairs, silently screaming and begging God not to let the flames reach her little girl. Then suddenly the rail changed and she realised she was there, at the top of the stairs. The fire raged and roared behind her, far too close for comfort, and she lurched forward, taking the steps two at a time, Orla held tightly in her grip.

As she got about halfway down, two pairs of strong hands suddenly grabbed them and pulled them to safety, two accompanying voices asking if they were OK, if they could breathe. The fire brigade had arrived. All Cat could do in response was shake her head, pulling the coat off Orla as they finally reached the blissfully cold air of the street, terrified at the sudden realisation that her daughter had gone quiet. Far *too* quiet.

Orla's mass of dark curls didn't move, and for a moment Cat's heart completely stopped in her chest. *Why wasn't she moving?* Had she inhaled too much smoke? Was she breathing? Cat opened her mouth to scream for help, but in that moment suddenly Orla stirred, looking up at her with tear-stained cheeks and a terrified sob.

'*Mummy.*'

'Oh, Orla,' Cat cried.

The knowledge that her daughter was OK sent her over the edge, and suddenly her knees felt too weak to hold her up. She dropped down to the pavement and squeezed Orla to her chest as though she would never let her go, and then she sobbed, deep loud sobs, as she let out all the fear and shock and adrenaline that had been coursing through her body.

'I love you so much,' she whispered through her tears into Orla's hair. 'I love you so much. I'm so sorry, baby. I'm so sorry you were scared.'

'That's OK, Mummy,' Orla replied into her neck. 'I knew you'd get us out.'

Fresh tears sprang to Cat's eyes as those words hit her square in the chest. Orla had so much faith in her. In her sweet young innocence, Orla believed her mother could do anything. She didn't realise yet that they'd just lost the last few remaining things they had in the world. She didn't know that her pathetically meagre bag of toys and books, and even her clothes, had gone. She didn't know that as of now, the pair of them very literally had nothing but the nightclothes and coats that they stood in.

'It's all gone,' Cat whispered in horror as she stared over at the burning building. All the windows were shattered, and flames licked out of every single one. The roof had fallen in and the entire building was engulfed. 'Oh my God, it really has all gone.' She felt sick.

'It's OK, Bunny,' Orla crooned, glancing round and then hiding her face in Cat's neck again. 'I've got you.'

Cat looked down to see what she was talking about and realised Orla still had her bedtime bunny clutched in her arms. It was as filthy and soot-coated as they were, but Orla didn't seem to care. She peeped up at Cat. 'I saved him,' she said simply.

'Well, that's something.' Cat managed a weak smile.

But this dropped as she moved her gaze back to the fire. What, or who, had started the fire? How had this happened? They would have died in that room had Orla not woken up when she did.

The sound of a car starting up pulled at Cat's attention, and as she turned she saw the dark saloon pull out of the street and round the corner.

Who was that? she wondered. *Had they been watching?* As the tail lights disappeared, Cat felt a cold tingle of dread settle in the pit of her stomach. Because whilst she had no idea who it belonged to, she'd seen that car before. She was sure of it.

THIRTY-SIX

Cat picked at the last little piece of her cold croissant and watched Orla quietly chomp away on hers in the passenger seat beside her. Their one saving grace had been that the car keys had been in her coat pocket still, but that really was *all* they had going for them right now. Everything else – their clothes, her phone, her wallet with her bank card – all of it had gone up with the B&B. Cat had thought she had nothing before, but this was another level of nothing entirely.

An ambulance and a police car had turned up shortly after the fire brigade, and after the paramedic had checked each of them out, one of the police officers had begun asking people if they needed help with sorting other arrangements, such as lifts to other locations or a shelter for the night.

Even in the midst of all the chaos, alarm bells had started clanging in Cat's head. Jeanie had threatened her with a call to social services. The last thing Cat needed, on top of all this, was for it to go on record that she couldn't even put a roof over her daughter's head. What if Jeanie really went through with it? They'd take Orla away from her for sure if they realised what dire straits Cat was really in. She'd hurriedly told the officer that they were fine, that they had a safe place to stay and a way of getting there. Then she'd rushed Orla to the car, ignoring the officer's worried protests. She would figure things out on her own, she'd decided determinedly. She wasn't sure exactly how yet. But she would.

After driving around the corner and tucking the car behind an overgrown bush, where it couldn't be spotted from the main road, Cat had finally let an exhausted Orla fall asleep in her arms, cradling her silently in the back seat as the night slowly made way for the day. She hadn't been able to sleep herself. Her mind had been too busy trying to understand how the fire had happened. Because the fire officers were stumped. They said they believed a curtain had caught fire in one of the rooms, as though a candle or lit cigarette had reached it, but the landlady had insisted that that room had been empty. All the other guests had insisted they were asleep, as it had been nearly three in the morning. One of them could have been lying, of course, in order to cover their tracks. But somehow Cat didn't think they were.

Her mind kept going back to the parked car down the street, but the police hadn't been interested in that. *Probably someone just off early to work*, they'd said. *Nothing to worry about*. It sounded logical enough, but something about it just didn't seem right. Surely someone off to work would have stopped to check that the people on the street outside a burning building were OK?

There hadn't been many guests in the B&B. Other than Cat and Orla's room, only three others had been occupied. In one, there had been a young couple who were zealously into clean living, who ate only organic foods and religiously took early nights and ice baths. An older man had been staying in another. He was a quiet soul. A dedicated churchgoer who spent most of his time at the soup kitchen and whose only vice was a good second-hand crime novel. The last guest was a woman in her forties who was loud and brash and liked a drink, no matter the time of day. But she'd been out with her friends, stumbling back well after they were all out of the burning building, and screeching in drunken shock as she'd seen what was left of her temporary home. The only other person in the B&B was the landlady, Mrs Marsh, and she lived in the basement flat. She'd have no reason to be upstairs in an empty room in the middle of the night, much less doing something that could put her home and business at risk. So how on earth had the fire started?

'Can I have a drink please?' Orla asked, clearing her throat and wiping the crumbs off her nightdress.

''Course, baby,' Cat replied, passing her the bottle of water they were sharing.

She'd found a packet of baby wipes in the glove compartment and had cleaned their hands and faces up as best she could, though they both still had a rim of soot around their hairline, and there was nothing she could do about the state of their clothes. Then she'd rummaged around various pockets of the car for change, managing to come up with a little over five pounds. It was a pathetically meagre amount, but it was enough to buy a pack of croissants and a couple of bottles of water at the local shop. That was something at least. But that wouldn't keep them going for long. She had a lot to sort out.

She'd deduced that she was now down to just two options, neither of which were particularly appealing. Without a bank card or her ID, it was going to be tough to get access to the money in her bank account. And she couldn't wait to get that sorted out. They needed shelter and food. They didn't even have clothes. She couldn't afford anything anymore, least of all pride. So she had to make a choice. Go begging to Greg for help, or go begging to her new employer. Even the thought of those scenarios made her cringe with embarrassment and shame, but she knew she had to put her feelings aside. Because if she didn't, her daughter would be sleeping in a car tonight, hungry and cold and dirty. And Cat would rather die than be the reason her daughter suffered like that.

'Come on – let's get you in your car seat. We're going to take a drive,' Cat said gently as she took the water bottle back from Orla.

'Am I going to school?' She looked down at herself. 'I can't go in my nightie.'

'Not today. We're going to go and see a friend of Mummy's, and then we're going to go shopping and get you a brand-new outfit. That sound like a good idea?' Cat asked.

'OK, Mummy.'

Orla clambered into the back, and Cat strapped her in, then she took off down the road. Sophia was the lesser of the two evils, in her current predicament, so she would start there. She just had to hope and pray that she wasn't overstepping so much that they'd turn her away.

* * *

Sophia sat down at the breakfast table and pulled her arm out of her sling, testing it. She winced at the shooting pain that still zapped through her wrist but noted that it was definitely better than it had been before. The cast they'd put around it was irritating her more than the actual injury at this point. Perhaps they would allow her to remove it soon. She carefully buttered her toast and glanced over the table at her eldest son. He smiled at her as he poured himself an orange juice, and she smiled back.

'Want a top-up?' he asked.

'No thank you,' she replied. She took a deep breath in before she continued. 'As much as I've loved having you here for breakfast these last few days, are you ever actually going to tell me what's going on?'

Alex pulled a look of confusion that she knew was fake. 'I don't know what you're talking about. Can a son not just want to enjoy breakfast with his favourite mother?'

'I'm your *only* mother,' she replied. 'And as your mother I know when you're *lying*. What happened? What has that wife of yours done now?'

Alex sighed and put down the toast he'd been about to put in his mouth. 'She's not done anything. It's me.'

'*You?*' Sophia asked, surprised. 'What could *you* have done?'

Sophia hadn't minded Bianca when Alex had started dating her, years before. She'd been happy for them when they got married, too, because Bianca made her son happy. But Bianca hadn't made him happy for a long time now, and what's more, she was now constantly causing trouble, embarrassing him in public, spending all his money, kicking off at everyone and anyone, and neglecting what Sophia saw as her wifely duties entirely. And it wasn't that Sophia expected her to act like some fifties housewife, doting on Alex every second of the day. But considering Bianca didn't work and wanted for nothing, she could have at least made a homecooked meal for him once in a while or been there a bit more for him. Because Alex was a good man and a good husband to her, and he deserved much better treatment.

'Well, I haven't *technically* done anything, but Bianca thinks I have,' Alex replied in a tired tone. 'She's got a bee in her bonnet about Cat. Think's I've been having it off with her.'

Sophia bristled. 'She's accused you of *cheating*? That cheeky mare! Who does she think she is? I can't believe she has the bloody nerve, I really can't! You're nothing like your—' She stopped short and closed her mouth, pursing her lips tightly. 'Well, you just ain't like that.'

Alex reached over and patted her hand, looking away. They both knew what she had been about to say. That Alex was nothing like his father. Sophia had loved her husband, and he'd loved her back, right until the end. But he'd still cheated on her numerous times in their marriage, and Alex had grown up watching the heartbreak and pain it caused her, every single time. He'd sworn many years before never to turn out like that. And he hadn't. So these accusations hit a very raw nerve for them both.

'She's just venting, Mum,' Alex told her. 'I'm sure she doesn't really believe it. She's just—'

'Oh, Alex, you've got to stop making excuses for her,' Sophia said, cutting him off. 'We've all been doing it for far too long.'

The doorbell sounded, and they both glanced towards the hallway. Alex made to stand, but Sophia put out her hand to halt him. 'No, don't get up. I'll go. I need to stretch anyway.'

She made her slow, awkward way through to the hallway and opened the door, expecting it to be the postman, still being so early. What she saw on the other side of the door, however, made her gasp and clutch her chest.

'Oh my God, what happened? What – wh— Sorry, come in. Come in.' Sophia stepped back, shaking herself.

'Mum?' Alex appeared, looking concerned, and his eyes flew as wide as his mother's had when he caught sight of their visitors. 'Jesus Christ, what happened to you?'

Sophia shut the door and took in the dreadful sight of the sorry pair. Cat and the little girl, who had to be Orla, were covered from head to toe in thick black dirt, save their faces and hands, which appeared to have been roughly wiped. Their coats were done up, but Sophia could see the hems of their night-dresses sticking out the bottom above bare legs. Orla was in Cat's arms, and the little girl didn't even have any shoes. Sophia saw the misery and shame on Cat's face, and she almost felt like crying for her.

'Love, what happened to you?'

'I am so sorry to come here like this, Sophia,' Cat started, barely able to look at her.

'What? *No!* I'm glad you did,' Sophia protested. 'But what's going on?'

'Here, may I?' Alex held his hands out to Orla, and to everyone's surprise she went to him without question.

'Thank you,' Cat mumbled, looking exhausted. 'The B&B burned down in the night. We got out, but we very nearly didn't. All I had time to grab was our coats. Luckily the car keys were in my pocket, but everything else...' She trailed off and turned her face away from them as a wave of grief washed over her features.

'Why don't we get you a drink, huh?' Alex asked Orla, his voice gentle.

'And why don't I make your mamma a strong coffee too,' Sophia added, reaching for Cat's arm. 'Come.'

'Thank you, but I really didn't mean to impose,' Cat protested as they walked through to the kitchen. 'I just wanted to ask a small favour. My wages for this week – if it's not too much trouble, could I get them a day early? And in cash?'

'Of course,' Sophia replied. 'But we'll get to that. Let's just get you sat down first.'

Alex placed Orla down on the kitchen side, keeping one arm across her as he reached for a glass. 'Now, what would you prefer? Milk, orange, beer or broccoli juice?'

Orla giggled, and Alex's face broke out into a warm smile.

'You're silly,' Orla said.

'Broccoli juice?' Alex asked. 'You sure?'

'No!' Orla giggled again. 'Milk please.'

'Ah, OK then,' Alex replied.

Cat was watching them, a small smile breaking through the stress on her face. 'You're a natural,' she said. 'Do you have kids?'

'No, not yet,' he replied. 'Maybe one day.'

'So, first things first,' Sophia said, pulling out everything she needed to make coffee. 'Where are you going to stay? And what do you need?'

'Oh, don't worry,' Cat replied, her cheeks immediately flooding red. 'I'll sort something out. I won't be able to work today, and I'm so sorry about that, but I'll get us sorted, and I'll be back to normal come Monday.'

Sophia frowned. 'But didn't you say before you had nowhere to go? A few days' wages won't cover much, and you need clothes and food and all sorts.'

Cat squirmed, looking thoroughly embarrassed. 'Honestly, I'll be fine. I really didn't come here to put all my drama on you.'

'Of course you didn't,' Sophia replied. 'You came here because you're trying to do it all on your own.' She tutted. 'Well, I hate to tell you this, Cat, but that ain't possible in this world. You can't do everything and be everyone all by yourself, all the time. Especially with that lovely little girl of yours. And you certainly can't go through all of *this* on your own.'

Sophia looked over at Orla, now quietly sipping her milk, comfortable in the safety of the crook of Alex's arm. She'd been lucky when she'd had her kids. She'd had a husband who, despite his faults, looked after them all well and made sure they wanted for nothing. She'd had her mother around to help – and her sister-in-law. Friends and neighbours. A whole community really. Cat had no one. And whether or not she'd admit it, she was drowning. Sophia couldn't even imagine how that must feel as a mother, trying to keep two heads above water, all alone. And now they'd just lost what little they had left. She looked back at Cat and made a sudden decision.

'No. No, you're not going anywhere,' she said firmly. 'You're going to stay here, with me. Both of ya.'

'What?' Cat asked, shocked. She began to shake her head. 'No. Oh, Sophia, I can't stay. I can't put you out like that—'

'You *can* and you *will*, Cat,' Sophia replied, her tone brooking no nonsense. 'I'm rattling around here on my own with four spare bedrooms. It would be a bloody sin to let you leave here when you ain't got anywhere to go.' She put her hand out to halt Cat's protests. 'No, I mean it and that's final. From this moment on, until you're back on your feet, you are my guests. And I'll sub you whatever you need to replace your clothes and bits. You just let me know, alright?'

Tears welled up in Cat's eyes, and she dropped her gaze to the floor, looking relieved and ashamed, all at the same time. 'Thank you,' she whispered. 'Thank you so much.'

'You're welcome. Why don't you take Orla upstairs for a bath and I'll find some things for you both to put on, just until we sort out some proper clothes, yeah?'

Cat nodded, wiping her tears away. 'Thanks, Sophia. I can't tell you how much this means.'

'Oh, I know, love,' Sophia said softly. 'I'm a mum too.'

'Cat, how did the fire start?' Alex asked.

'They don't know,' she replied. 'It started in what should have been an empty room. It's a bit of an odd one really.'

Alex nodded and something clouded his expression. 'Whereabouts in the room? Just out of interest.'

Cat walked over and picked Orla up. 'Er, it was near the window. They reckon the curtain somehow caught fire. Like as if someone had a candle or a cigarette. That's what's so weird about it. There shouldn't have been *anything*.'

'Yeah, strange,' he agreed, before turning to put the milk back in the fridge.

Cat shot Sophia one more grateful smile and then walked out of the room, towards the stairs. As soon as she was out of earshot, Sophia turned back to Alex.

'What is it?' she asked quietly.

He walked over to the island, where she was hovering, and

stared after Cat with a troubled frown. 'Hopefully nothing,' he murmured. 'But I've got to go. I'll be back later.'

'But...' Sophia trailed off as he walked out and then pursed her lips.

Some things she wanted to know and some things she didn't. And something told her that this was probably something she didn't.

THIRTY-SEVEN

The dark, stuffy hotel room reeked of stale cigarettes and sex. The curtains were closed, the sheets were in a tangled mess on the floor and the constant pounding boom of garage music assaulted their ears from the room next door, but Antonio didn't much care. He only cared about forgetting his troubles and enjoying some sweet instant gratification. A task that was becoming more and more difficult these days. It was almost as if the more he sought it, the harder it tried to hide from him.

He looked at the dark hollows under the eyes of his latest paid companion and reached over to his wallet on the bedside table. He pulled out a fresh bag of white powder and saw the interest sparkle in her eyes.

'What say we get back on the Colombian marching powder, eh?' he suggested. 'Go on, turn over. Get on your back.'

He tapped some of the powder out onto her naked pelvis, and then, covering one nostril, he leaned over and sniffed some of the small snow pile up his nose. He sat up and sniffed a few more times, savouring the tingle and the chemical taste as some of it hit the back of his throat, before reaching back for his wallet. He pulled out a card, and this time he neatened what was left into a small, thin line on the bedside table. The fifty-pound note was already rolled, from their earlier session, and he used it again now.

'OK, my turn,' the woman said.

He didn't even know her name. Not that he wanted to. He'd chosen her for two reasons and two reasons only. Her mid-length dark hair and her slight figure. He grabbed her wrist as she reached for the coke and pushed her back with a small smile.

'Oh no you don't. You've got to earn it first. So come on.' He lay back on the bed and thought about Cat, trying to imagine that it was her. 'Work for it.'

She let out a little giggle and then wriggled up the bed and straddled his legs. She took him in her hands, and he closed his eyes, his excitement starting to wake at her touch. As her rhythmic movements began to speed up, his breathing quickened too. He could picture her. Cat. Here with him. Touching him. Naked, in all her glory.

'Ahh, that's it. Good girl.' In a swift movement, he reached down and pulled her on top of him, plunging deep inside her and groaning with relief at the feel of her warmth. 'Yes,' he murmured as she bucked back and forth on top of him. He gripped her thighs and moved with her. 'Ah, Cat...'

'It's Stacy,' she breathed.

'What did you say?' Antonio barked, abruptly stopping.

His eyes snapped open and he glared at her, his lip curling back over his teeth. For a moment, she looked truly afraid, pulling back from his furious expression, then she seemed to gather herself.

'Sorry, love. Call me whatever you want.'

Antonio pushed her off him, and she fell off the bed with a thud. He leaped up and stood above her, glowering down.

'Yeah, that's right,' he growled. 'I'll call you whatever the fuck I want. And I'll *do* whatever the fuck I want *to* you.'

Fear flashed across her features again, and without missing a beat, Antonio pulled back his fist and slammed it into her face. She let out a yelp and covered her face, looking shocked. Antonio pulled in a breath, feeling momentarily exhilarated as he replaced her face with Cat's in his mind.

'That's right, bitch,' he muttered. He grabbed a fistful of her hair and yanked her forward until she was facing his erection. It was pulsating with his need to punish her. To degrade her. 'Go on then,' he ordered. 'Do what you're paid for.'

She whimpered but obeyed, just as he'd known she would. He tightened his grip on her hair, forcing himself further down her throat, over and over. She tapped his leg and then clawed at his hands, but he ignored her, and it was only when he felt her taps grow weak that he finally shoved her back away from him.

She gasped for breath, sobbing with fear, her eyes beseeching him. Blue eyes, he realised. Not brown like Cat's. He growled and grabbed her by the hair again, slamming her head into the wall. She faltered and fell, regaining consciousness just as she hit the floor.

'Wha— Please stop,' she begged.

But Antonio wasn't interested. '*Oh no*, Cat. You've got much more coming to you. *So* much more.'

Hours later, Antonio emerged from the motel room, closing the door quickly behind him. He looked around carefully as he shrugged his jacket on, then pulled out his phone and made a call. 'Danny. I need a small clean-up crew to a hotel room, on the down-low. Bring the doctor and some readies. We'll need to pay this one off. Couple of grand should do it. Mm...' He glanced back at the door. 'Make that five actually. And make sure she remembers who she's dealing with. That she needs to keep her mouth shut. Get here smartish, alright? I'll send you the address and leave the key at reception. Oh, and, Danny? Do *not* tell my brother about this.'

He ended the call and turned to hang the DO NOT DISTURB sign on the handle, then walked swiftly away towards his car. As he opened the driver's door, he felt a deep stab of annoyance at himself for what he'd just done. This wasn't him. He didn't want to do this to women. He *loved* women. He had a long-standing reputation as a skilled and generous lover, not as someone who hurt people like that. It was why sex workers and club girls all loved him. Because he always gave them a good time. But Cat had just made him so unbelievably mad that he'd lost all control tonight. He'd been consumed by the dark, angry frustration that had been building up ever since she'd said no, and it had burst out of him tonight.

It couldn't happen again. Not like that. His expression hardened as he revved the engine and slipped the car into reverse. He needed to stop this before he got any more out of control. And there was only one way that was going to happen. He was going to get Cat alone, and when he did – when he had her to himself somewhere that no one else could find her – he would finally release all the pent-up darkness inside of him and give her what she deserved, once and for all.

THIRTY-EIGHT

Maria crossed the road with her coffee and glanced at the smoky black glass wall of the building beside her. He was there again, the man she'd caught following her the other day. He was in his fifties with slicked-back, dyed-black hair and a black leather bomber jacket. He was quite hard to miss in the sea of suits that swarmed the area each lunchtime. She crossed the road again, and, sure enough, he crossed again too.

Taking a deep breath, Maria reached into her pocket and pulled out her phone. She switched on the camera and started filming, then sped up and began weaving in and out of the crowd ahead. She was a little restricted in her tailored skirt suit and heels, but she managed to keep up a good pace, and when she checked another reflection, he'd fallen a little further behind. As the road curved around, she quickly ducked into a small haberdashery and doubled around to the window.

She pulled back behind a stack of fabric rolls and pointed the camera at the window, then waited. Just a few seconds passed, then he was there, in plain view. He stopped right outside, looking this way and that, as he realised he'd lost her, and Maria finally got a good look at the man. There were no distinguishing tattoos or scars, and now that she was closer, she realised he was older than she'd initially thought. He appeared to be around mid-sixties, and the hair she'd assumed was dyed black now looked more like a wig. She frowned. Why would he be wearing a wig? Why go to so much trouble? The man moved on, apparently determined to catch up with her, and Maria ended the recording.

'Hello,' a chirpy voice said from behind her. 'Can I help you with anything?'

Maria turned to see a short, stout woman in her forties with bright blue hair smiling at her.

'Oh, no, thank you,' she said quickly. She touched one of the fabric rolls and pretended to size it up. 'I thought I saw something I need through the window but, um, it's not quite right. Thanks anyway.'

She moved towards the door with a tight smile.

'Are you sure? What is it you're looking for? Maybe I can help,' the woman called after her.

'No, no. I'm fine,' Maria replied as she opened the door. 'Thanks anyway!'

She paused outside in the doorway, taking a few seconds to check that the man following her really had moved on, then she turned and began making her way back towards her office. As she walked, she took out her phone again and forwarded the recording to Alex and Danny, along with a text.

Find out who this is. He's been tailing me all week.

She took one more cursory glance over her shoulder and then carried on, confident that she was now walking alone. So confident that she didn't bother turning back again. So confident that she entirely missed the second man leaning casually against a wall on the other side of the road, who quietly pushed off and fell into step a little way behind her.

THIRTY-NINE

Alex glanced sideways at Antonio, his critical gaze taking in the creased suit jacket and his sallow complexion. He watched as his brother sniffed, yet again, and looked around with eyes that were slightly wider than usual. More alert. More anxious.

'Are you alright?' he asked, stopping outside the tall white building. 'Seriously? You don't look well.'

'Oh, lovely. Thanks,' Antonio replied sarcastically. 'Well, you don't look like fucking Brad Pitt either actually.'

Alex tutted. 'I mean it. You don't look right. You been sleeping OK?'

'What is this?' Antonio asked defensively. 'I'm fine.'

'Yeah, fine and on the gear, right?' Alex replied, calling him out. It was obvious to anyone with any experience of the drug that he was coked up again today.

'Sorry, Mum,' Antonio declared. 'Didn't realise you were here.' He gave Alex a disapproving glare.

Alex held his hands up, knowing there was no point pushing him. 'Fine. But you look me in the eye now and tell me you're up to this today. Because I need you on form, and there ain't *no* room for you to go off on any tangents.' He eyed his brother – hard.

Antonio stopped and turned to face him, meeting his gaze. 'I promise you, I'm *fine*. Alright? I'm fine. I'm on form. I'm here to stick to the plan. Scout's honour.'

'You got thrown out of scouts,' Alex reminded him.

'Yeah, 'cause they were all fucking idiots,' Antonio replied.

Alex sighed. 'Just stick to the plan. I mean it. Not one fucking word outside of it.'

The pair of them walked into the Paddington hotel and across to the same lounge they'd been in before. It wasn't long until the sound of sharp footsteps clipped across the hall and Justin Sinclair made his entrance.

'Ah,' he said as he reached them. 'You're here. Have you got news for me?'

'Of sorts. But there's something we need to show you,' Antonio told him.

'Oh. Well, no thank you. I don't want to *see it*.' Justin paled at the very thought, pulling an expression of disgust. 'That's not my bag, I'm afraid. That's why I hired *you*.'

'It's not what you think,' Alex informed him. 'It's not done yet. There's a little hiccup with your dad's estate. See, we do our research before pulling a job. Make sure everything's gonna land the way it's supposed to. Not sure this one's going to land quite the way you think it will.'

Justin's expression turned to one of concern as his father's estate was mentioned. 'What do you mean? *No*. Just show me. You're right – it'll be easier. I'll get my coat.'

Nearly an hour later, after getting stuck in traffic with Justin harping on in the back about all the far-fetched plans he intended to carry out after his dad's death, they finally pulled into the driveway of Frank's house.

'And you're *sure* he's not here?' Justin checked. 'It's just, that's his car.'

'Got picked up by a mate,' Antonio told him curtly, clearly as sick of the man as Alex was.

'OK. If you're *absolutely positive*,' Justin replied.

'Yep,' Alex replied. 'Let's go.'

They walked to the front door and opened it, ushering Justin inside and through to the large, light-filled family lounge. There, sat on one of the cream sofas, was Frank, waiting for them, as planned.

Justin choked when he saw his father, his pale blue eyes widening in alarm. 'Er... oh-oh no. *No*, I— Dad, I meant to, er, I'm...' He floundered, looking around to Alex and Antonio in panic.

'Sit down, son,' Frank said in a weary voice. 'I think we need to have a little chat, don't you?'

'Er, a chat. Right. It's just that...' Justin tried to back out of the room, but Alex put a firm hand on his shoulder.

'Sit down,' he said in a hard tone that brooked no nonsense.

Justin swallowed hard and then did as he was told, his eyes flicking around nervously between his father and the two men who'd brought him here.

Alex sat down next to Justin and Antonio settled on the sofa between the one they occupied and the one Frank was comfortably situated in.

Frank had a tray of tea in front of him on the coffee table, and he gestured towards it as he picked up his own cup. 'Would anyone like one?'

Alex declined with a shake of the head.

Antonio followed suit. 'No thanks.'

Justin looked at the tray hopefully then sat back when he saw the look on his father's face.

'So.' Frank took a sip of his tea, his eyes never leaving Justin. 'I hear you hired these gentlemen to kill me.'

Justin's face flushed red and for a few moments he didn't respond, then when he did it was with an angry outburst. 'Well, what did you expect? You cut me off! You cancelled all my credit accounts, removed me from the company bank accounts – you were going to remove my bloody inheritance!'

'Yes, that's quite correct,' Frank replied, seemingly unaffected by the outburst. 'Because you were defrauding the company – *my* company – running up bills you couldn't afford to pay, even on the overly generous salary I was paying you, and you'd proven yourself unworthy of taking over. And what did I expect, you ask?' Frank sighed. 'What I *expected* was for you to wake up and realise that none of this was acceptable. What I *expected* was for you to change your ways and make an effort to prove yourself worthy again. Or at least that's what I *hoped*. But I can see now, from your despicable actions and from the news of your latest and *greatest* debt to date, that this was no more than a fantasy. I can't believe you were prepared to *kill* me. To kill your own *father*.' Frank shook his head in saddened amazement. 'Do I really mean that little to you, Justin?'

Justin huffed, offering him a bitter glare of resentment. 'You don't know even half of what you think you do. You don't know how badly I needed that money. How *my* life was in danger. It was either you or me. As a father, surely you'd *want* me to put myself first? Surely you'd *want* to protect me?'

'Wow,' Frank muttered. He looked ill suddenly, his face paling tiredly to a washed-out grey as all of his son's true colours were finally revealed. 'I love you, Justin. With all my heart. Which is why it breaks my heart so deeply to see you turn out like this.' He cast his gaze down to his cup. 'Your mother would be so ashamed of you.'

'Don't talk to me about my mother,' Justin spat.

He turned to Alex, accusation in his eyes. 'What *is* this?' he demanded. 'What, you wanted to make me face him before you go ahead? Well, *fine*! I've faced him. OK? Now go ahead and fucking *kill the bastard*. Go on. *Now*! I'm certainly bloody paying you enough for it.'

'Actually, there's been a change of plan,' Alex replied. 'You see, you left out a rather important detail when we made our deal with you. The hundred grand you owe The Raven.'

Justin's eyes widened, and panic flashed through them. 'OK, alright, *look*.' He held his hands out placatingly. 'I'm sorry about that. I didn't want to put you off the job, and, honestly, it makes no difference to the outcome. The Raven is the first person I'll pay off with my inheritance. It will have no bearing on you or your percentages whatsoever.'

'See, that's where you're wrong,' Antonio chimed in. 'Because your little fucking shark mates picked me up in a van off the street and gave me a good going over, not realising who they were dealing with.'

'They realise now of course,' Alex confirmed. 'And they were very sorry indeed. But sorry doesn't fix much, does it?'

'Oh, come on, surely things like that are par for the course in your line of work?' Justin responded arrogantly.

'Wrong answer,' Antonio said flatly.

'The *new* plan is a little different,' Alex explained. 'In the new plan we arranged with your dad, everybody lives happily ever after. Your dad goes on living his life, we take care of the hundred grand and in return we get twenty per cent of the hotels, along with a number of rooms we can call our own, no questions asked. It's less than we originally had planned with you, but we don't have to kill anyone, so...' Alex pulled a shrug-like expression.

'What? That's *absurd*! Twenty per cent is worth so much more than a hundred grand,' Justin spluttered.

'Oh, yeah, that's also payment for setting *you* up,' Antonio added. 'And, you see, *that* costs a lot.'

'What do you mean, *set me up*?' Justin demanded, real fear in his face now.

'We mean set you up elsewhere in the world, where you will be taken, never to return here again,' Alex explained.

'You'll have a new ID, new papers, new citizenship in Brazil and twenty grand to start you off,' Antonio told him. 'I personally think he should leave you with a tenner, but your old man seems to really care about you. *God* knows why,' he added.

'You can't be serious?' Justin looked around at the three men, his gaze coming to rest on his father.

'Deadly,' Frank said tiredly. 'You were given every chance here, and you never could make it work. You need a fresh start, and I need it to be somewhere you won't be tempted to kill me for my hotels again.' He pulled one corner of his mouth upwards in a humourless smirk. 'This is the last thing I will ever give you. And maybe one day, if you manage to make something of yourself, you'll see it for what it really is. A gift.'

'A *gift*,' Justin repeated with a bitter laugh. 'You keep telling yourself that, old man. And I'll tell *you* something.' He stood up. 'I'll make it. Wherever I do or don't go, *I will make it*. But when I do, I certainly won't be coming back to tell you or *thank you*. The only reason I will ever return here is to *spit* on your grave.'

Alex saw the older man wince at his son's hateful words and he had to look away. Some people deserved all they had coming to them, and Justin was one of them.

'Good luck, Justin,' Frank said. 'I hope one day you prove both of us wrong.'

Alex stood up and gestured for Justin to do the same. 'Come on. We need to get going.'

'What, *now?*' Justin asked, aghast. 'I can't. I have plans tonight.'

Antonio laughed. 'Did you think this was a pick-and-choose sort of situation? If so, you were sadly mistaken. We're going right now.'

'But I haven't *packed*. I have none of my things. This is *ridiculous!*' Justin exclaimed.

'You aren't taking anything of your old life,' Alex revealed, pushing him on towards the door as Frank gave him a nod. 'That's the point. You aren't Justin Sinclair anymore, so you won't be taking his things.'

'Come on – be reasonable,' Justin argued. 'Dad? *Dad!* Come on – let's talk about this. I thought you were *joking*. Dad, *please? Dad!*'

'Goodbye, son,' Frank called as they walked out through the front door.

Alex shoved Justin in the back of the car, still arguing and complaining, and tuned him out as they drove away from Frank's house in the countryside.

'Guys, please, *come on*. I'll *double* what he's paying you. Hell, I'll double what *I* was going to pay you,' Justin begged.

But they simply ignored his endless torrent of pleas for the following few minutes until they reached a small grove of trees and a secluded parking area tucked down the side of the road. Here they stopped next to a colourful flower shop van and got out of the car, dragging Justin with them.

'What's going on? Why have we stopped? Why are we out of the car?' Justin's questions continued until they reached the back of the van and the doors opened.

Two large men sat on a bench on one side of the van, and Maria smiled out at them from her seat at the back. Antonio disappeared around the side, walking away to the front of the vehicle.

'Justin, Maria,' Alex said, gesturing to each of them. 'Maria, Justin. Right. Now you're acquainted, let's get this moving, shall we?'

'Get what moving? Is this how I'm getting to Brazil?' Justin frowned at the van. 'I'm not sure you've thought this through.'

'Brazil?' Maria queried, raising one eyebrow at Alex.

'Brazil was the bedtime story,' Alex explained, shoving Justin forward into the van.

'Ouch!' Justin hit his leg on the bench and fell to his knees. The two men reached down and lifted Justin up, plonking him down on the bench between them. 'Hey! Be *careful*, will you?'

'Don't worry,' Maria remarked. 'None of it will matter soon enough.'

'What do you mean?' Justin asked.

'What she means, Justin, is that you ain't going to Brazil after all,' Alex explained.

Antonio returned, carrying a heavy bucket full of something grey and sludgy-looking. He carefully placed it in the back of the van and slid it across in front of Justin.

What was really happening seemed to dawn on Justin, just as the men either side of him seized his legs. He tried to jump up, but it was too late.

'No. *No*! Get off of me! Get off my legs! *No!*'

They forced him down into the bucket of cement, his weedy legs no match for their muscular arms, and he began to wail.

'I'm afraid you're what we call a liability, Justin,' Alex told him. 'And we can't have those running around. Let's face it, the minute you're set loose, you'll only run straight to the police. Spin it so you look like the victim. We can't have that. Plus, the second you get back, you'd just hire someone else to off your dad, and we can't have that either. He's under our protection now, being a business partner and all.'

Antonio took off the gloves he'd worn to mix the cement. 'Your dad will be told you got off safe and sound, just like we planned, so he won't be none the wiser. And you told him yourself that you'd never talk to him again, so that won't be much of a surprise either.'

Justin let out a strangled sound that sounded like words but that they couldn't quite make out through his tears of self-pity.

Maria jumped out of the van and stood beside Alex and

Antonio, dusting off her hands and nodding to the men. 'Knock him out before you drop him in. No need for him to suffer.'

Justin's cries grew louder, and she swiftly shut the doors, muffling the sound to almost complete silence.

Alex turned to Antonio. 'You sure you're good to drive?'

'Yeah, fine,' he replied. 'I'll check in after drop-off and then see you tomorrow.'

'And you'll stick to that back route?' Maria checked.

'Yeah, all good. Those new boots of his should be solid enough by the time we reach the boat. I'll have him at the bottom of the shipping lane in a couple of hours and it'll all be over,' Antonio confirmed.

Alex and Maria exchanged a strained look, but Alex simply nodded. They had to start trusting Antonio again. He was their brother. He'd been pulling jobs alongside them for years. So why did they suddenly feel so tense about him doing these things now?

Forcing himself to move, Alex clapped him on the back and caught Maria's eye, tilting his head towards the car.

'See you at home,' she said to Antonio, following Alex back to the car.

They waited there until Antonio was behind the wheel of the van and had pulled out onto the road, travelling in the opposite direction, then they set off themselves.

'You think he's OK?' Maria asked, looking troubled.

Alex glanced in the rear-view mirror at the fading light in the distance. 'I don't know,' he answered honestly. 'Something wasn't right tonight. Something's been off in general lately. I just wish I could figure out what.'

'I've been thinking the same,' Maria admitted.

Alex exhaled heavily and focused on the road ahead. 'Well, right now we just need to make sure he pulls tonight off and gets home in one piece. The rest we'll figure out later.'

Though how exactly they were going to do that, Alex really wasn't sure.

FORTY

The dull, thudding beat of the music reverberated through the thin walls of the club bathroom, and Bianca rested her head back against the wall of the stall as the young man she'd dragged in there dropped to his knees. She lifted her leg and grabbed his hair, guiding him to where she wanted his tongue.

'That's it,' she said throatily. 'There. No...' She frowned, frustrated. 'No, *there*. Up a bit. It's, *ugh*, never mind. Just get up here.' She pulled him up and kissed him, her frustration growing as she frantically undid his belt.

The young man was eager, just like all the others had been, and this gave Bianca a little thrill of excitement. She liked them young. They didn't tend to ask questions when a woman like her lured them into cubicles or down alleyways. No, they simply gave her what she needed. What she desperately craved. Sex, attention and blind admiration. Just for a short while.

She pulled him free from his underwear and lifted herself on, gasping with pleasure as he dove into her with fervour. He was big and it felt good. For the briefest of moments, she thought about Alex. About how incredible sex had been between them, in the early days. But she quickly shoved that thought aside and focused on the man currently inside her instead. Because Alex didn't deserve her head space right now. He hadn't touched her in *months*. These days he seemed more interested in his work, and in avoiding her, than having sex with her.

It was probably because he was shagging Cat, of course. Bianca was sure of it. It all seemed so obvious, now. This whole story of Cat coming out of nowhere and suddenly being part of the household, hadn't added up. But after all that Antonio had whispered in her ear, Bianca had started putting two and two together. Clearly Cat was Alex's side piece and giving her this job in his mother's home was his way of keeping her close.

Alex swore blind that this wasn't the case and Cat had yet to find proof but, when she did, she would make that bitch's life hell. Because Alex was *hers*. And this, what she was doing now, wasn't the same thing. Bianca cheating on Alex wasn't even slightly the same as Alex cheating on her. Because Bianca was only doing this to scratch an itch. To have her basic needs met, while her husband didn't bother meeting them himself. Other than physically, she was entirely loyal to her husband. She would never *leave* him. She would never value another man above him. But Alex *could* leave *her*. And the closer he got to Cat, the more danger Bianca was in of losing everything.

Her cubicle partner was speeding up now, ramming her back against the cubicle wall, again and again, and Bianca closed her eyes, giving in to the pleasure. She moaned and gripped his shoulders, grinding rhythmically against him as they both geared up to climax. And then suddenly, as she let out a cry of triumph, he did too, and it was over.

He stepped back with a grin and blew upwards to move a lock of floppy hair that had fallen over his eye. 'Wow, that was intense.'

'Mm,' Bianca agreed, grabbing a wad of tissues and quickly cleaning herself up. 'It was.'

She tossed the tissues in the toilet and pulled down her tight bodycon minidress. She hadn't bothered wearing any underwear, this being the main goal of her evening. Carla, the only friend she trusted to keep her dirty secrets – mainly because she kept hers in return – was waiting outside with her drink, keeping an eye out for any faces they might recognise, and now she'd been satisfied, Bianca was ready to get back to her. She tucked her boobs away, almost laughing at the disappointed look on the guy's face, and opened the door.

'Whoa, hey!' he protested, quickly doing up his jeans and following her out.

A couple of young women stood by the sinks reapplying their make-up and staring at them both knowingly in the mirror. Bianca ignored them, unfazed, but her companion flushed bright red.

'Er, sorry, ladies, just ignore me. Wait!' The last comment was directed at Bianca, and she paused, turning around with an eyebrow raised in question. 'Er, so, can I buy you a drink, or get your number...?'

'No,' she replied simply. 'Goodbye.' With that, she turned and left the club toilets, quickly losing herself in the busy room as she made her way back over to Carla.

Carla was waiting where she'd left her, looking bored, with two drinks in her hands. 'Ugh, *there* you are,' she commented as Bianca sidled up. 'Here's your drink. Get what you wanted?'

Bianca took the glass and had a quick sip before responding. 'I certainly did,' she purred.

The two of them exchanged a giggle.

'What our husbands don't know won't kill them, right?' Carla said sunnily.

'I completely agree,' Bianca replied.

Carla was right. What Alex didn't know wouldn't hurt him. But she'd make damn sure that she knew all of Alex's dirty little secrets. Because what Bianca didn't know *could* hurt her. She wasn't stupid. She knew she had nothing without Alex's power and status. And no one, especially not a woman like Cat, was going to get away with taking it from her.

FORTY-ONE

Sunday came around all too quickly and Alex was exhausted, having stayed up most of the night to make sure Antonio and their men got home safely and quietly. But there was no rest for the wicked. Especially on a Sunday. Sophia had decided to throw a big family dinner, and for once, rather than looking forward to it, Alex just felt stressed. Aside from all he had going on with work and Antonio, Bianca was still acting frostily towards him, behaving like everything was fine on the surface with that fake smile he *knew* hid some ulterior motive. Usually she hated these family dinners, but ever since she'd found out that Cat would be there, she'd been waxing lyrical about the whole thing, which just made him feel even more anxious.

He'd gone home Friday and demanded to know if she'd had anything to do with the fire at Cat's place, and she had seemed genuinely shocked. She also had an airtight alibi, having been out with friends all night, downing shots and causing carnage. He'd felt relieved when he found that out and then guilty for wondering in the first place. Bianca was a lot of things, but she wouldn't go as far as burning a building down while Cat and her daughter slept inside. He was sure of that.

They were all now sat around the long Italian-marble-topped dining table – Alex, Bianca, Sophia, Antonio, Maria, Cat and Orla. The table was laden with food, a roasted leg of lamb taking centre stage, and Sophia's special plates out for the occasion.

It was awkward as hell for an event that should have been relaxed. Cat was trying to make herself as small and as helpful as possible, clearly feeling out of place at the family gathering. Bianca was drinking like a fish and throwing eye daggers Cat's way at every possible opportunity. Antonio was in a foul mood, also glancing over at Cat whenever he thought no one was looking and giving Alex a distinct chill whenever he did. Maria, having picked up on all of this too, was sitting back and watching everyone, more reserved than usual because of it. And Sophia was trying to make up for the strange atmosphere by acting completely over the top.

'Right, everyone, help yourselves!' she shrilled, a wide smile on her face. 'Alex, can you carve up the lamb?'

Alex stood up and took the carving knife and fork she held out, and as he leaned over the table, Bianca placed a proprietorial hand on his back. It was the kind of gesture that would have been sweet if it was genuine. But he knew without looking round that Bianca was icing Cat across the table, and that it was purely a move to publicly stake her claim. She was still hung up on the idea that they were having an affair for some reason, though Alex genuinely couldn't work out why. Cat was luckily too busy looking after Orla to notice, but he saw his mother's eyes tighten slightly as she cast her gaze towards his wife.

'You know, Cat cooked most of this lovely meal today,' Sophia said brightly. 'Didn't you, love?'

'Oh, not at all; it was a team effort,' Cat replied, brushing it off.

'Don't be modest,' Sophia insisted. 'She's a *fantastic* cook, as it turns out. That beautifully cooked lamb you're carving was all her. Your favourite that, isn't it, Alex?'

Alex felt Bianca's grip tighten on his back and shot his mother a warning look that told her he knew exactly what she was doing, then he turned to Cat with a polite smile.

'It looks very nice, Cat.' He'd pay for that comment later, no doubt.

Why on earth was his mother fuelling the fire? He knew she enjoyed needling Bianca, but this was the last thing he needed right now. He continued carving, wishing he'd never told her that Bianca was convinced she'd been dangling Cat in front of him.

'I think I need a top-up,' Sophia mused, looking at her nearly empty wine glass.

'I'll grab a fresh bottle,' Cat offered, jumping up. 'You stay there.'

'Thank you, love,' Sophia gushed.

'Who else needs a top-up?' Sophia asked as Cat returned with the bottle. 'Maria? Antonio?'

'*I* would,' Bianca said pointedly.

'Oh, that goes without saying, dear,' Sophia replied smoothly. 'We all know to assume *you'll* want a top-up.'

Maria pulled both lips in between her teeth to bite down a smile, and Cat's eyes widened at the slight, but Bianca simply pursed her lips. Alex sighed and sat down, having done enough carving to last them a while.

'Meat, anyone?' he asked.

Maria put her hand up, and he passed the plate of cuts down towards her, sending a prayer up to the heavens as he did so that they all made it out of this meal alive.

* * *

After a very long and stressful meal, dotted with the occasional double-edged comment that referred to things she clearly wasn't privy to, Cat settled Orla down in their new bedroom upstairs for a nap and made a start on the washing-up. The family had retired to the lounge and were most likely talking about business now that she'd disappeared. She'd noticed that was often the case and therefore made a point of not hanging around unnecessarily. She was just soaking the bigger pans when she heard a noise behind her. She swivelled round, anxious that it might be Antonio. She'd been uncomfortably aware of him sitting just across from her for the entire meal, though admittedly he'd not made a move or comment out of turn all day.

'Sorry, didn't mean to startle you.' It was Alex.

Cat relaxed and smiled, glad to see it was him. 'You didn't.' She reached for a towel and quickly dried her hands, glancing over his shoulder to check that they were alone. If they were, this was her chance to bring up the bright idea she'd had, the night before the fire. 'I was hoping to talk to you actually.'

'Yeah?' he asked, sliding onto one of the island bar stools. 'What about?'

Nerves fluttered in Cat's stomach. 'Well, I have sort of a business proposal to put to you.'

'A business proposal?' The corner of his mouth hitched in amusement. 'OK. Sure. Shoot.'

Cat cleared her throat. 'You said you solve problems, right?' He nodded, the smile fading. 'I have a problem that I need a solution for. And I don't think I can do it legally. Or, well, I *could*, but it would take time and money, both of which I don't have, and even then, it's not guaranteed that I'd win.'

'Alright, what kind of problem are we talking about?' Alex asked, his expression serious now.

'Well, first off, let me lay out what I can offer you in return,' she replied.

She stepped forward until she was at the kitchen island

directly opposite him. 'My father has a – *had* – a successful medical technology company out near Brentwood. He's come up with all sorts of things over the years, but most recently he invented an incredible piece of tech that takes the images from an MRI and shows it in holographic 3D. It's still in the early stages, but it's already taking the world by storm.' Cat smiled, feeling the incredible sense of pride that she always did when she thought of her dad's life's work. 'He built his company from scratch, and when I left school, I went to work for him, looking after his accounts.'

Alex scratched his chin, looking confused. 'OK. Go on.'

'I never got any formal qualifications, but I worked his accounts for over a decade and I got pretty good at it. I learned some interesting tricks too, like how to hide money and how to move it to make it work better for us. I mean, not that my dad wasn't above board – he *was* – but with so much coming in and out of so many departments, things easily got lost. Sometimes it was easier to square it away myself. And I got really good at it. Never got caught out.' She bit her lip. 'I know you kept what you do vague when you explained it to me. And I understand why. If you can help me with my problem, and if the idea is amenable to you, then I'd like to offer you my accounting services in return as payment. No questions asked, no stories told.'

Alex frowned at her for a few seconds before answering. 'You're an *accountant* and you're here washing dishes?'

'Like I said, I never got any formal qualifications. And, for reasons that I'll explain later, I have no references now either.'

'I don't need an accountant right now,' Alex replied, after a long pause.

Cat's hopes dropped like a stone to the bottom of her stomach, and she nodded, trying to hide the misery from her face. It had been all she had to offer him. The only thing of value she'd had to give, and he'd rejected it. She was right back to square one with no way forward and no more ideas left in the pot.

'Sure. Yeah. No worries. It was just—'

'I wasn't finished,' Alex interrupted. 'I don't need one *right now*, but I am going to need one soon. I have a special business venture I'm starting up in the near future, and when I do, I'll need to figure out a clever way to move the money. I want to keep the circle small, so...' He flicked his gaze around her face as if searching for something. 'I'll help you. Whatever it is, I'll find you a solution. But you have to understand, once I do this, there's no going back. There will be no undoing anything, no matter what happens next. So make sure you really *do* want my help before you give me the green light.'

Cat nodded, her heart soaring. He *was* going to help her! He was going to get back what was hers and Orla's! As the thought registered, she suddenly felt like a weight rose up and off her chest, like she could finally pull in a full breath again, and she couldn't help the smile that widened across her face.

'Yes,' she breathed. 'Yes, of course. I understand. Thank you. Thank you *so much*.'

'Oh yeah? What's *my* wonderful husband done to deserve such enthusiastic thanks then, eh?' The sour voice broke through the moment, shattering Cat's elation like a brick through a stained-glass window.

Cat lowered her eyes respectfully and took a step back, remembering that however generous and friendly Sophia had been, she was still just the housekeeper here. Bianca, on the other hand, was married to Sophia's son. And although it sounded like Sophia would like the idea of bathing in a tub of rotten eggs more than she liked her daughter-in-law, Bianca was still family. And family ranked higher than the help anywhere.

'Oh, just some help with a problem I had,' Cat said demurely. 'I'd better get back to the pans.'

'Yeah, you do that,' Bianca said with a cold sneer.

'Hey,' Alex said, standing up. 'Come on. Let's go home.'

'No, actually, I think I'll stay and have a chat with *Cat* here,' she shot back, crossing the kitchen towards the other woman. She stopped right next to Cat, giving her no choice but to turn and face her. Bianca's face was like thunder, and Cat blinked in surprise. 'This what you get off on, is it?' she snarled.

'What?' Cat asked, confused.

'Bianca, stop it,' Alex ordered, walking over and grabbing her arm.

She shrugged him off angrily. 'No! Come on, Cat. This what you like, is it? Stealing another woman's man? Batting your eyelids and opening your fucking legs for someone who ain't yours – playing fucking families at his mum's? Eh?' She put both hands on Cat's chest and shoved her – hard.

'That's *enough!*' Alex shouted, yanking her back now. 'What the *fuck* is wrong with you?'

But before he could say anything else, Cat had shoved past him and thrust her face right up against Bianca's.

'I haven't *touched* your husband,' she growled furiously. 'I would *never* do that. I got cheated on right, left and centre by my own, so the *last* thing I'd want in my life is a man who's happy to do the same to someone else. Even if that someone else is as rude as you bloody are!'

'Whatever,' Bianca snarled, pushing her forehead up against Cat's, not ready to back down. 'I—'

'*You* are *done!*' Alex said, cutting her off. He swung her around and propelled her towards the door. 'Cat, I'm so sorry. I don't know what's got into her head, I really don't.'

'Don't worry about it,' Cat replied, stepping back, though inside she was still seething.

She took a couple of deep breaths to calm herself as she heard the pair argue down the hallway and out through the front door. She had no idea why Bianca thought they were together. They were certainly getting to know each other a little, now that she'd started working here, yes, but neither of them thought of the other like that. Neither of them had ever acted inappropriately. They were both on the same page, each respectful and friendly towards each other, the same way any two people in this situation would be. With one last deep breath, she shook it off, reminding herself that it didn't matter whether Bianca liked her or what she thought. Alex had agreed to help her, and now there was finally light at the end of the tunnel. Nothing could dampen the hope that this had given her today.

The new phone she'd had no choice but to buy with the money Sophia had subbed her buzzed in her pocket, and Cat quickly dried off a hand to grab it. It was Greg.

'Finally,' she muttered, picking up. 'Greg. I need you to pick up Orla from pre-school on Tuesday.' She heard him make a sound of reluctance on the other end of the phone, and her anger immediately rose. 'No, I don't even want to hear it. You and your bitch girlfriend have screwed me over on every front possible and you damn well owe me. And – not that you'll even care, Greg – but the place we *were* staying has burned down, with everything we had in it. So I don't care *what* you're doing on Tuesday, who you're screwing, what work you're pretending to do, what golf course you want to play, you *will* pick Orla up from pre-school so that I can go and see the one-bedroomed flat I've managed to get a viewing for. *OK?*'

She realised her voice had risen to almost a shout and she quickly shut her mouth, taking a deep breath in and closing her eyes as she waited for him to respond.

'Right, there's really no need for the dramatics, Cat. I'll move my afternoon around for you, as you've asked. Just this once though. I really do need more notice in future.'

Cat's free hand curled into a claw, and she raised it, imagining she was squeezing his neck. She gritted her teeth and tried to keep her voice level. 'You'll need the pass phrase to pick her up, as they don't know you. It's "hazelnut soup". Got that?' She refused to thank him, even though she knew that would be what he was expecting.

'Hazelnut soup. Right. Tuesday, yes?' Greg replied in a clipped tone.

'Yes. Do *not* forget.'

Cat ended the call, unable to listen to his careless drawl for even a second longer. He hadn't cared one jot when she'd told him about the fire. He'd not even asked if they were OK, if *Orla* was OK. What kind of man cared that little for his own daughter?

A sound by the door made her turn around expectantly, but no one was there.

'Hello?'

Footsteps hurried away down the hall and disappeared, and Cat frowned. Who had been listening in to her call? And why had they run off like that? She suppressed a shiver. She liked Sophia and her job, but she wouldn't be sorry when she could get out of this house and into somewhere of her own. There were far too many weird undertones here that she just didn't understand.

FORTY-TWO

Cat couldn't shake the feeling, all throughout Monday afternoon, that something was wrong. She couldn't put her finger on *what* exactly; she just felt a strange sense of unease. It was most likely the weather, she kept telling herself. The sky outside was black with angry, swollen clouds, and the rain had been pelting down mercilessly all day. As she stood by Sophia's kitchen sink, drying off the last couple of mugs, a great spear of light suddenly cracked through the dark sky, followed, a second later, by a deep booming rumble of thunder.

'Great,' she muttered.

Cat placed the last mug in the cupboard and then hung the tea towel on the rail before untying her pinny. She needed to get going. In this weather, the traffic would be worse than usual en route to Orla's pre-school.

Sophia hobbled into the kitchen as Cat turned to leave. 'Have you got an umbrella?' she asked. 'If not, take one from the cupboard, OK?'

'Thanks, Sophia. I have one in the car,' Cat replied with a warm smile.

She slipped out into the hall, put her jacket on and then legged it through the rain to her car, still thinking about Sophia. If someone had told her a few weeks ago that the hard, frosty woman she'd met would turn out to be her saviour, she would have laughed. But there was so much that she had to thank Sophia for now, and she didn't know where to start.

Sophia had tried to give them two rooms, after they'd arrived there filthy and broken, on Friday, but Cat had insisted they only needed one. Orla was still sleeping in the same bed as her while so much upheaval was going on. So instead, Sophia gave them the biggest guest room with a large en suite. It was twice the size of the one they'd been renting at the B&B.

But Sophia hadn't stopped there. The morning they'd arrived, she'd made a couple of phone calls in Italian, and a few hours later some of her friends had arrived with new clothes for them both. Sophia had paid for them all, refusing to let Cat contribute even a penny. The following day she'd even surprised Orla with some new toys and colouring books and crayons. It was such a beautiful act of kindness that Cat had cried, unable to stop herself. Orla had lost so much, and the joy on her face as Sophia had given her these gifts was priceless. Cat had tried to insist that Sophia at least discount some rent from her pay, but the other woman wouldn't accept this. She told Cat to save her money instead, to put it towards their next home.

Sophia had turned out to be the guardian angel that Cat and Orla so desperately needed. And Cat knew that no matter what she did to repay that, down the line, it would never be enough. Because Sophia didn't even really know them. Cat was just her housekeeper. Yet she'd taken them in without a second's thought. Offered them shelter and food and comfort, and the care and thought a mother might offer, even though none of this was her responsibility. That sort of kindness from one stranger to another – for that's what they practically were – when they had nothing to give back was priceless.

Cat made her way to the pre-school, the traffic slowed to a crawl and the sheets of rain making it almost impossible to see even with the wipers on full speed. The red brake lights of the car in front lit up, and she swore under her breath. She was going to be late.

Sophia's kindness had truly been a godsend, but it had also highlighted just how awful a person Greg was. He knew the B&B had burned down. He knew they'd lost the very few things he'd left them with and he'd not cared one jot. He'd not checked on Orla once. He'd not asked if she was OK, or if they needed anything, or even if they had somewhere to go. For all he knew, they could have been out on the streets. And it had amazed her, even now, even after everything, that he really could be so uninterested in the welfare of his only child. That he could be so cruel and cold.

She finally arrived at the pre-school and parked up a couple of car lengths down from the front of the building. Her hair was already soaked just from running to the car at Sophia's, but she took the umbrella anyway, to save Orla the same fate. After hurrying through the puddles and up the front path, Cat pressed the bell on the front, readying her apologies.

The door opened to reveal a harassed-looking Miss Shannon, who blinked at her in surprise. 'Oh. Hiya. Did she forget something?'

'Sorry?' Cat queried, confused. 'What do you mean?'

'Orla,' the woman replied. 'Did she forget her jumper again?'

Cat stared at her, trying to understand what she was missing. 'I'm sorry, I don't follow. I'm just here to pick her up.'

The pre-school teacher's eyebrows shot up, and she took a half step back. 'But she's already been picked up.'

'What?' Cat frowned, alarmed, and rubbed her forehead. 'Who picked her up?'

'You didn't know about this?' Miss Shannon visibly paled as her eyes darted around. 'Hang on. Let me check who picked her up.' She turned to look over her shoulder. 'Adel? Can you come here a minute?'

Cat's heart began to thump painfully in her chest. What was going on?

'Yeah?' A girl of maybe eighteen walked over with an expectant smile.

'Adel, who picked Orla up?' Miss Shannon asked.

'Oh. Er, it was her dad, I think. He asked for her by name and he had the password.' She shrugged then bit her lip, looking worried.

'Alright, was anyone else with you?'

'No, everyone was busy, but I did double-check the password,' Adel insisted.

'OK. Thanks, Adel,' Miss Shannon replied, dismissing her. She turned to Cat. 'Sorry, she's new, so she don't know all the faces yet.'

'No, that's OK,' Cat replied, realising what must have happened. 'It's fine. It's my ex. He's supposed to pick her up tomorrow, not today. He must have got the days wrong.' She managed a tight smile. 'Sorry about that.'

'No worries,' she replied sunnily. 'See you tomorrow.'

Cat waved and turned, irritation running through her. It was typical. She'd asked Greg for nothing but this *one* thing and he couldn't even do that right. She pulled her phone out of her pocket as she trudged back down the path and dialled his number.

'Yah?'

The short, affected, pompous greeting was like nails on a chalkboard to her ears, and she gritted her teeth. The background was busy with other similar voices and sounded more like he was in a pub than at home with their daughter.

He had better not be in a pub with Orla, she thought angrily.

'Why did you pick up Orla today?' she snapped.

'What? Hang on, can't hear you,' he replied. The background noise lessened slightly. 'Right. Did I pick up Orla?' he queried, mishearing her question slightly. 'No, of course I didn't. You said Tuesday. And if you got the date wrong, then tough, I'm afraid. I'm in a meeting and I can't leave.'

'*What?*' Cat stopped as she reached the pavement, his words hitting her like an invisible force to the chest. 'You don't have her? You haven't picked her up?'

Greg tutted, sounding annoyed. 'No. You said *Tuesday*, so I'm picking her up *Tuesday*. It's *your* job to pick her up today. So I suggest, if you muddled that up, that you get a move on. Sharpish.'

Cat felt a swell of panic and terror and confusion rise within her like a balloon, filling up every single space in her body. It left no room for anything else. It left no room for his words to dry-shave her nerves; it left no room for her to be angry at him or to take in any other aspect of this situation at all. Because for some awful and horrifying reason, her daughter was out there somewhere she didn't know, and with someone she didn't know.

'Cat?' Greg's voice broke her out of her frozen state, and she ended the call without responding to him.

She dropped her umbrella, no longer caring about the ceaseless rain pelting down on her, and turned to face the pre-school. They wouldn't have any answers – that was clear from the conversation they'd just had. The new girl didn't know anyone yet, and they'd been so busy no one else saw who'd taken her little girl. But they'd had the pass phrase. How on earth would someone have that? Her mind reeled as she stood there, getting drenched, her pale face now grey with fear.

She had to call the police, she realised. That's what she'd do – she'd call the police. But as she looked down at her phone, she saw a text there, waiting. A text from an unknown number. A text that said just six, heart-stopping, world-shattering, awful words.

Call the police and she dies.

FORTY-THREE

Alex sat back in the executive leather chair behind his desk in their library office and tapped his fingers over his mouth as he listened to Danny.

'There have been many things over the years, as you know, that one or the other of you have asked me to do discreetly. Keep between us. And I have. Every time. That's my job,' Danny said, visibly stressed. 'But I— *Ugh*. This is— I just...' He scratched the back of his head. 'Things are getting out of hand and I can't in good conscience keep hiding these incidents from you. It's putting the firm in danger. It's putting *all of us* in danger.'

'Tell me,' Alex said simply, knowing already from Danny's face that he wasn't going to like this.

Danny swallowed, his Adam's apple bobbing before he spoke. 'I got a call from Antonio, asking for a clean-up crew at a hotel room. He asked for the doctor too, so I think perhaps she was still alive when he left her.'

Alex's frown deepened and he sat forward. 'Who?'

'Stacy Fraser her name was. She was a tom he'd hired for the night. I don't know what went down, but he, er...' Danny cleared his throat and looked away, trying, not very successfully, to hide his disgust. 'Well, he'd beaten the living shit out of her, to be honest.' He looked back at Alex and shook his head. 'It looked like it was while they were, you know. That things got taken up a level. But he didn't stop. She was covered in bruises and scratches, and...' He scratched the back of his head again with a grimace. 'Well, it weren't pretty.'

'*Fuck.*' Alex wiped a hand down his face and exhaled a loud breath in shock. He couldn't believe it. His brother was a lot of things, but he'd never in a million years thought he'd do something like this. 'What have you done with her?'

'We've dealt with it. She won't be found,' Danny said quietly, sadness on his face. 'But I need to be straight with you. I'm loyal to you and to this firm, and you have that loyalty and my silence till the day I die. But if your brother keeps going as he is, I'll have to walk, Alex. I'll have to leave the game. 'Cause I can't keep burying these girls like this.'

'Keep?' Alex repeated, his stomach dropping. 'How many have there been?'

Danny sighed. 'This will be the second I've buried. There was another we had to patch up and pay off.'

Alex's eyes widened as horror flooded through him. 'Tell me that ain't true?'

Danny's gaze dropped to the floor. 'I wish I could.'

'Oh my God,' Alex uttered.

He couldn't believe it. His mind reeled, and he suddenly felt incredibly sick. How had he missed this? How had Antonio turned into such a monster, right under his eyes? Two completely unnecessary bodies. Two girls just doing their jobs and trying to live their lives, dead. *Murdered*. By Antonio.

They weren't *good* people, the Capellos. They'd long ago given up their tickets to heaven in order to buy a better life first, here on earth. That was something Alex had come to terms with a long time ago, so he never looked at his brother through rose-tinted glasses, by any means. They'd killed before and they'd kill again. But they only killed when it was absolutely necessary or required by a contract. And they only took a contract like that if the payout made it truly worth it. That was business. It wasn't personal. It wasn't something they just did because they wanted to. Because they got caught up in the moment and felt like it. They didn't *enjoy* it.

It was what separated men from animals. Men killed when they had to. Animals killed whenever the urge took them. Because they simply *wanted* to. Just because they *could*. That kind of behaviour in a person was dangerous. And that kind of behaviour in a person as powerful as his brother was nothing short of terrifying.

'You were right to tell me,' Alex said after a long, stunned silence. 'So, these girls. What's the fallout? Are they down as missing?'

'No,' Danny replied. 'The first one seemed like she might have been here illegally. There was nothing I could find on her, and if anyone looked, they stayed very quiet about it. This one, there's a roommate texting the phone, but Joe replied, faked her leaving the UK with a new boyfriend. Roommate seemed to buy it. The one that survived, we paid her off. She knows who she's dealing with, so she won't talk.'

Danny couldn't keep eye contact, and Alex could understand why. This wasn't the work of respectable criminals playing the game and living to a code. This was shameful. None of them had signed up for this.

'I'll deal with him,' Alex promised. 'Leave it with me. I'll speak to Maria, and we'll figure it out. If anything else happens, you come to me straightaway. Understood?'

'Understood,' Danny confirmed.

Alex stood up and Danny did the same, turning and walking back out of the library office. Alex walked with him to the hallway, wondering how on earth he was going to tell his sister all of this. Danny opened the front door and gave Alex a respectful nod before lifting his jacket over his head and jogging back to his car.

Alex glanced up at the black furious sky and was about to close the door when another car suddenly shot up the driveway and screeched to a halt at the bottom of the front steps. The door was flung open, and a sopping-wet Cat jumped out, running up the stairs towards him, not even bothering to close the car door behind her. Her wet face was stricken, and she was shaking as she reached him.

'Whoa, whoa, what is it?' he asked, alarmed.

'It's Orla,' she wailed, pulling out her phone and shoving it at him with trembling hands. 'It's— Someone's taken Orla. Someone's taken my baby,' she sobbed. 'Look. They sent me this. I don't know what to do, Alex. I don't know what to – where to – I – what do I do? *Please help me*,' she begged.

Alex read the text, and a cold ball of fear sank to the pit of his stomach. He gripped Cat's arms and looked into her wide, terrified eyes. 'You need to tell me everything that's happened and everything that you know.'

FORTY-FOUR

Alex slammed his car onto his drive and ran into the house.

'*Bianca!*' he yelled, his anger having grown on the way over. '*Bianca!*'

'*What?*' She sounded annoyed as she called back from upstairs.

Alex took the stairs two at a time and came face to face with her as he reached the landing. Bianca looked dishevelled, her eyes puffy and only half open, as though she'd just been woken up.

'What have you done?' he demanded, towering over her with seething rage. 'Where is she?'

A flicker of guilt flashed over her features then disappeared, and Alex suddenly felt certain, in that moment, that he was right. Bianca had taken her. His heart fell and almost disintegrated in his chest as he stared at the woman he'd once loved so dearly, knowing she'd now crossed a line they could never come back from.

He stepped backward with a deep, heartfelt groan, all fight seeping from his body. 'Oh, Bianca... *Why?* Where is she? Please give her to me,' he begged.

Bianca frowned now, a spark of anger igniting in her eyes. 'What are you *talking* about? Who? Who is *she?*'

'Don't play with me, Bianca,' Alex said strongly. 'This ain't the time. She's just a child, for God's sake.'

Bianca pulled back, looking puzzled. '*Who's* a child? What are you *on* about, Alex? Seriously, I've just woken up. If this is some sort of joke, it's *not* funny.'

Alex stared at her, his mind working as he studied her face. She shrugged at him as he scrutinised her, and he narrowed his gaze.

'You really don't know what I'm talking about?' he asked.

'No!' she insisted, sounding more than a little peeved.

'Where have you been today?' Alex demanded.

'Seriously? Jesus fucking Christ, the Spanish Inquisition was less hassle than this,' Bianca declared. 'Alright, I slept in till about nine, went and got my nails done, had lunch with Carla, got back an hour ago and went for a nap. Think I popped to the ladies' room about one thirty, if that helps ya,' she added sarcastically. 'What's this about anyway? Why you all flustered?'

Alex ran a hand back through his dark hair, resting the other hand on his hip as he stepped back. 'Cat's daughter's been taken from pre-school. Cat got a text saying, *Call the police and she dies.*'

'*What?*' Bianca's mouth dropped open in shock, but then she quickly shut it as her expression darkened. 'Of course,' she hissed. 'Of *course* you'd run to her fucking aid, and of *course* you'd think it was *me*.' She let out a bitter, incredulous laugh. 'Unbelievable. Taking that skank's side against your wife. As if I needed any more proof of your feelings for that little bitch.'

'Ugh, *Bianca*! *Listen* to yourself!' Alex cried. 'There's a *kid* missing. Cat's kid. I am *not* sleeping with her. I do *not* have feelings for her. But Cat's one of our own now, for fuck's sake, and her kid's been taken! Orla's *three*, Bianca. She's probably terrified, and God only *knows* what she's been put through.'

Bianca pursed her lips, her expression still angry but the logic of his words enough to make her stop fighting him for a moment. 'I'm sure she's fine,' she said eventually. 'But if you really expect me to believe you ain't lusting after that slag at your mother's house, then you give my intelligence even less credit than I thought you did.' Looking him up and down, Bianca gave him a challenging sneer and waited for him to deny it.

Alex looked at her, *really* looked at her, and he realised with a deep sadness that he truly hated the woman his wife had become. The woman he'd married had been fun and warm. A teammate. A woman who cared about people and who shared her love with him in so many ways, every day. *This* woman, the one before him now, didn't resemble her at all anymore. For so long he'd blamed himself. For not being there enough, for not giving her what she needed, for not finding her something to better occupy her time. But as he looked at her now, he realised it wasn't him who was to blame for her actions at all. It was just who she was now.

He'd just told her that a three-year-old child, an innocent child she'd met and spent time around, had been kidnapped. And she'd just looked back at him with cold, empty eyes and an ugly sneer, still focused on nothing but herself and her own bitter insecurities.

Alex stepped back and began to shake his head slowly. 'I don't know who you are anymore, Bianca,' he said quietly. 'I really don't.'

'Huh! Well, maybe that's 'cause you're too tied up with your *other* woman to notice your *wife* these days, eh? Maybe, if you spent more time—'

'No.' He cut her off. 'No, Bianca. You're not the woman I married. You're not someone I even like these days. And, honestly...' He cast his gaze away from her, his expression sad and heavy. 'I don't know if I can even do this anymore.'

There was a stunned silence as Bianca blinked in shock. Whatever she'd been expecting from him, that clearly wasn't it. Alex suddenly needed to get out of there before she found her tongue again because he didn't want to hear whatever she decided to throw at him next. He backed away from her and then turned.

'I have to go,' he told her as he reached the door. 'Just do us both a favour and give me some space, Bianca.'

As he stepped back outside into the storm, he barely felt the rain. He barely felt anything at all, a strange numbness taking over. But as he reached the car, he pushed his wife from his mind completely. He had much bigger things to focus on right now. Orla had been taken, and they needed to figure out why and by who – before it was too late.

FORTY-FIVE

Cat drove fast, frantically overtaking other cars and beeping her horn at everyone who got in her way, but when she was about halfway there, she suddenly slowed down. The last thing she needed now was for the police to see her and pull her over. She couldn't tell them what was going on, even though she itched to do so. It was just too risky.

Go back to the pre-school, look and see if there are any cameras around the front that we could get into. Traffic cams, video doorbells across the road, anything pointing that way, Alex had told her after she'd shared everything she knew so far with him. *I know a guy. We can hack into the footage. I just need to know what we're looking at. Ring me once you're there. And when they reply.*

They'd tried the number, but it had gone straight to voicemail, so he'd told her to text and ask what they wanted. The reply hadn't arrived yet, but she had the phone on loud so that she'd hear the instant it arrived.

She'd racked her brains trying to figure out who it might be, who might have taken Orla from her like this, but she couldn't think of anyone. It could be someone she *didn't* know, but she prayed it wasn't. Because whatever way she looked at it, that was worse. If someone didn't have a personal reason to take her child, their intentions weren't something she could bear thinking about. The only possibility that she kept coming back to was Greg. Was he playing with her? Was he just trying to mess with her head? Or was it Jeanie perhaps? Trying to send a message, flexing her power and showing off just how far she was prepared to go to get what she wanted. At this point, either of those options would be preferable to the alterative. At least Orla would be with people she knew, who'd keep her safe. She wouldn't be scared or hurt or... She stopped the thought there, unable to complete it.

Turning the corner into the road the pre-school was on, the loud beep of a text arriving caught her attention. She pulled up to the kerb quickly to read the text. It was the reply she'd been waiting for.

> *Well done. You passed the first test. Now it's time for the second round. Come directly to the address below. Do not tell anyone. Do not collect £200 as you pass Go. And remember – if you want the chance to win, you have to play by my rules.*

A deep feeling of dread pooled in Cat's stomach as she read the words through carefully again. What *was* this? What kind of sick, depraved person kidnapped a child and turned it into a game? What could someone possibly want from her?

But just then it all suddenly clicked with the most dark, dreadful clarity. All the warmth seemed to evaporate from her body, and her breath caught in her throat. Because she suddenly knew exactly who had her tiny, precious, helpless daughter. There was only one person that she'd heard would go to this kind of extreme to get what they wanted.

Wetting her lips as she watched the screen, she tried to weigh up the options until she came to the stark realisation that she had none. Who would even believe her? Then, ignoring the fresh fear gripping her insides, she turned the car around and headed for the address in the text.

It took nearly half an hour to drive out to the address she'd been sent. At first Cat hadn't been sure she was in the right place. The building was clearly abandoned with weeds growing up through the cracks in the concrete surrounding it, windows boarded up with wood and a metal fence erected all the way around with NO ENTRY signs attached to it here and there. But then she saw the gate had been left open a crack, the chain unlocked, and as there were no other buildings close by, she knew this had to be the one.

She'd searched the car for some sort of weapon, finding an old screwdriver in the bottom of the door pocket, which she slipped up her sleeve so that he couldn't see that she had it. She was still clinging on to the desperate hope that she might not have to use it, though she knew, realistically, that she probably would.

As she crossed the empty space between the road and the front door, Cat suppressed a shiver. The place gave off dark, ominous vibes, like it held the worst secrets in the world behind its rotting window boards, and she didn't think she'd ever felt more scared in her life. It was only the thought of Orla that kept her moving forward and fighting the urge to flee.

The building looked almost like a very large house, or a short row of houses that had been merged together, though she knew it had to have been something else. Something commercial. There was a large, square space above the double door where a sign had once hung, four holes in the brick where the screws must have been.

Her phone beeped once more, and Cat glanced down at the screen. It was a message from Alex, asking if she'd had a reply.

She wanted, so desperately, to respond, to tell him where she was and who was inside. But she couldn't. Too much hung in the balance. She couldn't risk it.

Hesitating only a fraction of a second more, as she reached the front door, Cat swallowed her terror and put her phone away, walking determinedly into the darkness within.

FORTY-SIX

As her eyes adjusted, Cat covered her mouth and nose with her scarf. There was an overwhelming smell of damp and decay, and the dust she'd disturbed upon entry now floated lazily in the air around her. She was in a large reception area, the circular desk station still in place, random wires sticking out from somewhere beneath, the items they'd connected to long gone. There were double doors either side of the room and a set of stairs leading up at the back. Cat tried the door to the left first and found it locked. The other was locked too. Which meant they had to be on the next floor.

Moving as quietly as possible, Cat crept up the stairs. She knew it was probably pointless. He had to know she was here. Her car would have made enough noise, and he'd most likely watched her walk up from wherever he was in this godforsaken building. She strained her ears, listening out for any sign of him or of Orla. The stairs doubled back on themselves, and as she neared the top, she could suddenly hear the sound of muffled sobs.

'Orla,' she muttered under her breath.

Her heart lifted, and both her hope and her fear increased at the same time. She was close. She was *so* close. And Orla was alive at least. That was something. She just had to find her and get her out. But *he* was here too, she reminded herself. And he'd made it very clear that this was a game. So what was his next move? And what could she do about it? She rolled the screwdriver around and gripped it a little tighter beneath her sleeve.

'I'm coming, baby,' she whispered, reaching the hallway at the top of the stairs.

It was almost pitch-black, and she had to squint to see down it. The hallway was long and straight in both directions, a number of doors leading off it, most of which were slightly open. Which one was he behind? Which one hid him as he lurked in the shadows, lying in wait for her? She glanced backward, now wishing she hadn't so blindly followed his instruction to tell no one. But she'd had no choice. If he found out that she hadn't done as he'd asked, and he hurt Orla, she would never forgive herself.

Biting her lip, she forced herself forward, down the hallway to the left. That was where she could hear the sound of Orla's sobs. She wanted to call out to her, to ask her to be a little louder so that she could find her quicker, but then he'd know where she was. If he didn't already. Every cell in her body was screaming at her to run from this place. Every hair stood on end, as though sensing his evil. Or perhaps it sensed something else, too, because it certainly felt like nothing good could ever have happened here.

As she passed each room, she glanced fearfully through the open cracks, not quite brave enough to go inside. Most rooms had bedframes, some with old mattresses tossed on the floor nearby, as though the inhabitants had left in a hurry and dropped them on their way out. In the hallway, there were a couple of upturned medical trolleys and old papers scattered on the floor. She shuddered as she came across a discarded needle bin, the contents strewn across the floor. It had to have been an old medical facility, though what kind she had no idea.

Orla's sobs were closer now, and she hurried her pace as she realised which door the sound was coming from. She glanced back down the hallway, feeling hopeful as she saw she was still alone there. She tried the door handle, but it wouldn't budge. It had been locked. The sobs inside instantly changed to frightened whimpers at the unexpected noise, and she kneeled beside the door, putting her mouth to the keyhole.

'Orla, it's me. It's Mummy,' she whispered. Instantly, Orla let out a shrill shriek of relief, and Cat winced. '*Shh!* Shh, baby, we must be quiet now, OK?' she begged quickly. 'Be a good girl now while I get you out, alright?'

Orla just continued crying, but at the lower volume she'd been sobbing at before, and Cat could picture her nodding in response.

'Good girl. That's my girl,' she crooned. 'Orla, are you on your own in there?' She held her breath.

'Yes. And I'm scared, Mummy,' Orla replied with a shaky voice.

'I know, baby,' Cat replied, her own voice not much stronger. 'I'm going to get you out, OK? Hold on.'

She slipped the screwdriver out from under her sleeve and eyed the keyhole. She'd seen people pick locks a hundred times in films and on television, but it wasn't something she'd ever had need to do herself. It couldn't be that hard, could it? She tried to think how they did it in those scenes. Someone always put something like this into the lock and then tried to manoeuvre it into the right position from the inside. She tried it, inserting the screwdriver and digging around a bit, but nothing moved.

'Hang tight, baby,' she whispered. 'I'm nearly there.'

A low chuckle from somewhere close behind made her yelp and jump nearly out of her skin. The screwdriver went clattering to the ground and skidded out of reach, back towards the stairs. She swivelled round, pressing her back to the door, her hands still on the handle as if trying to protect it. And there, in front of her now, in all his hateful glory, was the man who'd kidnapped her daughter.

Antonio Capello.

FORTY-SEVEN

Maria looked over the latest batch of fifties that were hot off their printing presses and slipped one crisp note out, holding it up against the light.

'See – we've improved the watermark now.' The woman who spoke stepped forward and pointed out the detailing. 'Here, look. It's a sharper edge than before. Practically identical. They'd be hard pushed to ID one of these as fake.'

Maria nodded and rubbed the material between her thumb and forefinger. 'And the weight?' she asked.

'As close as we can get it,' the woman answered. 'Crude machines won't be able to tell, but some of those new expensive ones the banks have...' She pulled her face to one side in a grimace. 'We can't test them yet, for obvious reasons, but there's a small chance those might still pick it up.'

'Then we keep improving until there's *no* chance,' Maria told her.

'Of course,' the woman replied hurriedly.

'But good job,' Maria added. 'These are looking good. Our best batch yet.'

She walked over to the small makeshift office at the side of their crude basement money factory and closed the door behind her. Two of her men were waiting inside. As she sat behind the desk, her phone rang, and when she saw it was Alex, she picked up.

'Hi. What's up?' she asked.

'Where are you?' he demanded. 'And who are you with?'

'The paper hub.' She answered with the code name they used for the place. A safety precaution in case anyone was listening in who shouldn't be. 'And I'm with Jeb and Ollie. Why?'

'Put me on speaker,' Alex told her.

Maria frowned and did as he asked. 'OK, go ahead.'

'Orla's been taken from pre-school, and Cat got a text saying, *Call the police and she dies*,' Alex said, cutting straight to the point. 'She came to me for help. I sent her back to look for cameras while I checked something out, but she's disappeared now too.'

'What? Oh my God!' Maria exclaimed, exchanging glances with the others. 'Who's taken her?'

'That's what we're trying to figure out,' Alex said with a sigh. 'But now she's nowhere to be found and her phone's going to voicemail, and I don't like the look of it. She text them back asking what they wanted before she left me. She said she'd be back in touch when they replied, but nothing.'

'You think they've told her to go somewhere and not to tell anyone,' Maria deduced.

'Yeah, it's standard shit, ain't it? And she won't know better,' Alex replied.

'*Shit*,' Maria cursed. 'Where's Antonio? Is he on this?'

'Can't get hold of him. His phone's been off all day,' Alex replied. 'But I'd rather leave him out of this anyway. There's some other stuff going on that Danny brought to me today.' He made a sound of reluctance. 'I'll tell you about it later.'

Maria watched her two men exchange a knowing glance and narrowed her gaze. 'OK. What do you want me to do?'

'I'm not sure. Send everyone out looking. We don't know much, but we have to try. I'll contact Bill, see if he can track Cat's phone.'

Maria nodded. 'Good idea. And I'm on it. Call me if you hear anything.'

'Ditto.' Alex ended the call, and Maria slipped her phone away.

She folded her arms and looked at each of the men before her in turn. 'Are you going to start talking, or are you going to make me ask?'

'Well...' Jed cleared his throat. 'We were told not to say nothing, which is why we didn't.'

'By who?' Maria asked with a frown. 'You work for *me*.'

'And your brothers,' Ollie reminded her with an apologetic grimace.

'We got called into a clean-up job recently,' Jed admitted. 'One of Antonio's.'

'*Three* of Antonio's,' Ollie corrected.

Jed nodded. 'Yeah. There were three.'

'And?' Maria prompted when they both began to study the floor.

'Two of the times there were bodies, which we dealt with. The other, Danny paid her off,' Jed told her reluctantly.

'Bodies? *More* bodies?' Maria blinked, surprised. 'Why? What happened?'

Jed scratched his neck, and Ollie clamped his jaw shut in a stubborn line. Eventually it was Jed who continued.

'Your brother got a bit carried away with these women. It's been, er, getting pretty crazy. Danny spoke to Alex about it earlier today. I'm sorry, Maria. First time, we turned a blind eye. The second, we stayed quiet too, but this one... I don't know. We're worried that Antonio's starting to lose it.'

Maria watched them, her blood running cold as she took in what they were saying. She pulled a sharp breath in and looked at the wall above their heads as she sat back and processed it.

'Right,' she said after a few seconds. 'Right. OK. I'll deal with that later. Right now, we need to find Orla and Cat. Though *fuck* knows how.' She ran her fingers through her long, dark hair as she tried to work out where to start.

'Um...' Jed pulled a strange, contorted expression as though warring with whether to say something or not.

'What is it?' Maria asked.

'It's just...' He bit his bottom lip. 'The girl Danny paid off. The one that survived...'

'What about her?' Maria waited, unsure where this was going but trusting Jed enough to know it was worth hearing if he felt it was worth sharing.

'She was chattering on about what had happened, when we got there,' Jed told her. 'One thing she said stuck out. She said he'd got angry over her name.'

'Her name?' Maria frowned. 'Why would that matter?'

'She just said that's when he got angry, when he asked her name and she answered,' Jed replied. 'He told her she had to answer to a different name. That she had to be someone else for the rest of their time together.'

Maria felt an icy trickle of realisation creep up her spine at Jed's words. 'Who?' she urged, wishing she didn't have to ask. Wishing she didn't have to know what was about to be confirmed about her brother.

Jed met her gaze. 'He told her she had to call herself Cat.'

FORTY-EIGHT

'You've never picked a lock before, have you?' Antonio asked as he watched her from just a few feet away. 'Did you really think it was going to be that easy?'

Cat's dark brown eyes darted to the screwdriver once then twice, and as she held his gaze in the next moment, she tensed, ready to jump for it.

'Ah, ah, ah,' he said, stepping in between her and the object she so desperately wanted. 'You know, if you're going to try and flip the tables like that, you should really learn how to hide your moves better.' He leaned towards her and cupped his mouth, continuing in a stage whisper. 'You made it really obvious what you were about to do.'

She gave him a withering look of loathing, and he couldn't help but laugh at her expression.

'Oh, *Cat*!' he exclaimed loudly, his smile still wide. 'You do serve to entertain most *wonderfully*, now that you have no choice, don't you?'

'Mummy?' The scared voice came from beyond the closed door.

'It's OK, Orla,' Cat replied, trying hard to keep her voice steady. 'Mummy's here. I'll have you out soon.'

'She *will*, Orla,' Antonio confirmed. 'But not just yet. Mummy's got a few things to do first, so you sit tight.'

The wails started up again, and while they annoyed him significantly, they worried Cat more, and the heightened panic was clear on her face. He laughed again, thoroughly enjoying this.

'Oh, kitty Cat, you don't like that at all, do you?' he said in a sing-song voice.

'Let her out, Antonio. *Please.*' Her last word was forced through gritted teeth. 'Why are you doing this? She's terrified.'

'But so are you, aren't you?' he replied. With a smile, he bent down and picked up her screwdriver, slipping it into his jacket pocket. 'Here's the thing, Cat. I quite like you scared. Do you want to know why?'

'Because you're sick?' she hissed quietly, clearly trying not to let her daughter hear.

'No. Well. *Maybe*,' he admitted, thinking about it. 'But it's mainly because you've been driving me up the fucking wall for *weeks*.' He smiled at her then, as though they were two friends sharing a joke. 'You see, in all my years – and, thinking about it, this shocks me probably about as much as it does you – you're the first woman to *ever* turn me down. Can you believe that?'

Cat didn't answer; instead she just glared at him with pure hatred.

'I mean, a couple played hard to get,' he continued. 'I had to work at it a little bit, but I wore them down eventually. *You* though. You weren't having *any* of it.' He blew out a little breath and raised his eyebrows, shaking his head. 'You didn't want to know. Acting all snooty and better than you really are. Turning *me* down.' He placed a hand on his chest and raised his eyebrows at her again, as if imparting something utterly shocking. 'Just the fucking *cheek* of it was enough to rub me up the wrong way. I mean, someone like you should be falling over your fucking feet trying to get my attention, and you *turn me down?*' He barked out a laugh. 'I thought maybe I just wasn't your type. You know, that you were into your own kind perhaps. But then I realised you had a kid and a husband, and that you really were just *snubbing* me. I mean, it's just fucking *rude.*'

'Antonio,' Cat said carefully. 'Please let Orla go.' She wetted her lips nervously. 'I'm very sorry that I offended you. I didn't mean to. I appreciate the flattery, and I'm so sorry that my response to it came off as rude. I sincerely apologise.' A tear rolled down her cheek as she glanced back at the door. 'If you can see past my poor behaviour, then perhaps we could grab a coffee or something together, once we're back home.'

'*Coffee?*' Antonio blurted out with a loud laugh. 'I don't want to grab *coffee* with you. I want to *fuck* you.' He stepped forward menacingly. 'And that's exactly what I'm going to do here today. Every which way possible, for as long as I can manage. Which, from experience, is a few hours at least. And guess what? Here's a spoiler for you...' He leaned closer to her with a dark glint in his eyes. 'It's going to fucking hurt.'

Cat let out a sob, and she bit down on her lip, hard, trying to quell her fear.

'Oh, shhh now, don't start. It's a good thing.' Antonio took another step towards her, watching her press herself back against the door as tightly as she could. 'Because do you know something else? You've made me do some bad things, Cat. Some truly terrible, awful things. And I need to get you out of my system before I do anything else. Do you understand?'

She didn't respond, but then he didn't expect her to. She didn't know what he was talking about.

'And here's the thing, Cat. You ain't even gonna fight me. You're going to come willingly and do as you're told. Because if you *do*, if you please me, then I'll let you leave afterwards. Intact and with your daughter. OK?'

'And if I don't?' Cat asked.

He smiled coldly. 'Roll the dice and find out.'

Another tear slipped down Cat's cheek, and her mouth trembled, then, after a few seconds, she closed her eyes and nodded.

'There you go!' he exclaimed. 'That wasn't that hard, was it? You should have just let loose and had some fun with me before. We wouldn't have needed to get to this point, would we? Eh?' He stepped back and gestured to the open door behind him. 'Come on then. What are we waiting for?'

* * *

Cat walked into the room, shaking with fear, and looked around. It was much the same as the other rooms she'd passed, except this one had a double bed in it and the mattress was still on the frame. There was a lamp on the bedside table, and Antonio switched it on, showing her the base as she frowned in confusion.

'Battery operated this one,' he explained. 'No actual electricity in the building – it's been cut off.'

Cat's heart bled for Orla, who she could still hear crying across the hall. She must be completely terrified in there, alone in the dark. This place was scary enough for a fully grown adult, let alone a three-year-old.

'We bought this place a while back. Going to knock it about to make flats, just waiting for Maria to sort the planning on it,' Antonio continued, as though they were having a normal discussion in a normal situation. There was a short silence, and then he placed his hands on his hips, facing her. 'Well go on then. Take your clothes off. Actually, no. Let's go slow, shall we?'

He strode across to her, and before she could register what he was even doing, he grasped her by the neck and lifted her off the floor, slamming her back against the wall. She let out a short shriek and then silenced herself, horribly aware of how close Orla was to them. Of how much she could hear from there.

Antonio buried his face in her neck and sniffed deeply. 'Ahh, you smell good,' he murmured. 'I bet you taste good too.' He opened his mouth and suddenly bit down hard on her shoulder.

Cat couldn't help the small, high-pitched whimper that escaped as she tried not to scream, and she struggled under his grip, trying to get away. It was no use though. He was much bigger and stronger than she was.

'Do you want to know what annoyed me the most?' Antonio asked, his free hand now roaming down her body.

No, she screamed silently. *No, I don't!*

'The fact you were up for it with my *brother*. Ugh.' He sounded angry now.

'No – no, I— Nothing happened,' she squeaked urgently.

'Yeah, but you wished it did,' Antonio growled.

'No, I didn't,' Cat protested.

It suddenly registered in the back of her mind somewhere that this must have been why Bianca had been so convinced of their affair. Antonio must have been whispering in her ear, stirring up trouble.

He pressed himself against her now, and Cat closed her eyes in disgust as she felt how hard he was. How could anyone get off on this? How could this actually turn someone on? His hand was too tight around her neck, and she was struggling to breathe, but nothing she did seemed to make him loosen his grip.

'Showed yourself up for the whore you really are there. Clinging to him in your bath towel. Trying to tempt him away from his wife by getting naked in the house like that,' Antonio taunted, running his mouth down her neck to her chest. 'Well, I might not be him, but I'm about to give you what you were asking for.'

Antonio grabbed hold of the high neckline of her black top and yanked downwards, ripping it open and exposing her bra. Tears streamed down Cat's face, and she squeezed her eyes shut as she gasped for air, praying for the strength to endure whatever was about to come, so that she could get to her daughter. Orla was all that mattered now. Nothing else. Nothing but getting her out of here and away from this evil, dangerous being.

But just as she prepared herself for the worst, there was a sharp clang, and Cat's eyes flew open just in time to see the door bounce back off the wall and Maria storming in.

'Get the *fuck* off her!' Maria bellowed.

Two men appeared from behind Maria and started towards them. Twisting round with a growl of frustration, Antonio suddenly let go of Cat's neck and stepped back. She fell to the floor, coughing and gulping in deep lungfuls of air.

'What are *you* doing here?' Antonio demanded. '*Oh no you don't.*'

Cat had been trying to crawl away from him, but her head was suddenly whipped back as Antonio grasped a fistful of her hair and yanked her upwards. She cried out as she ended up on her knees, facing the ceiling, with her own screwdriver suddenly pointed at her neck. Her breathing grew rapid as panic set in even stronger than before.

'Or-Orla,' she cried to Maria, pointing towards the hallway.

But Maria and the men were now completely still, watching Antonio with the focus one might have when watching a snake about to strike.

'Easy now,' Maria said carefully. 'You don't want to hurt her. Not really.'

'Oh, I do,' Antonio replied with a short laugh. 'But that's beside the point. You already know I *want* to. You're trying to figure out if I really *will.*'

'I know you *can*,' Maria countered. 'I know about the others.'

This seemed to set Antonio back a bit. He faltered, and Maria took the opportunity to step forward.

'Three of them,' she continued calmly. Her face was serious, and she nodded slowly. 'I know you, Antonio. Better than most. I know you have this thing in you that when you've set yourself to something, you can't change it. You have to reach that destination, that goal. But here's the thing. Sometimes you need to adjust the journey. It isn't Cat you want. Not really. You did want her, but you wanted a version of her that wanted you back. And that version doesn't exist.' She took another step towards them as Antonio scoffed. 'No, it's *true*. And you know it.'

'You don't know what you're talking about,' he spat.

'I do. Because I'm the same way, Antonio. I just learned how to deal with it better,' she admitted.

Cat watched them, the pain in her head so strong she felt she might pass out if Antonio didn't release her soon.

'Just let her go, Antonio,' Maria said gently. 'This won't end well otherwise.'

Another tense few seconds passed, and then suddenly, with a growl of frustration, Antonio flung Cat away from him.

For one brief, wonderful second, Cat thought it was over. She thought she was free and clear, finally able to get to Orla. And then suddenly her head connected with something hard and sharp, and before she could figure out what it was, she was plunged into a whole new world of darkness.

FORTY-NINE

It was the searing pain that pounded through her head as though she was being sliced open by a hot laser that woke Cat up. It took a few seconds to think of anything but the pain, her brain unusually sluggish. When she did, she forced her eyes open and attempted to move, but she couldn't seem to do more than simply stir. Why were her limbs so heavy? Why did she feel so out of it? What had happened?

She tried to think back, and after a moment she remembered the fall. She'd been knocked out. A strange, slow sense of panic set in. She had to get to Orla, she realised. Looking around and trying to blink away the blurriness in her vision, she tried to work out where she was. It was so dark she couldn't make out anything other than the fact she was in the bed. Then a cold, sinking feeling settled into the pit of her stomach as she realised what this meant.

She hadn't left that room. She was still here. Somehow he'd overcome his sister and those men, and he'd tied her to the bed. Her nightmare wasn't over. It hadn't even yet begun. Tears welled up in her eyes, and she began to moan softly.

'*No.* No, no, *no, please,*' she cried pitifully. '*Orla!*'

'Shh, shh, it's OK. It's OK.'

The deep, husky voice made her jump, and her cries increased with her panic as she realised he was still there too.

'No, oh *God*,' she whimpered.

She tried to sit up and managed to get onto her elbows somehow, the world spinning around her as she moved, disorientated. He moved too then. She could hear him get up from a seat across the room and walk towards her. Her breathing hitched, and she prepared to scream, to beg, to cry out for help, when suddenly a light switched on beside her, and the scene before her shifted.

It wasn't him. It was Alex's face looking down into hers, concerned. It was his hand on her arm, trying to calm her. And the room was her room, at Sophia's house. The relief hit her so hard that it was almost a physical pain, and she began to sob.

'Orla?' she asked him. 'Where is…?'

'She's here,' Alex said, pointing to a small mound snuggled up under the covers, right beside her. 'You're safe. You're both safe now.'

'Is she OK?' Cat ran her hands over her sleeping daughter, frantically searching for any damage. 'Was she hurt? Did he hurt her?'

'No, I promise you, she's fine. Physically at least. We had the doctor check her over, and one of us has been here, all night, to watch her while you were out,' Alex reassured her.

Cat lay back on the small mound of pillows she'd been propped up on and laid a protective hand over Orla, releasing a long, exhausted sigh. Alex sat down on the bed beside her and hunched over, resting his forearms on his thighs and staring gravely down to the floor.

'Cat, I can't even begin to tell you how sorry I am,' he started.

'No.' Cat frowned then closed her eyes as the action sent a

fresh wave of pain through her head. 'No, it wasn't you. It's not your fault.'

'He's my brother,' Alex replied. 'I should have protected you both from him. I should have realised sooner.'

Cat sighed, too groggy to keep arguing. 'What happened?'

'Well, after you hit your head, Maria got you and Orla out pretty quickly. Antonio disappeared, but we'll deal with him later.' Alex sighed. 'He'd been treading on thin ice for a while. Causing problems, acting recklessly. Maria and I were already on the verge of taking action – it was just family loyalty keeping the hope alive that he'd sort himself out. But he didn't. What he did to you, to *Orla*, that was the last straw.'

Cat didn't answer for a moment, trying to process it all. Her mind still felt thick and slow. 'Did he drug me?' she asked suddenly.

'Oh, no, that was the doctor. He gave you a pretty strong painkiller. Said you'd feel groggy when you woke up,' Alex informed her.

'That makes sense,' Cat replied. She looked down at her sleeping daughter and stroked her hair. 'She must have been so scared,' she whispered, tears falling down her cheeks as her heart broke afresh.

Alex nodded. 'She was,' he admitted. 'But we've fixed that as best we could for now. Maria carried her out of that building with you and told her she was safe. And Mum gave her a bath and some hot milk and made her laugh before she came to bed. I read her a bedtime story. She seemed a lot more peaceful when she fell asleep.'

Cat stared at him, seeing his natural gentleness shine through his usually hard exterior. 'Thank you,' she whispered. 'You really are incredibly kind.'

Alex shook his head. 'I'm not. It was the least we could do after what Antonio did. Anyone else would look after her the same way in those circumstances. But now you're awake, if you're OK, I need to leave.' He stood up and picked up his suit jacket from where it hung at the end of the bed.

'Oh, yes. Of course,' Cat replied. 'You'll want to be getting back to your own bed, no doubt.'

Alex stopped and looked back at her from the doorway. 'I'm not going home, Cat,' he told her. 'I'm going to make things right. Even the scales a bit.'

'What do you mean?' she asked, confused. 'You need to rest now, surely? It's the middle of the night.'

She just caught the brief half-smile in the small amount of light coming from the hallway as he turned away. 'There's no rest for the wicked, Cat. At least, not if I can help it.'

FIFTY

It was the shrill scream that woke Greg, and he frowned, groaning with annoyance. 'Come on, Jeanie – go back to sleep.'

'N-N-No, wake up,' she stammered in a shaky, high-pitched voice.

'Yeah, Greg. Wake up.'

This voice made him jolt upright with a start. Because it wasn't Jeanie's; it was a man's.

'*What the fuck?*' Greg blustered.

A large man holding a heavy-duty hunting knife sat on the edge of the bed, closest to him, and Greg shuffled as far as he could over towards Jeanie. He expected her to move up, or even to get out of the bed entirely, but he was met with resistance and realised that she was pushing up towards him in the same way. He followed her terrified gaze and saw a second man standing nearby, on her side. He was also armed. Greg's heart leaped into his throat, and his insides turned to ice.

'Please,' he begged. 'Take what you want – we won't stop you. You want money? The code to the safe is seventy-one forty-four. Take it all. Please, just don't harm me.'

'*Us!*' Jeanie exclaimed.

'Us,' Greg quickly corrected, holding his hands out in front of him as though to shield himself from an imminent attack. 'Please don't harm *us*.'

He glanced at Jeanie then, wondering if perhaps *she* was what they were after. Wondering if they wanted more than just material gratification. It was a bit odd for burglars to wake up the people they were burgling. If that was the case, then they could *have* her, he decided. He certainly wasn't going to die for the sake of some girlfriend. His life was far more valuable. Realising he couldn't say this out loud, Greg shifted away from her slightly, hoping the distance made it obvious that she wasn't important to him.

The man sitting on the bed let out a low chuckle under his breath. 'You really are something, aren't you, Greg?' he asked. 'We don't need the code to the safe, and we won't be stealing anything either. Mainly because you don't actually have anything to steal. Because none of this is yours, is it?'

Alarm bells began ringing in Greg's head. The man had used his name. 'Who are you?' he demanded.

'You can think of me as your local friendly solution man,' came the answer. 'I fix problems that the law and other people can't.'

Greg's stomach did a small flip of unease, and his gaze flickered to the knife. 'So what do you want?'

Jeanie had fallen silent, watching everyone with wide eyes, with the covers pulled up to her chin.

'What I *want* is to ensure my client gets back what's hers,' the man said in a low, deadly voice.

'Cat hired you,' Greg said in a disgusted tone. 'Well, I have no idea what she's paying you with because she doesn't have a *penny*. I, on the other hand, have plenty.' He sat up straighter, knowing he had to try and take control. 'And I could use someone like you on the payroll. You can name your price. I'll make it worth your while.'

The man laughed again, but this time there was no humour behind it. 'That's the thing with people like you, isn't it? You think you can just steal and bargain your way to the top. But you see, that's not a very good business strategy. All you've built is a house of cards. And I'm here to blow it down.'

'Listen, I really don't know how you think this is—' Greg started, but the man cut him off.

'There are two ways this can go, and to be clear, I'm perfectly comfortable with either.' His dark eyes glinted at him through the darkness, and Greg felt a cold rush of fear run through his body. 'You *will* be giving Cat back everything – and I mean *everything*. You will have it all back in her name, the way it should have been, and you will be out of this house before dawn.'

'*What?* No!' Greg exclaimed. 'I don't know who you think you are, but this is my home, and I will not be bullied by some fucking strangers who broke in – illegally, I might add – in the middle of the night.'

'In that case, we go to the other option.' The man seemed unfazed by Greg's outburst and turned to signal something to the other man, who still stood silently on the other side of the bed.

'Wait, *wait*. What *is* the other option?' Greg asked, feeling his panic rise as the second man pulled out an even bigger knife than the first.

'We kill you both and make it look like a lovers' tiff turned into a double homicide,' the man said casually. 'These things happen. It'll be an open-and-shut case, and then Cat will inherit everything without the stress of having to deal with you. It's the same outcome either way.'

'What?' Jeanie shrilled, pushing herself further up the bed head with wide eyes. 'No, no, I'm not any part of this. This is an issue between husband and wife. You can't—'

'Well, that's not true now, is it?' the man asked, moving his cold gaze across to Jeanie.

'Wh-Wh— I don't know what you mean,' she stuttered.

'I think you do,' the man replied.

Greg glanced at her face and saw the guilt there. 'Jeanie? What's he talking about?'

'Nothing!' she exclaimed. 'I don't know! He – he's a madman, Greg. Don't listen to him.'

'Did it not occur to you that it was a bit odd, your father-in-law leaving it all to you?' the man asked, now looking back at Greg.

Greg frowned, his gaze flicking between the man's face and the large knife still in his hand. 'No, not really. Well, maybe a little, but it made sense. I work there; Cat hadn't for years.'

'Exactly,' Jeanie piped up. 'So you can't come in here and—'

'Be quiet,' the man demanded, raising the knife slightly, and Jeanie fell silent. 'He didn't leave anything to you,' he continued. 'Your girlfriend here faked the will for her own gain.'

'Wait, what?' Greg asked, looking at Jeanie confused. 'Jeanie?'

Jeanie was crying now, her hands shaking as she held the covers up over her, like a useless shield. 'I just wanted to give you the freedom to be with me out in the open,' she told him. 'I wanted to give you what you deserved and make it so that *we* could run the company together, like we're doing now!'

Shock zapped through him. 'So it was true? Everything Cat told me? Oh *God*, Jeanie.' He groaned.

'She can't prove it,' Jeanie replied hurriedly. 'She can't prove it. And *you* can't make us do anything either,' she added, directing her newfound braveness at the man with the knife. 'I mean, come on. You're not *really* going to *kill* us. You'd go down for murder. Surely a client isn't worth *that*.'

The corner of the man's mouth lifted in amusement. 'You're

assuming we'd be caught. We wouldn't,' he confirmed. 'We're professionals.'

Greg groaned again, seeing everything around him begin to crash down. '*Come on*. Look, there must be another solution here,' he said. 'You can't just extort me like this, blackmail me into handing my life over!'

'I'm not,' the man replied. 'I gave you a choice. It's up to you which option you choose.' He shrugged. 'I really couldn't care less which way you go, but I've not got all night, so hurry up and decide, or we'll have to go straight for option two.' He stood up and bent over Greg with the knife, moving it towards his throat.

Jeanie yelped as the other man did the same, and she grabbed Greg's arm across the bed.

'*OK, OK!*' Greg shouted, holding his hands up. 'I'll do it.'

The two men immediately backed off.

'Good choice. Less messy,' the first one told him.

Greg ran his hand through his hair, his eyes darting from one to the other and back again. 'I don't know how you expect me to do this,' he admitted. 'It takes time. Papers have to be drawn up, lawyers need to get involved. It's not as simple as just *handing it all over*.'

'Actually, yes, it is.' The man reached into his inner jacket pocket and pulled out a rolled-up sheaf of papers. 'You invalidated Cat's father's will with the fake one you had drawn up. We could waste time unpicking that, but there's a more streamlined solution. This is a new fake will that post-dates *your* fake one. It leaves everything to Cat and nothing to either of you two. It's been drawn up by a lawyer and the signature has been witnessed by Danny, here, a close family friend who Cat will swear to have known for years, and a Mr Caleb Wright, one of the company's oldest and most loyal employees.'

Greg grabbed the will and cast his eyes down to the bottom of the page. Sure enough, all the signatures were there. Some lawyer called Capello, a Daniel Turner and the security guard who had always hated him, Caleb Wright.

'That traitorous *shit*,' Greg seethed.

'I wouldn't go calling the kettle black too loudly there, Greg,' the man replied.

'So why are you here?' Greg asked, shoving the papers back at the man. 'You've clearly got what you wanted without any input needed from me.'

'Because you needed to understand how this is going to go,' he replied. 'You won't fight it. You won't delay. You won't mutter a word about your own fake will or question the validity of this one. Because if you *do*, I'll be back. And next time I'll just slit your throat in your sleep. You won't even know it's coming. Are we clear?'

Greg paled and swallowed hard, his Adam's apple bobbing. 'Crystal,' he confirmed.

'Good. Now get up,' the man demanded. 'Put some clothes on. You're leaving this house now, and you won't be welcome back.'

'It's the middle of the night,' Greg protested. 'Look, I understand, OK? I'll pack and get out first thing in the morning. The house will be Cat's again by lunchtime.' His truculent tone made it clear exactly how much he hated the idea, but he knew he had no choice. He'd been cornered and he'd lost.

The man leaned in closer with a low growl. 'You'll get out *now*. And you'll do it because I fucking say so.' He pulled the knife upwards again, and Greg raised his hands higher.

'OK, OK. Now it is,' he agreed hurriedly.

'Get your clothes on, both of you, and get in the car,' the man ordered.

'Where are you taking us?' Jeanie asked shakily.

The man simply glared at her, and she lowered her gaze, hurrying up as she shimmied into her skirt.

Three minutes later, the whole party was outside, and the two men ushered them towards a waiting black saloon. Greg now clung to Jeanie, his arm wrapped protectively around her shoulder in a show of care, despite his simmering anger at what she'd done. Or rather, at the fact she'd been so careless to let slip to Cat what she'd done. He couldn't afford to be angry with her right now. Not now he was losing everything of value he'd ever had. It had occurred to him, as they dressed, that she was all he had left now. He'd lost his home, his income, his business. And Jeanie would soon be fired too, no doubt. But at least she still had a house that he could live in with her, and she had the ability to get another well-paid position quickly, with her experience and skillset. She would be able to provide for him while he figured out what he wanted to do next. Jeanie had become his last lifeline. So he had to keep her sweet.

'It's OK, my darling,' he told her bravely as they got in the back of the car. 'We'll get through this together. As long as we have each other, that's all that really matters to me. Money is nothing compared to what we have.'

'Oh, Greg, do you mean that?' she simpered.

He forced a smile. 'Of course, my love. You mean everything to me.'

Greg wasn't sure but for a moment he thought he caught a look of amusement pass between the two men in the front. Well, they could laugh all they wanted, he decided. He had to do what was necessary to look after himself, even if he did sound like a pillock in the process.

They drove for several minutes in silence, and Greg stared out of the window uneasily. 'Where are we going?' he asked.

'Somewhere I think you'll like,' the man who'd sat on the bed replied in a strange tone.

This didn't serve to make either of them feel any less anxious.

A few minutes later, they turned down a street Greg knew all too well, and as they slowed down to turn into the cul-de-sac he'd driven into himself, so many times, he tensed.

'What are we doing? Why are we here?' he asked, his words much more urgent now.

'We thought we'd drop you at a friend's for the night,' the man replied. 'You know, as one last kind gesture.'

Greg's eyes widened, and his heart began to beat worryingly hard against the front of his ribcage. He licked his lips. 'Please, not here. Come on, guys,' he begged in a desperate tone.

'What's wrong?' Jeanie asked. 'Who's this friend?'

The car came to a stop, and the two men in the front got out. Greg groaned as realisation hit hard and disintegrated all the hope he still had left.

'Greg?' Jeanie prompted. 'Talk to me. What's happening?'

The back doors were opened, and the two men forced them out of the car. The first gripped Greg's upper arm tightly, pressing the knife into his back as he marched him up the front path to the small, semi-detached red-brick house. The second man didn't need to use such force with Jeanie, simply ushering her along behind.

'Please, turn us around,' Greg begged. 'Come on, man – you're *killing* me!'

'No, I'm not. Not today at least,' he replied, lifting his hand and knocking loudly on the door.

'Shit,' Greg cursed. 'Shit, shit, *shit*.'

'Greg, what's wrong?' Jeanie asked, a little sharper now, as she moved to stand next to him.

The door opened, and a slim, pretty, young blonde of no more than twenty peeped her head out, rubbing her eyes.

'Greg!' she declared happily before frowning in confusion at the rest of the small group of people. 'What's going on, babe?'

The man who'd forced him here now had a wide, gleaming smile plastered across his face. Whoever he was, he was apparently enjoying this immensely, Greg realised. Jeanie, on the other hand, had frozen, her eyes wide with shock as she stared at the woman behind the door. Greg watched in horror as his young mistress held her hand out towards his girlfriend and only hope left in the world with a friendly smile.

* * *

Alex watched it all unfold with glee. Watched the man flail like a fish out of water. Or perhaps more like a fish who'd been caught and was about to be thrown on the fire.

'I'm Rachel,' the blonde said to Jeanie sunnily. 'Nice to meet you. You guys been out on the lash or something?' She moved her quizzical smile back towards Greg, who simply hung his head and closed his eyes.

Alex stepped back next to Danny and watched for a few seconds, feeling a sense of immense satisfaction. This part hadn't really been necessary, but since he'd got to know Cat, and after what she'd done to help him, he'd wanted to help her get just that little bit of extra revenge on her cheating husband and his thieving girlfriend. Because she deserved it.

'You fucking bastard,' Jeanie shouted, finally finding her voice. 'You absolute *fucking bastard*! You told me it was a *lie*, that Cat had made it up! That you'd *never* cheat on me!'

'*Cheat* on you?' Rachel exclaimed, her smile disappearing instantly. 'How can he cheat on *you*? He's with me! We've been together for over a *year*.'

'A *year*?' Jeanie screeched.

To Alex's delight, she pulled back her fist and punched Greg in the face with all her strength, sending him sprawling into a bush. As he tried to get up, all hell suddenly broke loose, both women trying to shout over the other, each equally angry with Greg, as well as each other, and Alex and Danny melted back into the shadows, their work done.

They walked back to the car and drove off, leaving the rowing trio to their drama.

'That was brilliant,' Danny commented, as they rounded the corner. 'Proper karma that one.'

'Yep,' Alex agreed. 'What goes around comes around. Sometimes you just have to give it a little nudge.'

FIFTY-ONE

Maria paused outside the front of the run-down pub, staring at its old green-and-black tiles and grimy windows, and shook her head. 'This place is just one big fucking health hazard,' she murmured.

Danny nodded his agreement beside her. 'Sure you don't want me to take care of this?' he asked.

'No.' Maria's response was resolute. 'I made a promise to personally see this through, and I intend to keep it. Come on.'

She stalked forward, shoving her hands deep into the pockets of her long red coat as she entered the squalid building. The stench of BO and dirty beer trays assaulted her from the second the door was opened, and she fought against wrinkling her nose as the group of men inside all stopped what they were doing to look at her in surprise. She'd come prepared this time, leaving Joe with the two young men in the alleyway, making sure they didn't sneak up the back to warn anyone of her impending arrival.

She smiled, the action cold but unthreatening. 'Where's your boss?' she asked.

The door to the back room opened, and The Raven

appeared, looking a touch startled. 'Miss Capello.' His eyes darted around each of his men in turn before returning to her. 'This is a surprise. Here for a drink?'

'No,' she replied. 'I'm here to settle an outstanding debt.'

The Raven considered her for a moment. 'This about Justin Sinclair?' Maria nodded, and The Raven smiled. 'Lovely. Won't you come this way?' He gestured towards the back room with a flourish.

Maria walked through, checking her watch as she did. 'I can only stay a minute,' she warned him. 'I have somewhere to be.'

''Course, 'course,' The Raven replied amiably. He sat down and offered her a chair opposite.

Maria looked at it and ignored it, pulling a small rectangular package out of her pocket. It was well wrapped in black plastic and tied up tightly with twine.

'Our arrangement with Sinclair changed a little, since we last spoke. I won't go into detail but he's now dead,' she announced.

'What?' The Raven blurted, his smile instantly disappearing. 'Nah. Nah, nah, nah, he can't be.' He ran his hands over his balding head, and his expression grew stricken. 'He owes us a lot of money. And, hang on, what do you mean by *he's now dead*? As in *you* killed him?'

The corner of Maria's mouth twitched up. 'I'm not going there. All you need to know is he's dead, so he won't be able to pay off his debt to you after all.' She weighed up the package in her hand and glanced at it. 'Before he died though, his dad gave us twenty grand. It was supposed to buy him a new identity. I figure it should go to a good cause.' She dropped the package on the table in front of him and watched his face as his gaze rested on it.

'Twenty grand,' he repeated, blowing a long breath out through his cheeks. 'Well, it ain't gonna solve all our problems now he's dead, but I guess it's a start. Thanks.'

'No need to thank me, Raven,' Maria said, holding his gaze for a moment with a cold expression. 'I've always believed in paying debts.'

With that, she turned and walked away, Danny falling in right behind her. They didn't stop as they walked through the main pub, nor on the pavement outside. Instead, they carried on walking quickly up the road until they reached the entrance to the small alley where Joe was still watching the two young homeless men.

'All sorted?' Joe asked, as the two of them approached.

Maria and Danny turned to face the pub down the road.

'Yeah,' Maria replied. 'I'd say so. Give it a minute.'

The trio stood in silence watching the pub while the two homeless men sat warily watching them. After a minute or so, a loud resounding boom cracked through the air, followed by a spray of debris spewing out from the old pub. Glass tinkled and glittered as what remained of the windows clattered over the street and great clods of brick began thumping down to the ground. The front door opened, and some of the men ran out coughing and spluttering, then finally the flames started creeping around the side of the walls from the back, letting off puffs of thick black smoke.

'What – what happened?' one of the homeless men cried, looking stricken.

Maria turned to look at him. 'I made good on a promise.' She reached into her pocket and pulled out two brown rectangular envelopes, holding one out to each of the men. They shied back, distrustful. 'It's OK. It's money, not another bomb. Ten grand each. You're a much better cause than what it was intended for. Just use it wisely, yeah? Sort yourselves out.'

They took the packets and peered inside, looking shocked when they saw she was telling the truth.

'What the... *wow*. Thanks,' one of them said, in awe.

Maria eyed him hard before turning the same stare on his

friend. 'You didn't see us here today. Or the last time. Do we understand each other?' she asked.

They nodded hastily.

'I mean it,' she reiterated. 'We've got your faces, and you can't hide in this city from us. Got it?'

'Got it,' one of them replied. 'Can we go now?'

Maria nodded. 'Yeah. Go. Go on, get out of here before Old Bill arrives and wants to ask you questions.'

She watched as they hastily gathered their few belongings together and scarpered, then turned and walked on down the deserted road towards her car.

* * *

He watched as the Capello woman walked away with her men, and quickly took a few more photos as she got into her car. He knew he should be horrified by what she'd just done, and part of him was, but he still couldn't help the smile that crept over his face as he realised with glee that he'd finally got her.

Dialling the number of his most high-priority client, he barely waited for the call to connect before blurting it out.

'We've got her. I've got it all on camera. I'll get the photos developed, then I'll head straight over, but, Malcolm...' The grin spread even wider as he recounted his lucky stars again. 'We've *got* her. We've got her on something so bad, there's no way in hell she could wriggle out of it. Not in a million years.'

There was a pause and then a deep victorious chuckle. 'Ahh, Maria. You really should have been more careful.'

EPILOGUE

By Sunday, almost everything had changed for Cat. When Alex had come back and told her what he'd done for her, she could barely believe it. It had seemed too good to be true. And when he'd told her about the final icing on the cake, introducing Jeanie to Rachel, and the subsequent punch she'd delivered to Greg's face, she'd laughed until her sides hurt. When she'd gone to him for his help, she hadn't realised quite how effective that would be.

How can I ever repay you? she'd asked.

You will, he told her. *You owe me an accounting favour, remember?*

True to his word, Greg hadn't returned to the house. Though Cat suspected this was more to do with his fear of Alex than any honour he felt to keep to a promise. She'd boxed up everything of his – and of Jeanie's, who'd already taken over two drawers – and had dumped them unceremoniously on his mother's driveway, where he was now staying. He hadn't been in touch, not even to ask about Orla. This hadn't surprised her.

Cat had walked back into her father's building on the

Thursday, and after thanking Caleb for what he'd done for her, she'd promptly had him remove Jeanie from the building; amazingly, she'd had the audacity to keep coming in to work. She'd promoted the other executive assistant in the office and had immediately set about looking into what she needed to do to keep things running smoothly.

It was on the Friday that she'd found her father's original will in Jeanie's safe, along with a letter addressed to her. She'd cried as she'd read his final words to her, and, to her surprise, his release of her obligations to the company.

My dearest Cat,

You were the greatest gift I was ever blessed with. A beautiful daughter with a brilliant mind and the biggest heart, who not only made my days on earth wonderful with her company but who truly became my very best friend. You and Orla are the entire universe to me, and my only regret is that I didn't get to spend longer with you both.

If there is a heaven, or something similar, know that I'll be looking down on you both with love, and I'll be waiting at the gates when it's your time. We will see each other again. But for now you need to focus on living. For me. For Orla.

I'm proud of the company I built and the technology I developed there. But it's not in that that I live on. It's in you. So I don't want you to hold on to it. It was never your dream; it was mine. But now, it's worth a great deal of money, and I want you to sell it and use that money to follow your own dreams. Whatever they may be and however they shift and change. Let that be my last gift to you, my dearest.

With love for eternity,
Dad xx

That afternoon she'd contacted the company lawyers and informed them that she wanted it put up for sale. They'd agreed to do just that and had promised to come up with a plan and more details for her by Monday. That same day, she'd called an estate agent's and put her house up for sale too. She didn't want to be there anymore. There were too many bad memories, and she needed no help remembering the good ones. She planned to start afresh with a new home and new plan. What that plan was she wasn't entirely sure yet. But she quite liked it that way.

Antonio hadn't been seen since he'd fled the abandoned building on that dark and fateful Monday. Warnings had been issued to him through various channels, but whether or not he'd heard them was anybody's guess. He had to know though, Alex had told her, that he'd gone too far this time. This time there would be consequences, and lines had been drawn.

After much deliberation, Alex and Maria had decided the best thing to do was split the business. Antonio could keep the drug lines, seeing as they'd mainly been set up by him anyway. And they would keep the counterfeit money and the reputation for solving problems. They wouldn't go against Antonio, but he was no longer welcome in the family firm or at Sophia's.

Sophia was, understandably, devastated about the turn of events. But when she'd heard he'd kidnapped a three-year-old child, and what he'd had planned for Cat, she'd been the one to ban him from their home. She couldn't look at him, she'd said. She couldn't look at the monster who'd taken over her son.

But even despite this, Sunday lunch had turned out to be a warm and happy affair, as the rest of them sat around the table and ate and drank and tried to instil some sort of normalcy. Even Bianca had been less sharp for once, which Cat had been grateful for.

As the day came to a close, Cat walked to the hallway and picked up her coat, bidding Orla to do the same.

'You're sure you won't stay just another week?' Sophia asked for what seemed like the hundredth time.

Cat smiled. 'You've been so kind to us, Sophia, but I think

it's time Orla and I move to our own space.' Now she had access to her money again, she'd paid for an Airbnb nearby for a couple of months. Just until they decided where to buy. 'I'll be back tomorrow though.' She smiled.

After all the family had done for her, Cat had decided to stay on as Sophia's housekeeper, until her wrist and ankle had fully healed. She owed it to them. And, if she was honest, she wanted to stay close. Sophia, Alex and Maria had been so good to her and Orla. They'd treated them like members of their own family, throughout everything, and it had felt really good to feel cared about. They might not actually be family, but now her dad was gone, these people were as close to family as she and Orla had. And that counted for something.

Just as Cat finished tying up Orla's shoelace, Alex appeared in the hallway. 'You guys off?'

'Yeah.' Cat pushed a stray lock of hair behind her ear and looked down at Orla. 'You going to say goodbye, Orla?'

'Bye,' Orla said with a shy smile.

'Well, it's not really goodbye, is it?' Alex asked, smiling at her then looking up at Cat. 'We have unfinished business after all.'

Cat smiled back. 'We certainly do. Anyway, we'd best be off. I'll be seeing you,' she said sunnily.

'Stay safe,' Alex said, raising his hand in goodbye as Cat and Orla picked up the last of their belongings and walked out the door.

* * *

Bianca felt the hot strain in her chest as she watched them through the crack in the kitchen doorway. The bitch *still* had her husband in her greedy little grasp, even now. Even now she'd finally left the house. She was *sure* Alex followed her every move with his eyes, like some stupid puppy dog, and she couldn't *bear* it. As the anger boiled inside, she wanted to rage at him, punish him, force him back into line. But she knew she wouldn't get anywhere with Alex like that. Especially after their last heated exchange at home. For a moment, she'd really thought she'd lost him. That he was finally going to utter the words she knew he'd wanted to for a while. *I want a divorce.* Well, she wouldn't give him one. She wasn't letting go of her status as a Capello *that* easily. Alex was *her* husband. His bank balance was *hers* to spend, and his reputation was *hers* to use. She had not come this far in life only to be demoted, and so she knew she was going to have to change tactics. And though it pained her to act like some soppy little weakling, she knew exactly what buttons she needed to press to ensure he stayed in line. To ensure he still saw a future with her.

He walked down the hallway towards the kitchen, and she moved away from the door, quickly picking up one of the dirty dishes still on the side. She pretended to be cleaning it, feigning surprise when he walked in.

'Oh, hey. There you are.' She offered a small smile. A gentle one.

Alex hesitated then smiled back. 'Alright?' he asked, already looking away, clearly uninterested in her answer.

Bianca swallowed the sharp retort she'd usually shoot back at his lack of interest and forced a gentler voice. 'Not really.'

'Oh?' He glanced back at her. 'What's up?' He sounded guarded now, knowing her all too well. Knowing what she really wanted, right now, was a fight.

But instead of creating one, she walked around the kitchen island to him and looked up into his face with wide, serious eyes. 'Alex, I know we've been distant lately. And I know it's my fault.' Her stomach churned with disgust at her own words, but she pushed on. 'I've not been a good wife to you, but I want to be. I want to get back to *us*, you know?' She touched his arms and pulled him closer to her. 'The us we used to be. Because I love you, Alex. I always have. I loved you through the good times and the laughs. The hard times and the bad.'

She lowered her eyes for a moment, knowing that this reminder of her loyalty over the years, on top of her apparent vulnerability, was what would tip the scales. Because Alex was too good a person not to feel the guilt she'd just subtly plastered on. Sure enough, a second later, he pulled her into his embrace, sighing into her hair.

'I know, Bianca. And I want that too. You're my wife. We're a team,' he said heavily.

That's right, she thought. *Whether you want to be or not.*

'We really are,' she breathed.

Alex cupped her face in his hands for a moment then bent down to kiss her. It was a determined kiss. A hard kiss. But one full of promise. And she smiled, genuinely, knowing she'd got him right back where he belonged.

'You go back to your mum,' she offered, feeling generous. 'I'll clear up here.'

Alex winked at her and disappeared, and Bianca picked up the two empty wine bottles. She slipped her feet into the sandals Sophia kept at the back door and walked out to the recycling bin she kept down the side of the house. She was about to put the bottles in when something suddenly moved in the shadows, and she instinctively gasped, nearly dropping them, before she realised who it was.

'Oh, *Jesus Christ*, Antonio.' She sagged with relief and held a hand to her chest. 'You scared the shit out of me. What are you *doing*?'

He leaned in towards her face, a dark expression on his. 'I'm banned, remember?' he hissed. 'But you and I need to have a little talk.'

Bianca searched his face, suddenly wishing she hadn't come out here at all. 'What about?' she asked.

'*What about*,' Antonio repeated with a humourless snort. 'Well, I imagine you didn't tell the rest of the family about *your* part in all the business with Cat. Eh?'

'Shh!' Bianca glanced round at the door worriedly. 'Anyone could hear you.'

Antonio grabbed her neck and squeezed it a little. 'Maybe I want them to,' he snarled through gritted teeth. 'Because why the fuck should I be the only one who goes down in flames for it, eh?'

'Please,' Bianca whispered, her eyes darting back to the door. 'Stop. Just stop.' She gripped his hand, and he allowed her to loosen his grasp. He wanted something from her, otherwise he'd have already told them, she realised. She cut to the point. 'Tell me what you want.'

Antonio nodded. 'You always were smart. Too smart for my brother at least. So here's what you're going to do, Bianca.' He pressed his face right up against hers, his dark eyes wild as his gaze bored into hers. 'From here on out, you're going to be my little spy. You're going to do and say everything I tell you to, and you will find out everything I want you to. Because if you don't...' His face contorted, and Bianca felt real fear fizz through her. 'I will tell them *everything*. I will tell them who gave me the passcode to pick up Cat's daughter that day. I'll tell them how closely you stalked her, and I'll even tell them who whispered her address to me and suggested I start that fire.'

Bianca's face paled. 'Alright, alright, just *shut up*. Please,' she begged. 'I'll do that, OK? No need for threats.'

'Damn right you will,' he snarled. 'Because I'm not disappearing with my tail between my legs like they expect me to. I'm taking it all from them. And you're gonna fucking help me.'

The sound of feet in the kitchen momentarily drew Bianca's

scared gaze back to the light of the door, and suddenly Alex appeared.

'What are you doing?' he asked.

She choked and froze, like a rabbit caught in headlights. But as she cast her eyes back towards Antonio, hoping he had some sort of explanation that she couldn't find, she realised he'd gone.

A LETTER FROM EMMA TALLON

Dear readers,

Thank you for picking up my book! Whether this is your first venture into my version of the London underworld or whether you've followed me here from the Tyler or Drew series, I'm so glad you're here. This is the start of a brand-new series, and I have lots planned to unfold in the books ahead, so I really hope you stick around for the ride!

If you'd like to join my mailing list to find out about my next book, please sign up here. You can unsubscribe at any time, and your details will never be shared.

www.bookouture.com/emma-tallon

If you'd like to follow me on social media, all my links are below, and if you liked the book and can spare a few moments to share a review on Amazon, I would appreciate it more than you know. I read every single review, comment, email and inbox message that comes my way, and I always love to hear what my readers liked or found funny or want more of, so please do reach out if you have anything you'd like to let me know! In the meantime, and until the next book, stay safe and keep smiling!

With love,

Emma x

KEEP IN TOUCH WITH EMMA TALLON

- facebook.com/emmatallonofficial
- x.com/EmmaEsj
- instagram.com/my.author.life
- tiktok.com/@emmatallonauthor

ACKNOWLEDGEMENTS

Firstly, I would like to thank *you*, reader. Because without you, I wouldn't be able to write these stories and bring all these characters out of my head and into the world through the pages of my books. Every time you buy one of my books, borrow one from a library, share a recommendation to a friend or through social media, or leave a review or follow one of my socials, you're showing incredible support. And I value and appreciate that, very much.

Secondly, I'd like to thank my wonderful editor, Helen Jenner. This one hasn't actually been too painful! (She declares, not even halfway through edits...) As we know, some books are just harder to pull together than others, and although I've had my wobbles with this one, you've given me the most positive and steadfast support, and you've boosted me right through those rocky moments. And I'm just very grateful to have you as an editor and overall brilliant teammate. Sixteen books and going strong!

My next thanks are reserved for two of my closest, dearest and most wonderfully murderous friends, Casey Kelleher and Victoria Jenkins. You are two of my favourite people and my absolute tribe. I don't know how I got through all the years prior to meeting you and cannot imagine life without either of you now for even a second! You're the funniest, fiercest, most incredible friends I've ever known – and the first people I'd go to for help if I ever needed to bury a body in real life. (Probably shouldn't put that in print, but there we go.) Never change, you two.

And lastly, I want to thank my beautiful children, Christian and Dolly, for giving me the motivation every single day to create more, do better and reach further. You are the most important people on the planet to me. You are my universe and my reason for living. One day, when you're older and curious about my books, I hope you see this and feel just how much love for you goes into every word I write. I love you forever and always.

PUBLISHING TEAM

Turning a manuscript into a book requires the efforts of many people. The publishing team at Bookouture would like to acknowledge everyone who contributed to this publication.

Commercial
Lauren Morrissette
Hannah Richmond
Imogen Allport

Cover design
The Brewster Project

Data and analysis
Mark Alder
Mohamed Bussuri

Editorial
Helen Jenner
Ria Clare

Copyeditor
Jon Appleton

Proofreader
Laura Kincaid

Marketing
Alex Crow
Melanie Price
Occy Carr
Cíara Rosney
Martyna Młynarska

Operations and distribution
Marina Valles
Stephanie Straub
Joe Morris

Production
Hannah Snetsinger
Mandy Kullar
Ria Clare
Nadia Michael

Publicity
Kim Nash
Noelle Holten
Jess Readett
Sarah Hardy

Rights and contracts
Peta Nightingale
Richard King
Saidah Graham

RAISING READERS
Books Build Bright Futures

Dear Reader,

We'd love your attention for one more page to tell you about the crisis in children's reading, and what we can all do.

Studies have shown that reading for fun is the **single biggest predictor of a child's future success** – more than family circumstance, parents' educational background or income. It improves academic results, mental health, wealth, communication skills, and ambition.

The number of children reading for fun is in rapid decline. Young people have a lot of competition for their time, and a worryingly high number do not have a single book at home.

Our business works extensively with schools, libraries and literacy charities, but here are some ways we can all raise more readers:

- Reading to children for just 10 minutes a day makes a difference
- Don't give up if children aren't regular readers – there will be books for them!

- Visit bookshops and libraries to get recommendations
- Encourage them to listen to audiobooks
- Support school libraries
- Give books as gifts

Thank you for reading: there's a lot more information about how to encourage children to read on our website.

www.JoinRaisingReaders.com

www.ingramcontent.com/pod-product-compliance
Ingram Content Group UK Ltd.
Pitfield, Milton Keynes, MK11 3LW, UK
UKHW041859200625
6512UKWH00002B/89